J. A. BOULET

The STRONG AMONGST us

Published by J. A. Boulet.

Book cover design: Emily's World of Design

Book layout and typesetting: IsaDesign.net

ISBN: 9781777211219

Note to Reader

This is an artistic work of fiction. I am not a historian, nor do I pretend to be. I stumbled upon the 1875 immigration story in Gimli, Manitoba and was enthralled by the chronicles. I instantly developed strong fictional characters in my head and felt compelled to write this saga and tell the world. I have written this novel primarily as fiction, adding facts only to propel the story and give it life. What you are about to read is a fictional saga of joy, tragedy, perseverance and resilience. It should be read as such.

J A Boulet March 27, 2020

For my two awesome kids,
always follow your dreams and grow up
to be men who live with passion.

PART ONE

1875 - 1877

CHAPTER 1

The boats pitched and swayed in the violent lake. Nathanael Olason thought they were all going to die trying to find the new land they had dreamt about for so long. They had already named it Gimli, which meant paradise in Icelandic. As far as he was concerned, currently, it was nothing close to heaven.

Nath watched with trepidation as the lake swelled ahead of them. The dark clouds scowled threateningly. He was certain they were heading into a nasty storm. Nath felt his stomach lurch as the seasickness waved over him. Several passengers had already vomited, but thankfully the putrid smell was hurled overboard. Nath grit his teeth and peered over at his father. His dad's face was robust and steady. The square of his jaw conveyed that they were strong people, they will make it, and nothing will stop them now.

Nathan grabbed hold of whatever he could. He looked at his father and pointed towards a small railing to his left. His father nodded in agreement and carefully walked over to the banister, the boat swaying with every step. The older man temporarily lost his balance and Nath braced himself to rescue him immediately, but thankfully, it was okay; his agile father had regained his footing.

His father made it safely to the small railing, gripping it fiercely. Nathan smiled. His father was as tough as nails. They both leaned down in a half-crouched position, knees bent, bracing themselves.

Suddenly, the boat sloped to the right, sliding some personal belongings dangerously close to the water. Several people clambered to catch them before the lake swallowed their meagre possessions in its giant mouth. Nathan watched helplessly as a bag flew into the swells, a large splash claiming the belongings. A robust woman screamed and then was pulled back by her husband.

Nath held onto his bag securely, the waves lulling momentarily, offering a tiny reprieve before the storm ahead.

This was not what he had expected. This new land had been nothing but hardship, far from any kind of paradise, and it just kept getting worse, although Nathan wasn't sure there were any other options.

The forces of nature had given the Icelanders little choice but to seek a new country. The volcanic eruptions, of his homeland, had forced vast amounts of his people to flee. Then a man named Sigtryggur Jonasson had come up with a plan. The Icelandic entrepreneur had returned to Iceland with news of a beautiful country called Canada and began organizing mass boat trips to save his countrymen from the volcanic rumblings.

Nathanael's family refused to leave initially. His mother and father were intent on staying until the ground finally shook violently. When the ash spewed in clouds from Mount Askja in

March 1875, it was horrific. The volcano had killed most of their livestock and destroyed their land, coating everything in thick ash. The property was useless, nearly impossible to cultivate. There wasn't much left to farm or eat; their entire livelihood had vanished in a plume of ash. Thankfully, no family members were injured, but there was simply nothing left. Home had become a desolate land of destruction.

Leaving wasn't easy; there were many problems, and it took months for them to decide. The cost of the boat trip to Canada was so expensive that they could only afford to send his father and himself. His mother and sisters were left behind. Some of the more impoverished families had decided that they would send the strongest, hardiest women, men and children. Nathanael did notice some of his cousins on the boat as well, so that was comforting. Nath was turning eighteen in a few months, and he was rapidly changing into a man, eager to begin a new adult life. He felt the challenges ahead were just part of becoming an adult, although it was much harder than he had ever imagined.

It had been a harrowing trip immigrating to Canada so far. Initially, they had travelled by boat to Kinmount, Ontario. They spent a few months there, working long gruelling hours, with little pay. Conditions were brutal; lots of women and children had died. Nathanael had lost 10 pounds in the first few months. On his 6-foot frame at 155 pounds, he was very slim. But he still felt strong, very much so actually. The hard work had changed him into a tougher man.

The railroad work they had commissioned to complete became suspended because of a lack of funds. The project could not continue. There was no more work in Kinmount, no more food and the soil was not suitable for farming. They began to plan as a group where they would travel to next, but the Icelanders would have to go soon before they all perished in the isolated community of Kinmount.

Rumours went around that Sig Jonasson was currently living in Riverton, just north of Gimli. A group came back telling them of the beautiful beaches there. Lord Dufferin, Governor-General of Canada, had called this expansive piece of land New Iceland. Rumours said that this land was given to the Icelandic people. Icelanders just had to create a settlement there. The Dominion of Canada would help them with additional financial aid and travel.

They made a collective decision to join an expedition to travel to Manitoba, across land and sea. All of the Icelandic people in Kinmount left, some to Nova Scotia, the remaining to Manitoba. Kinmount was a ghost town. They moved on September 21, 1875. The group travelled by rail to Sarnia, then a barge overseas, train and boat again. They journeyed across Canada into the Americas, then back into Manitoba. It was an arduous, month-long voyage, but they remained committed.

It was now October 21, 1875. The strange flatboats that they were travelling on were approximately thirty-six feet in length and quite narrow. There was an entire fleet of these flatboats. They had been travelling by steamboat for several days with nearly two hundred and fifty other Icelandic explorers. But when they left Winnipeg, it was October 16, and they were all transferred to the flatboats. Initially, they simply floated along the Red River current. The beginning of the trip up the Red River from Winnipeg was pleasant but chilly, although arduously slow. It took four long days of drifting. But so far, their luck was holding up. They all knew it was risky for them to travel during the fall, but the settlers were determined to claim their land. They discussed it as a group several times since leaving Kinmount, and they concluded that the risks far outweighed the present options. Similar to Mount Askja, they had little choice but to leave.

Upon arrangement with the Hudson Bay Company, the steamer Colvile came to tow the fleet of flatboats from the mouth of the Red River this morning. At first, they were excited and energized. They would finally be arriving at their wonderful Gimli land today!

Then the bad weather started.

Nathanael and his dad ate dried meat for lunch, sharing a flask of cold water, while the boat began to pitch again. "What do you think Gimli will be like, Pabbi?" Nathanael asked between chewy bites.

The gruff father chuckled, "It will surely be better than what we've had to live with so far."

Nathanael nodded. They had been through some tough times, he thought, surely it could only get better.

"Do you think it will be beaches and paradise?" Nathan asked. "Lord Dufferin called it such."

"I would like to hope so, Nath," Pabbi replied. "I tend to think more realistically. Better to keep expectations low, work hard for what you want, never expect it to be handed to you as a paradise." Pabbi gulped down water and wiped his mouth on his sleeve. "Something tells me we should be prepared for a long hard winter. Look, the wind is picking up already."

The wind swirled ahead on Lake Winnipeg, and the temperature felt several degrees colder. They wrapped the heavy fur coats tighter around themselves. A freezing fog blew over the lake ahead, obscuring visibility.

Nathanael quickly ate the rest of his dried meat and secured his belongings onto his back. "Pabbi, hurry up and eat, we need to get ready for some bad weather. Look, up ahead."

His father quickly stuffed the remaining dried meat away and secured his backpack. A gust of freezing wind blew onto the flatboat, swirling the first flakes of snow across the boat.

Lake Winnipeg churned up angry white caps in response to the increasing winds, creating a misty whitish fog rising above the seascape. The boat began to lurch and rock front to back again.

"Looks like we might be heading into some lake swells." Pabbi pointed north.

Nathanael watched as the lake rose menacingly and swelled directly ahead of the boats.

Five minutes later, they were amidst the swells. The boats pitched dangerously, tied together; they threatened to capsize each other. The boats banged alongside one another, lightly at first, then increasingly harder. Nathanael motioned for his dad to follow him to the railing. They gripped the rail and stationed their feet firmly, bracing themselves. Gusts of wind blew steadily across the boat, splashing water and snow onto the deck.

They noticed the captain of the steamer Colville talking loudly then shouting. He was gesturing to several deckhands towards the back of the ship. Several minutes later, the deckhands cut the ropes to the flatboats. The Colville was turning around and returning to Winnipeg! Nathanael couldn't believe their terrible luck. The captain had obviously determined that the risks were too high. The boats being tied so closely together in the storm all the way to Gimli would surely cause them to capsize. But they would be safer being blown across the lake!

The flatboat he had been living on was now rocking violently and travelling at dangerous speeds across the lake. This was undoubtedly the end. They would all end up in the frigid waters.

It was late afternoon, as he watched his father bracing himself against the post, the wind blowing his beard across his face. "We will be alright, son," he shouted. "We didn't come this far to be defeated. Get your rope out and wrap it onto something, son. Like an anchor. We don't want to be hurled into these cold waters."

Nathanael wedged himself against the post, holding onto it with an iron grip, unravelling the rope from his backpack and began securing it onto the small rail, watching as his father did the same. Blustering waves of thick icy fog gusted over the boat, reducing visibility. He tried to work as fast as he could, but the freezing humidity was forming ice onto his beard and lashes. The flatboat jerked and rumbled. He looked up at his father. Then the boat sharply hit something. The impact was enough to send people overboard. Nathanael lost his grip momentarily, but recovered quickly and clambered back to the posts. Bodies scrambled overtop each other. When he looked up, his father was gone! He panicked. He saw his father sliding on the flatboat, feet first towards the water. He prayed for strength and tied the rope more securely into a tight knot from his waist and pushed towards his father.

The boat was slick with water, his feet slipped, and he crashed into his dad, grabbing hold of him at the same time, sliding further, until the rope saved them both from the freezing waters. He gripped his father's hands onto the line, and they both climbed up until they were once again near the small rail. His father had some cuts on his forehead, but he seemed alright.

Many people were groaning and complaining. Some were splashing in the water. Nathanael used his father's rope to lower it into the water.

"Grab the rope!" He shouted to a young man in the water. "The rope!! Grab the rope!"

Finally, the young man swam to the rope, gripped it and pulled himself aboard. Wet and shivering, the man thanked Nathanael. The freezing man pulled his damp hair back, and Nathanael noticed it was his second cousin! "Viktor!!" He slapped him on the back. "You should really be more careful!" he laughed.

"Damn boat!" Viktor laughed. "What did we hit?"

His father pointed in the distance. Trees were dotting the landscape, showing themselves between the waves of fog. "We hit land, my boys! We did it! Welcome to New Iceland!"

Roars of laughter rose over Willow Point. The Icelandic explorers had reached paradise, approximately 20 miles from their intended destination.

CHAPTER 2

They awoke the next day to snow. It was cold. They had hastily set up tents last night so they could sleep. There were no people anywhere for miles. Just trees and bushes and water, lots of water. Everyone arrived safely. The flatboats hit the sandy beach at Willow Point. A few settlers had fallen into the lake, but it was so shallow, only some bumps and bruises were the resulting injuries.

They were cold and exhausted from travelling for so long. Being dumped on a shoreline named Willow Point was akin to heaven in their eyes. They would travel to Gimli soon by foot, although, the immediate concern was shelter.

"We need to build some homes quickly," Pabbi said. "Before this winter gets worse, Nath."

Nathanael looked up from the woodpile he was chopping. "Yes, Pabbi. We can start by using some of this dead wood and our tents. Any home is better than nothing. I will build a fire for warmth and cooking first. Let's eat." He put a bowl of hot water on the fire then added some dried meat and potatoes from Winnipeg. "We need our energy. A hot stew would be just what the doctor ordered."

They ate the crude breakfast and then started building tent huts. The strongest men came together to build the homes for the families. They began dismantling some of the boats that afternoon, utilizing the wood to construct the makeshift huts. Some of the other homes were just hastily erected tents.

They aimed to build as many as possible in the next two weeks because the weather was growing increasingly colder. The snow continued accumulating on the ground as they worked. They were running out of time.

It was physically demanding work. Nath and his father worked all day and night, only managing to get one hut built. "Pabbi, at this rate, we will freeze to death. We need more wood, more tools, more food. What do you think about sending a group to find Sigtryggur Jonasson or maybe someone else closer in Gimli? We will ask them for supplies. I can go with Viktor. We can find others. We will come back with a wagon full of tools, food and wood." Nathanael wiped his forehead with a dirty hand, smearing his face.

His father nodded, "Yes, that is a good idea. Gather five young men together and leave in the morning."

Nathanael put down the axe, wiped his hands on his pants and stomped, in his fur-lined boots, over to a group near the communal firepit. "Hey, Viktor," Nath said, punching his cousin playfully in the shoulder.

Viktor grabbed his shoulder and hugged him. "Nath! You are as strong as a horse!" Viktor shouted. "Wish we had a few horses actually, then we could get more wood, maybe some food. We tried hunting but failed horribly. Do you have any ideas, Nath?"

"Actually, yes, I do," Nath replied. "Viktor, you and I, will travel to Gimli to find someone to help us get more supplies. Let them know the Icelandic settlers are here!"

A round of raucous laughter erupted from the young men.

"But listen!" Nathanael said, waving his hand up. "We need a group of young men to go, about five people would do. We need to bring back tools, food, horses, wagons and some wood. Any volunteers?"

"Yes. I will go," Aron, Nathanael's third cousin, said, raising his hand gruffly.

"I'm in, too," Gunnar said, joining in. He was a young thirteen-year-old boy, but already six feet tall.

"You can count on me, too," Kristjan, Viktor's brother, said, standing to join the group. "When do we leave?"

"We will leave tomorrow morning before sunrise," Nathanael responded. "Bring clothes, rations and warm footwear. I don't think we are that far from Gimli, but just in case."

The men sloshed cans of water together, pretending it was beer. "Let's do this!" They all shouted. Nathanael joined in, they slapped his back and hugged him. He smiled; they were a rambunctious group.

"Ok, I need to get back to finishing the hut," Nathan said. "Viktor, enough breaks, come help me!"

Viktor followed Nath. "Hey, Nath," he said. "Good idea about finding someone in Gimli to help us. You should be in politics."

Nathanael laughed, "Maybe one day! Who knows what the future has in store for us?"

Pabbi stood up as his son approached. "What was that ruckus all about?" he said, laughing.

"Just having fun!" Nath replied. "I have five men together. We will leave before sunrise tomorrow."

"Good job, Nath! You are really good with people," Pabbi stated.

"Funny, that's what Viktor said. He said I should be in politics!" Nathanael pushed the smaller man's shoulder.

"Ah, don't take it as a compliment!" Viktor shouted, alongside the hut. "It might be harder work than building huts." He grunted as he moved the log upright against the cabin, muscling it into place. He was not a large man, several inches shorter than Nath, but he had surprising strength.

Nathanael laughed gruffly. "You might be right!" He grabbed the next log with Viktor and moved it into place. "We need better nails and hammers to secure these logs. The nails we brought are not long enough."

Viktor agreed. "We will make a list tonight."

"Good idea, Viktor," Nathanael made a mental note that his cousin was also smarter than he appeared.

Pabbi joined the young men, picking up a hand saw and started framing the doorway. "We will succeed," the older man said. "I know it. Nothing will stop us."

❦ · · · ❦

As nightfall descended, the forests became a greyish blue in the dark, and the lake changed to entirely black; it was like nothing Nath had seen before. A feeling of accomplishment spread warmly through his body as he settled into his tent. He left the finished hut for the younger boys. Not many women or young children had made it this far, most perished in Kinmount. The few that made it to Manitoba had mostly decided to stay in Winnipeg. The hardships of travelling to a new country had exhausted most of the people's reserves, except the 200 or so people now on Willow Point. Mostly men!

Nathanael loved his cousins and his father, but he was truly missing the women. They fed him better, they hugged him more warmly, and their kisses stirred his loins. He was a virgin, never having the experience of bedding a woman. He felt like an outsider, assuming correctly that many of his cousins had already bedded many women. Nath had kissed a woman in Kinmount, but she was not someone that genuinely made his desires go wild. Oh, sure, his body responded instantly, in fact! But it just didn't feel like love. Her name was Katrin. She stayed behind in Winnipeg with the other women. She was strong and healthy, so she had survived Kinmount, but he was just not that interested in her.

Nathanael stared out of the tent flap at the blackness engulfing the beach. It was breathtakingly beautiful, even in the dark. The snow had stopped earlier in the evening. The skies were so startlingly clear; he could see a million stars! And the moon! It was only a crescent moon, but it rose dimly above the horizon as if floating on the lake. Nath felt a sense of belonging as if the lake was welcoming him home to this strange new land. Shivers raced up his spine; he had a strange feeling of knowing wave over his body. Knowing what he did not know, but it was a warm feeling, a wholesome, positive intuition, that he was on the right path, that everything was going to fall into place. But there was something else. An even more odd feeling that some things would be more challenging than he had ever encountered before. He knew resilience better than anybody! After immigrating to Canada, working on the railroad in Kinmount, starving, he expected things not to be easy. But this feeling was different; it encompassed joy and sorrow in one. This, he did not understand. But what he did know is that he wanted a woman to warm his bed soon, someone who would love him every night and every morning, someone he would have a child with, build a home with, share every passion, hardship and joy with for the rest of his life. He hoped one day he would meet her soon. But where he wondered? Certainly, not in this jungle of men on Willow Point! Maybe he would meet her in Gimli?

He laid back and imagined his woman, a shadowy figure, with long hair, moving her slender body overtop of his. Her hair smelled like flowers and the lake. She slid her hands all over his chest and kissed his mouth eagerly. She suddenly grabs at his pants, pulling them down urgently, to reveal his large erection, bouncing out to greet her. Nathanael moved his hands along his thighs and grasped his penis. He curled his fingers over it, running his hands up and down slowly, trying not to wake his father. Nath tried to focus on keeping his grunt quiet. This was difficult; it sometimes escaped from his mouth before he could stop it.

The shadowy woman moved over top of him, reaching down and grasping his penis. She positioned her hips above his swollen groin, circling her slender hips above him until finally, she lowered herself onto him. The wetness made him slide effortlessly into her. He imagined exploding inside her womb, grunting as his penis twitched with each spurt of fluid, over and over again, until he lay exhausted.

He grunted involuntarily. He tried not too, but he was too aroused. He looked over at his father, the large man groaned and moved onto his side.

Nathanael looked up at the stars with his hand in a wet towel on his abdomen.

Nathanael's eyes drifted closed as he breathed in the beautiful New Iceland air. His breathing slowed as his mind began to wander. It had been a long, physically demanding day. He was exhausted and began to drift into a deep sleep.

A distant rustling sounded in the forest. Then it moved closer.

His eyes bolted open. What was that? It was slight. Maybe a nimble deer? Or a human? Perhaps one of his cousins?

He listened hard.

Another rustle. And a murmur.

He immediately pulled his pants on and rushed out of the tent into the black night. He couldn't see anything! He remembered the words of his mother. Keep your eyes open and wait for the night to adjust your vision. Be patient; it will happen, then you will be able to see the night.

He crouched by the tent and opened his eyes wide, waiting patiently.

Another rustle. Very close! On the east side of the tent.

Finally, his eyes began to adjust, and he could see everything in a bluish-grey world, so different than daytime, but just as beautiful.

Another rustle!

He stood and peered over the tent. Someone was there. "Viktor? Is that you?" Nathanael called out to the darkness.

Silence.

"Hello? Who's there?" Nathanael asked.

Then another rustle, farther away, this time.

He was sure that it was human, not animal. Maybe it was the way it stealthily moved, not bolted like a deer would. He stared into the bluish world of trees, knowing that whoever had visited was gone now, their physical absence noticeable. Strange, he thought.

Who would come at night like that? Jonasson would not, he thought. He would arrive at daylight with horses and wagons. There were no other people in New Iceland as far as he knew, so it must have been an animal. His cousins would have said something about other humans being in the area, he thought.

But something inside of him, intuition, knew deep down that it was human. And that it was cautiously friendly.

Shivers ran up his spine again. He shook it off and crawled back into his fur blanket. Through the slit in the tent flap, he stared up at the expansive New Iceland stars, wondering who the strange human was. Part of him was apprehensive, but the other part was glad. He felt almost happy, actually.

He remembered his last thought before drifting off to sleep. Cautious but happy? Very strange, Nath, very strange, he thought.

CHAPTER 3

Viktor poked his head in the tent at 6 am, "Nath! Get up! Get your belongings together! We are all ready to go to Gimli."

Nathanael groaned and rolled over, grabbing his pants. "Ok, ok, I will get dressed. Give me 5 minutes!"

Nath stuffed extra clothes in his backpack, some dried food, extra gloves and a knife, just in case they were lucky enough to hunt for some food. He tied up his favourite boots, the ones he had brought back from his homeland. They were a unique design, a warm one-piece sheepskin boot with attached woollen socks inside. They were so much better than anything Canadian people wore, Nath thought. He tied it securely around his lower calves, circling the sheepskin laces around and around until he tied a small knot. Nath pulled on a heavy woollen sweater and, lastly, a full fur coat over top. He would stay warm, for sure.

"Nath!" Viktor yelled. "We are leaving without you soon!"

Nathanael opened the tent flap and crawled out. "I'm here! Carry on, let's keep moving forward!" He joined the already moving group to the trees.

They trudged through the forest and snow. Branches snapped, the snow cracking under their heavy footsteps. The normally serene and peaceful forest became alive with rabbits scurrying away and a few deer leaping into the distance.

"Deer!" Gunnar shouted. "We need to learn how to catch them! They are so swift here."

Nathanael nodded his head in agreement. "I think I heard one last night in the bushes very close to my tent." He kept his thoughts about thinking that it was a human, to himself. He was afraid that his peers would think he was crazy. There were no humans here. "We will figure out a way to hunt these swift deer! Maybe we could ask Jonasson or someone for help."

Kristjan waved his hand towards the deer, "Hopefully, it will only be a day trip or two before we reach Gimli. We are running out of food rations quickly at Willow Point."

Gunnar jumped over a log eagerly. "Maybe we could jump on the deer and kill it with a knife!"

Viktor laughed wholeheartedly. "If we could only catch it first!" Viktor said, smiling.

All the men laughed, as another deer jumped out of a nearby bush, sailing effortlessly 10 feet into the air and gracefully landing on the rough gravel horse road in the distance.

Aron chuckled. "He must have heard us scheming to catch him!" Aron said. "Although he is the one that is mocking us with his agility and speed!" He pointed in the distance.

Nath followed his gaze towards the rough horse road. "Maybe we should follow that deer," Nath said. "It looks like he knows this land better than us." He pointed to the road.

"That looks like a horse road. It should be easier to travel than this snowy forest. Let's check it out. It is heading north, towards Gimli."

The group trudged through the snow until they reached the weathered packed road. Nathanael was right; it was much easier to travel on gravel, rather than snow and branches. Someone, or a group of people, had cleared the road, so humans must exist here, Nath thought. The bushes were trimmed, and some fallen trees removed. Maybe the explorers in Gimli had cleared the road? He thought.

As the wind blew more harshly on the open road, Aron tugged and pulled his hat down over his ears. "Colder here," he said. "But, it will propel us to travel faster."

Gunnar bolted ahead and picked up some small stones. "Who made this road?" he said, asking the question everyone was wondering.

"Good question, Gunnar," Viktor answered. "I would speculate that the Gimli explorers created this so they could travel to Winnipeg by horse. There are no other inhabitants here, other than our Icelandic comrades. The only explanation I can think of."

Gunnar pointed out horse droppings up ahead. "Look, it's definitely a horse road!" he laughed boyishly.

Nathanael laughed, "True. That does look like horse dung!"

The group continued walking for quite a distance as the sun rose over the tree line. It was a sunny day, but cold and windy. They immediately curled the coats tighter around their bodies and turned their heads down to face the wind, keeping the swirling wind out of their eyes. They grew silent as time went on. An hour of travelling passed without another word. The only sounds were the crunching of the gravel road beneath their feet.

A rustling in the forest caught Nath's attention. That wasn't a deer. It was the same rustling he heard last night. He didn't want to raise the alarm with his peers, so he said nothing, although, he glanced cautiously towards the forest. He wanted a glimpse of this strange human that was spying on them.

He strained his eyes into the distance, but could only see slightly swaying branches occasionally. Whomever it was, this human was stealthily quiet, almost undetectable. But somehow Nathanael knew, his instincts picking up the presence of this human again. He had a peculiar feeling that the human was somehow interested in him, not the group. Why would this be? Nath thought. Maybe the human thought Nath was the ring leader and was assessing the threat. Possibly, just play it cool, Nath reflected. His instincts told him the human was not immediately threatened, just curious and cautious at the moment. He tried straining his eyes again to get a clear picture of the human, but nothing. It was too sly.

He decided to scare it away. "Hey! Kristjan! Do you have some water? I am getting low," Nath bolstered loudly to his cousin, who was in the front of the line.

"Geez! You scared me, Nath!" Kristjan shouted, handing the water behind to Nath. "Here you go. Don't drink it all!"

Nathanael grabbed the water flask, drank a swig and stared through the sunlit forest. His eye caught a quick, silent movement, a small body, maybe a boy? Nath was excited! It had worked! So, it was a curious Icelandic boy! But where were his parents? A boy surviving in this cold, snowy forest alone? It didn't make sense, he thought. He ran up to Kristjan and handed the flask back, slapping him on the shoulder. "Thanks, cousin!" The forest was unmoving now. The human had scurried away.

Nath shook his head in bewilderment and tried to forget about the stranger in the forest.

"Look!" Gunnar pointed up ahead at a hastily built outpost.

All the men cheered and laughed heartily at the short journey.

"Hopefully, it is an Icelandic cabin!" Aron shouted.

They picked up their pace, walking determinedly towards the cabin. Within 10 minutes, they arrived on the stranger's parcel of land. An older man lumbered out of the front door. "Hallo, strangers!" the older man shouted. "Where do you come from?"

Nathanael laughed warmly. The man was Icelandic! "Hallo, comrade! We come from Iceland! Two hundred fifty of us landed here two days ago!"

The man laughed, rushed up to Nath and hugged him warmly. "You tell the truth? Fellow Icelanders? My prayers have been answered!" The older man looked up to the sky and raised his hands. "My name is Fredrik. We heard the news of an initial explorer group! You are them! My heart lifts! Oh, my God. Come, come, I will feed you all some warm soup!"

The group of men laughed, and they all hugged the older man one by one. "We would very much appreciate that, Fredrik! You have no idea how long we have been travelling. Warm soup is like heaven right now!" Viktor said, gratefully.

They all followed Fredrik to the backyard, where a fire was blazing in an enclosed pit. "I will go get some soup!" Fredrik announced gaily. He went inside the log house and returned with an iron pot, wooden spoon and ingredients for the soup.

He positioned the pot over the fire on a metal grate, cut a few potatoes, some onion, salt, spices and deer meat. The aroma was intoxicating. The men all became very hungry at this delicious smell. They rubbed their hands and pestered the older man, stealing a potato here, a piece of meat there. "You are like my sons, back home!" Fredrik shouted playfully.

The men all laughed. Nathanael helped cut up the deer carcass. "How did you hunt the deer, Fredrik?" Nath asked.

"Oh, an Indian helped me to learn how to hunt the animals here. I traded blankets for these valuable lessons. He also showed me how to make a bow and arrow. That is what I use to hunt deer now."

"Indians?" Nathanael asked.

"Yes," Fredrik nodded. "Originally, we thought nobody else was inhabiting this land, but we noticed them hiding and watching us. They are very cautious but friendly. You will notice them when you get to town. They don't speak good English, but they are trying. They are wary, though, so please don't scare them when you are in town. They have been valuable to us, teaching us about the land."

"Interesting," Nath nodded as he helped stir the soup. "How long before the soup is ready, Fredrik? We all have been living on rations for weeks."

Fredrik waved his hand over the pot. "It should be ready in a half-hour, maybe less." He clapped his hand, and a long-haired mutt dog came running out. "Grover, here," Fredrik said, throwing a deer bone over to the mutt. He laughed as the skinny dog bit into the bone and dragged it to the side of the house. "That dog is my only companionship out here, except for Jonasson and the group in Gimli."

"Do you know Sigtryggur Jonasson?" Viktor exclaimed.

"Oh, yes! Of course, we arrived here together in a group last year. Jonasson is my sister's husband's brother. So, brother in law, I gather. I've known him for ten years! Adventurous fellow! Never stops to think; he just does things before anyone has a chance to complain!" Fredrik chuckled. He looked up at Nath. "You are here to meet with him?"

"Yes, we settled at Willow Point just a few days ago. We need food, horses and supplies to build more homes before the winter comes. It seems like it might be a cold one."

Fredrik hugged Nath roughly. "You will be able to get assistance from Jonasson definitely, but he is in Riverton, much farther away. He has an associate in Gimli named Carl Arnason. I will draw you a map to his house after lunch. I can't go with you; my leg won't make it that distance, unfortunately. But he will help. It's not far, just a 20-minute walk." He pointed northeast towards the lake and then hugged Nath again, laughing. "I'm so glad that you all made it! We were praying that our comrades were going to follow us! You have no idea how happy I am to see fellow Icelanders. Its been a long, lonely year with only a dog, an Indian and a few relatives, that's all."

"Well, we are glad to be here finally," Aron shouted. He raised his water flask and clinked with the other men. "New Iceland!" They all shouted together, slapping each other's shoulders and laughing heartily.

❦ · · · ❦

They walked along the horse road with full warm stomachs. The group was in good spirits. They will succeed; they were determined. The trail veered off to the east; then it ended abruptly at a clearing. Another road, packed with rough stones and broader, travelled straight east. It was a well-travelled road. "This must be Main Street in Gimli," Nath exclaimed.

A few people were seen at the back of some houses, tending fires. Smoke rose, the clouds billowing upwards, contending with the colder air. They continued walking as some people stared, obviously wondering who this group of young men were.

They waved to a few villagers, and some waved back, others just looked at them like they were from a different planet.

Finally, the road ended as it met the lake. The wind blew forcefully in their face, almost daring them to get closer.

As they travelled closer and closer, the magnificent lake spread out before them. Acres of sand sprawled alongside the shoreline to the north, continuing beyond for miles. The view was breathtaking. The men all slowed down their pace, silently taking in the vista. But it was colder here, something about the energy from the lake made Nathanael shiver. It seeped into his bones. It felt like a harsh winter was threatening to come. The waves curled angrily up, stealing the sand with every wake, daring someone to break the riptide current. The lake was a force to be reckoned with, Nath thought. He felt it's furious potential. This area was his home now, and he already loved it, regardless of its angry nature.

Viktor was the first to speak. He pulled his hat over his head, shivering. "The wind is worse here, but, my God, that lake renders me speechless!"

"I agree," Nath replied, among the nods from the other men.

Aron examined the map and pointed north along the shoreline. "Look, I believe that may be Carl's cabin. According to the map, it should be just north from the sand. Let's talk to the man."

There were a few houses along the outer side of the sand, built on more solid clay ground. Some were still under construction. A few people milled about, chatting. There was a group by the lake, pulling a boat back in from the rough waters. A trading house had been set up by Hudson Bay already, although it looked like it was under construction as well. Gimli was just a small settlement, so far. No more than 20 people milled about in the center of town.

Nathanael and his men trudged along the sand, travelling north. It was difficult walking through the sand; it sank under their feet and slowed their movements considerably. They complained gruffly, but it wasn't far, so they continued until they were at Carl's door. The house was painted white, with thick timber planks as siding. It formed a steeple on the roof, making it look like a church. The paint was peeling already, giving it a rough rundown appearance. There was mould already forming on the edges of the roof, the humidity evident.

Nathanael knocked on the thick wooden door. "Carl Arnason? Your fellow countrymen are here!"

They heard boards creaking, and the door creaked open, roughly, as if it didn't open too often.

Carl Arnason was a tall, lanky man, with a large barrel of a chest. His beard was long and greying, hanging down to almost his collarbone. His hands were rough, cut, bleeding in spots and calloused. "Who is it?" he asked hastily.

Nath extended his hand, "We are 250 settlers from Iceland, arrived in Kinmount originally, then we left almost two months ago on a journey to settle here in Gimli, although, we crashed in Willow Point instead. It is where we are settling, for now, trying to build homes before the cold winter is upon us. We have come for your assistance. We need horses, wood, food and longer nails."

Carl laughed heartily, he reached out, grasped Nathanael's hand, hugged him and kissed him on one cheek. "Nath! I was in Kinmount briefly. I remember you! A strong young, competent man; you came with your father, I remember. And who are all these men?"

"Mostly, my cousins," Nath laughed, as he introduced each one to Carl.

Carl shook hands heartily with all the men, then gestured towards Main Street. "Let's go talk to the fishermen. We will see if we can get a letter to the Dominion of Canada. The government had offered some financial assistance in the form of a long-term loan to the Icelandic settlers when we were in Kinmount. We will request the remaining monies right away. Then we will go to the farmers for horses and supplies. I have some money, but it will have to be considered a debt and repaid."

Carl grabbed his fur coat and trudged out of the house. As the door opened, Nath noticed an exotic young woman sitting on a bench in the house, with a swollen tummy, knitting. "Is that your wife?" Nath asked.

"No, her name is Nita. My friend, Tom, met her here in Gimli. She is an Indian." He nodded to the house. "They are both staying with us until they finish building their home. She doesn't come out much, very wary of us settlers. The town folk don't care for her either. The Indians first appeared a few weeks after we arrived. At first, they scared us; we didn't know if they were a danger or not. Over time, they have slowly become friendly but remain very cautious." He pointed towards the fisherman along the shore. "Some fishermen are Indians too. They have become valuable to us; some have taught us how to fish and hunt for deer." Two indigenous people, a man and a woman, gathered by the boat with a few Icelanders, pulling the fishing vessel onto the sand. "We trade clothing and blankets for their assistance. Many of the townsfolk are critical about mingling too much with the Indians. As a result, they have frowned upon my friend marrying an Indian."

"She is beautiful, though," Nath commented.

"Yes, she has a certain way that is so different from others," Carl replied. "So, what is a man to do? There are very few women here! She is pregnant with his child."

"Please send Tom my congratulations!" Nath smacked his back gruffly, as the other men nodded their approval.

"Yes, I will," Carl replied. "We will see how it goes with the town folk. So far, they are very resistant in accepting her into our tight-knit community of friends. So, she stays in the house a lot."

Nathanael was astonished that such thoughts of superiority infected the Icelanders. "That's not fair. Why would they discriminate?"

"Honestly, I don't know. Without the Indians, we may very well have perished." Carl pointed towards the fishermen group. "Garth!" he shouted at one of the men pulling the boat in. Garth looked up; he had a large round weathered face.

"Carl! Who are these groups of men?" Garth responded in a gravelly voice.

"The settlers from Iceland have arrived, comrade!" Carl exclaimed. "They have around 250 in Willow Point!"

"Oh, thank the heavens!" Garth wiped his slimy fish hands on his pants and stuck out his hand for a handshake. "Welcome, my comrades!"

Nath shook his hand roughly, trying to hold his breath from the stench of fish emanating from the man. "Good to meet you, Garth! My name is Nathanael. We are here for supplies and to send a message to the Dominion government."

"He's right; we need to send an urgent letter, Garth." Carl described the contents of the letter they would draft this evening and the urgency of delivering it to the Dominion government in Winnipeg. "We will have it finished by morning. Do you have any boats going to Winnipeg tomorrow?"

Garth squinted into the fierce wind. "This lake is awful right now. Cannot travel on the lake until the wind calms. But the lake is very unpredictable. It could be calm by morning.

Meet me here at 6 am, and we will see what the weather brings. Make sure you talk to Yuri, the farmer, in case you must send the letter by horseback."

"Good!" Carl said, shaking hands with Garth, while the two Indians watched and listened. "Yes, we were on our way to Yuri next to get some supplies for the new settlers."

The woman Indian was staring at Nathanael, curiously. She was small but strong, her hair hidden in her hat so that he couldn't see her hair colour, but he guessed it was black. Nath nodded friendly to her, saying hi with his gestures. Her eyes gleamed with knowing intelligence. She acknowledged his salutation with a curt but friendly nod; then her eyes glanced demurely down.

She was quite pretty, he thought.

Soon, Garth and Carl wrapped up their plans, then Nath, Aron and the men all left, acknowledging the fisherman and his helpers. "Good day, Garth and your Indians! We will talk soon!" Carl shouted.

The native people enthralled Nathanael. They seemed intelligent and responsive, wary, but friendly. The young woman had an exotic look that he had never encountered before. As they walked towards the farmer's property, Nath saw a few more natives, scattered mostly as helpers. "Do they talk English?" Nath asked.

"They talk a bit of English. They come from a tribe called the Swampy Cree. They have their own language, but it is complicated to learn. So, they have been slowly adopting our language," Carl replied. "The woman fisherman is Garth's adopted daughter; her name is Anwaatin. Her father died at an early age. Garth married Anwaatin's mother." Carl looked down as he walked, deep in thought. "Poor girl. But she is also the best fisherman in town." Carl coughed. "Look, we are almost there."

"That must be Yuri now!" Viktor shouted as they approached the farmer's homestead.

Yuri was an elder with a huge Icelandic family; Carl told Nathanael. He was a local now, raised his children in Winnipeg, then moved north to Gimli in search of vast farming property. "Yuri has been here in Gimli the longest. He is a fixture here. But he's also a tough negotiator. You can't get anything for free from him. Nath, you will need to offer him a price on loan for the horses and supplies. Tell him about the Dominion government loan, that will make him more amicable."

Yuri slammed the gate behind him and approached the group. Nath smiled and stuck out his hand. "My name is Nathanael. We are part of a much larger group of Icelanders that have recently settled on Willow Point. We are here to ask for your assistance."

Yuri laughed. "My assistance? Nothing is free in this life or the next." He shook Nathanael's hand. "What kind of assistance are you speaking of?"

"I assure you the money will come from a Dominion of Canada loan. We are not asking for any free handouts. But we do need horses, food, wood and building supplies, long nails preferably. The loan application is being drafted tonight and sent to the Dominion government tomorrow morning. I will show you a copy of it if you wish."

"What's the conditions?" Yuri asked, skeptically.

"The condition is that you sell us the supplies now, with a signed legal agreement. But we cannot pay you until we receive the loan money from the Dominion of Canada."

"So, I give you an interim loan?" Yuri chuckled. "How is this a good deal for me? I lose horses and supplies for a signed document!"

Nath stood straight, tall and robust. He ran his fingers along his thin moustache. "Well, what else would you need from us?"

"Hmm, good question," Yuri deliberated, silently. "You all look like a healthy group of robust men, skinny but strong." He pointed at Aron. "You leave me the strongest man to work on my farm for no wages until your purchase is paid in full. He will be provided with warm meals and shelter at no cost. He will be free to go back to your settlement after your account is settled with me."

The group of men all turned to Aron. He shuffled his feet, clearly deciding the risks and benefits. "I might consider this," he said.

Yuri smiled. "Well, Nath, if your friend agrees, then we have a deal."

"He's my cousin, actually," Nath replied, then turned to address Aron. "Do you want to take the job, Aron? We could find someone else if you don't want to."

"Food and shelter sounds perfect! I will do it." Aron responded, with a grin. "I will stay here at the farm while my cousins return to Willow Point with the horses and supplies. One of the men can return here, bringing my belongings."

Yuri clapped his hands joyfully. "Well, then we have a deal!" Yuri shook hands with Nathanael and Aron. "Come inside! We will draft the purchase agreement!" Yuri slapped Nath on the back and gestured for him to follow into the large farmhouse. "How many horses will you need, son?"

Nathanael laughed. "I was thinking two horses, one for pulling, one for riding. I also need a trailer for the supplies, some saws for the wood, long nails, food and oil paint, if you have some."

"I can provide you with all of this! Welcome to Gimli!" Yuri shouted happily.

CHAPTER 4

The morning sun rose along the horizon of the cold lake. Nathanael had trouble sleeping, he awoke in Carl's quiet house and walked outside to watch the sunrise amidst the crisp autumn weather. It was still breathtakingly beautiful, despite the cold October wind, although the wind had died down since yesterday. He sat on the sand, filtering it through his fingers, loving the way the land felt in his hands. This was his land! And his Pabbi's, and his cousins! He would send for his mother and sisters when he had enough money. They will cultivate the land, hunt and fish, sell their hard labour for cash or trade for goods. It was a dream come true, finally.

Nath felt a wave of gratitude wash over him. It has been tough travelling, wondering where his home was, wondering what the future holds. But now, he could envision the future. It still might be difficult; of that, he did not doubt. This harsh cold start to winter was ominous, although he just knew deep inside his soul that he and his family were going to survive and prosper.

He stared at the beautiful sun, peering over the horizon of gentle waves. The wind blew gently in his face. The coldness stung, but he embraced it. The lake was much calmer today. He loved it actually; luck was on his side. They would most likely be able to send the funds request of the remaining five-thousand-dollar loan to the Dominion today by boat.

A movement caught his eye. Someone was pulling in a larger boat. He stood and used his hand to shelter from the sun. He squinted into the bright rays. It was just one person, pulling in the boat. He strapped his boots on and scurried over to the dock.

"Hey, do you need a hand?" Nathanael shouted as he approached.

A woman's voice lilted into the air, gentle but full of strength. "No, I am okay."

"No, I must! Let me help you," Nathan insisted.

She looked at him stubbornly, shook her head and relented. "If you must."

Nath grabbed the rope and helped pull in the boat, anchoring it along the sand. "Is this the boat that will be taking the letter to the Dominion for us today?"

"It is, yes," she replied. "Sorry for my English. I am still learning."

"You are native to this land?" Nath asked. "How long have you lived here?"

"Forever," she laughed. "Ma and Pa were born here, so was I."

"Interesting," Nath replied. "It is a beautiful land. And a beautiful lake."

"Yes, Nath, it is."

"You remembered my name?"

"Yes, I did. Is that wrong?" she asked.

"No, no. Just a surprise, that's all," Nathan answered.

They both sat down on the sand and quietly watched the sunrise. It was captivating. Every second the sun rose further and further into the sky. It almost appeared as if a line was painted, and the sun was yearning to grow over the line. Nath sifted his fingers through the sand again, looking down. "Gimli is beautiful."

Anwaatin looked at his handsome face. "I love this lake. It is in my blood."

"I heard that you were the best fisherman in town," Nath commented admiringly.

"Yes, Garth says this," Anwaatin nodded. "I have not done much else, though. It is all I know. And some deer hunting." She removed her fisherman's hat and let down her long black hair. Thick wavy hair cascaded down her shoulders, framing her face exotically.

Nathanael's penis twitched briefly. He closed his eyes and looked at the sun, wishing his imminent erection away. "Could you show me how to fish sometime, Anwaatin? I can pay you," he asked.

"You can call me Anwa," she stated. "And yes, I could do that. No need for money, we can work something out."

"Thank you," Nathanael replied. "It is much appreciated."

They sat silently in the sand, watching the sunrise, both content with the silence, both appreciating the magnificent scope of the lake. The breeze lifted Anwa's hair several times and her smell wafted over to him; she smelled wonderfully musky.

Anwa pointed to the south. "You landed on Willow Point? You and many more Icelanders?"

"Yes," Nath replied. "There are two hundred and fifty of us at Willow Point."

"Many deer over there," Anwa stated.

"Yes!" Nath exclaimed. "We saw lots of deer jumping out on our way here. I wish we could catch some. That would be excellent meat."

"I can show you how to hunt the deer," Anwa offered. "My family has been eating deer meat for centuries. We use bow and arrows for the deer."

"I would love that." Nathanael looked at this small strong woman and was amazed. She knew how to fish and hunt this land better than anyone, and she was half the size of some of his Icelandic cousins. "I think that's pretty amazing that you are so experienced in fishing and hunting, Anwa. It is rare for a woman to know such things."

Anwa looked up; her large brown eyes shone with achievement. "Thank you, Nath. No one has ever said anything like that to me before."

"No?" Nath replied. "Well, I can't see why not. You are resilient, resourceful and also very beautiful. I would think every man would notice."

Anwa's face lit up in the most beautiful smile he had ever seen. Nath smiled back. She smiled more, and so did he. Then they broke out laughing. It was silly, but oh my, it felt good, Nath thought. He felt very comfortable with this woman. It was almost strange because he could sit and watch the sunset in silence with her, be silly with her and call her beautiful, without even once being a bit nervous.

"Thank you. I don't really think I am beautiful. I think I am wilder woman than some men like," Anwa replied, her thick native accent slurring her words.

"Oh no, you have that wrong, men like wild!" Nath said, laughing. "All men like a bit of a wild woman."

Anwa burst into laughter again. She laughed so hard that tears began to well in her eyes. Nath grabbed her waist and tried soothing her, although he started laughing too. Anwa's hand fluttered down onto his lap as he held onto her waist. They both took deep breaths, trying to calm down the laughter bubbling up inside of them. Then they burst into laughter again. They forgot what they were even laughing about all along! It was so silly! She loved the way this man made her feel, Anwa thought. It was like she had nothing to hide from him. It was indeed a wonderful feeling.

Nath's hand moved up and down her back, trying to soothe the laughing fit out of her. Finally, she calmed down and started breathing heavy but normal. Nath sensed something; he was not sure what, but it felt like he should kiss her. She looked up, and their eyes locked. The heat was building between their bodies at an amazing rate. Her hand stayed firmly on his leg. Nath felt his head swim, and his penis hardened instantly. Hopefully, she doesn't notice, he thought. Right at that moment, as if on cue, she looked down. Yes, she just noticed, Nath thought. He pulled her body a tiny bit closer. He needed to kiss this woman; something was pulling him to her with an incredible energy that he couldn't describe. He lifted his other hand to her chin. She was breathing heavily.

"Anwa! Where are you?" Garth's voice boomed over the beach.

She jumped up as if stung by a scorpion. "Oh my, that is Garth, my stepdad! I must go help get the boat ready!" She bolted and ran away across the sand towards the dock. She turned back once and waved at Nath. "It was so nice meeting you, Nath!"

Nath stood, dumbfounded, watching her run away, feeling like someone had just taken away his favourite toy. He waved back to the disappearing Anwa, Miss Wild Woman, her beautiful long hair flowing behind her. "Yes! It was a pleasure meeting you as well, Anwa!" His hand floated in the air, wishing he could pull her back here to where they were and finish what had happened. What had happened, he thought? He was going to kiss her, that's what!

He stood rooted to the sand for several moments, willing his erection to go away. It persisted valiantly, so he slumped down and sat in the sand. He watched the sun while his erection softened. Wow, he thought, he really likes this woman! It was the first time he had experienced such a thing, was it called chemistry? Or just raw attraction. He didn't know, but whatever it was, it felt amazing, he felt like he was floating! He smiled, bent his knees, wiped the sand from his pants and began to walk back to the house. His heart lifted, and he felt like his steps were somehow lighter. In no time, he reached Carl's home. He had been running! He didn't even realize it! He felt so happy.

He burst into the cottage, and all the men turned around, they were packing up their things to get ready for the day trip back to Willow Point.

Aron looked up from his bag. "Nath! You look so happy! Why are you smiling like that? What happened?"

Nath ran his fingers through his hair and looked down. He didn't realize that he had a permanent grin on his face. "Nothing. I just chatted with the fishermen. The boat is getting ready! We have our wish; the loan documents are going to be delivered this morning! Let's get ready!" Nath said excitedly.

Gunnar and Kristjan had their packs on the quickest and were at the door. Aron and Carl followed.

Gunnar looked at Nath, "Hey, are you okay, Nath? You look flushed."

"Yes, I am fine. I was running across the sand. The sun was beautiful, rising over the lake this morning. I stopped and met with the fishermen. They are getting everything ready for us. Who will deliver the letter?"

"I will," Carl replied.

"Thank you so much, Carl!" Kristjan replied.

"No trouble at all. I know where to go. I would do this, ten times over, for my fellow countrymen."

They packed up and left the house. By the time they had arrived at the wharf, Anwa was already inside the boat, clearly busy getting the vessel ready for the trip. Their eyes met once, briefly, but she looked away as if she was embarrassed. This confused Nathanael. He was sure that she had wanted to kiss him. Everything began to happen quickly; before they knew it, Carl was on the boat, and Anwa was steering it southward down the lake, disappearing into the horizon of the lake with the letter.

"Nath!" Aron slapped him on the shoulder. "Wake up, let's go! We have a whole lot of supplies to pick up this morning! And I have my first job to go to." Aron laughed heartily.

Nath followed the group down Main Street towards Yuri's farm. His head still felt light, like something important just happened, something that he would not forget for a million years.

The horse road was rough, even for the horses. The trailer was overloaded with supplies, almost too heavy for one horse. The other horse was a riding horse Kristjan rode this one, while Gunnar ran up ahead, and Nathanael carried extra carts of food. They were halfway back to Willow Point. The weather was holding up, so they were all glad that the loan papers would reach the government safely today. Travelling by boat was so much faster, they all agreed.

They travelled back the same way they had come, dropping Aron off at Yuri's farm and then even stopping by Fredrik's house and wishing him well. The older man was glad to see them, hugging and praising them on a job well done. Deer occasionally darted through the bushes, although Nath did not see the native boy in the bushes on the way back. The trip back was short. They knew where they were going, and the horses quickened everyone's pace to keep up.

The group reached the Willow Point settlement by noon. A crowd ran up to them, surprising them all. Many of the older men were very pleased with Nath, Viktor and the group.

Pabbi came over, hugged and kissed his son. "Nath. I heard Viktor telling his family that you had applied for the remainder of the five-thousand-dollar loan from the government. That's wonderful news! You must tell me all of the details later tonight." Pabbi started unloading the trailer and hauling materials over to the building sites. "We need to start building more houses this afternoon. This weather may not hold. We must take advantage of it while we can. Jonasson had warned that the winters could be tough here."

Fifty men began systemically unloading building materials, food and supplies from the trailer. Other men started building. The sound of hammers filled the beautiful lakeside settlement. Nath, Viktor, Gunnar, Kristjan and Pabbi all worked together on one house. Several other groups worked on other cabins.

After several hours, Nath noticed his Pabbi sweating and losing energy. "Pabbi! Rest and have some food! We brought some deer soup from our old friend Fredrik. He insisted that you have some." Nath warmed the soup over the fire in an iron pot. "Pabbi, you must not overexert yourself. Your health is important to us."

"You sound like your mother. I miss my Margret, son. She is in my thoughts every day now." Pabbi drank a long swallow of weak beer. "I look forward to the day when we can send for them, and the rest of our family can join us here in New Iceland."

"It will be soon, Pabbi, soon. I miss Mamma too. I miss my sisters too." Nath sipped a weak beer as well. "Actually, I miss all females!" he laughed. "It is somehow so much warmer with women around. And the food is better!" The younger men overheard the conversation and laughed heartily. Nath chuckled and thought about telling his Pabbi about meeting Anwa early this morning. He was just about to say something when Pabbi interrupted him.

"Nathanael, I have some concerns that there may be other inhabitants here on Willow Point. I noticed someone in the bushes when you left. Did you see this?"

Something told Nathanael to keep this a secret. "No, I did not."

Viktor sat down by the fire. "There are Indians in Gimli, Pabbi. They are native to this land. They will teach us fishing and maybe even hunting someday. Maybe that was who you saw in the bushes. We didn't notice anything on our travels, though."

"I thought so," Pabbi announced, stroking his beard. "Are they dangerous? You must keep your distance from such folk, Nath."

"No, they are not dangerous, Pabbi," Nath replied, unsettled that his Pabbi showed disdain over a people that he had not even met yet. "They are wary and cautious, but they have great skills from living on this land for hundreds of years. We can learn much from them."

"Still," Pabbi announced firmly. "I would prefer that we just use them for what we need and not become friends with such folk."

Nathanael's heart sank. He really liked Anwa. She brightened his day this morning with her laughter, her smell and her friendliness. She was not wary and cautious around him. And she was certainly not someone that he wanted to distance himself from because his father wished it so.

Pabbi squinted at his son, picking up on Nathanael's change in demeanour. "What is it, Nath?"

"Nothing, Pabbi," Nathanael countered. "I just don't feel these natives are bad people. We should not fear them. We should learn from them and share the land with them."

Pabbi bolted upright. "No!" His remaining beer toppled on the ground. Pabbi's face turned slightly red, and you could feel the anger emitting from him. "This is our New Iceland! We are conquering this land. It is ours. Even the Dominion thinks so! They are loaning us money. They agree to name it New Iceland. These natives will not share it with us. That's preposterous! This land is ours!"

Viktor and Nath fell silent. They sipped the rest of their beers and stirred the soup, not speaking at all for several minutes. Pabbi sat down wearily, obviously overexerted from his outburst. Finally, Nath grabbed his father a bowl, poured some soup into it and handed it to him. "Eat your soup, Pabbi. It's warm and tasty."

"Thank you," Pabbi said, taking the bowl and eating the soup in silence.

Nath looked at Viktor and stood. "Pabbi, we are going to get back to work. Please take a break. The rest of the men and I will finish what we can today."

"Ok, son," Pabbi replied.

Viktor nudged Nath on the way back to the partially built cabins. "What do you think that was all about?"

"Old people just think that way, I suppose. I am not going to worry about it too much," Nathanael replied.

"Alright, then. Let's get back to work." Viktor handed Nath a hammer and grabbed several nails for himself. He looked around at the cabins, some missing roofs, some missing doors, but all were very close to being finished. There were eight cabins in total now, five partially built, and the other three completed first upon landing; the rest were mostly tents with wood stakes for stability. "I want to get some of these cabins built before nightfall! Let's get to it!" Viktor waved his arms across the lakeside at the cabins, gesturing at the expanding community. "We have New Iceland to build!"

Nathanael joined the group. They worked continuously, running very late into the evening, until the night cascaded over the land, blanketing everything with black darkness.

CHAPTER 5

They had built almost twenty cottages in total over the past week. Nathanael awoke stiff and hungry; he had been working relentlessly. Only a few of the homes were complete cabins. Most were makeshift tent cabins, nothing more than tents with some walls, roofs and tent flaps, but they were complete, and the cabins would help them survive through the winter.

Carl had arrived back during the week and travelled to the settlement himself to meet everybody. He had announced the good news that the Dominion of Canada had granted the loan. The funds would arrive within the week. Some of the settlers left to Gimli with Carl the next day, accepting jobs in the town and several others agreed to move to Gimli once the loan proceeds arrived to help build the community. Some settlers also chose to build homes closer to Gimli, away from the cold wind. Some were considering moving to Winnipeg.

Less than 50 people now inhabited Willow Point, but it was still a strong community, everyone helping everyone.

That number would dwindle once the loan proceeds arrived. Many people spoke of moving to Gimli. Nath didn't care, as long as he was near the lake, the smells, everything. It filled him with an awe-inspiring feeling like he had some greater purpose in life; like the wind, sea and sand all formed a part of who he truly was.

Nathanael grabbed his weak beer and walked along the sand, waving at his Pabbi. "I'm going for a hike along the beaches. I will be back!"

The sun was bright in the early morning, but it was cold. He wrapped his fur coat around him and shuffled his feet in the sand, feeling the frigid wind bite at his nose. The cold didn't matter to him. It was his New Iceland, and he loved it with a passion that he couldn't describe. It filled him with a definite purpose and clarity that he truly loved.

He stopped and turned to admire the lake. It was a rare calm day. The lake looked like glass; only small ripples broke its surface. The gentle lapping was the only sound he heard, except for the occasional eagle. He was amazed at the beauty of it all.

He noticed a slight movement at the edge of a cluster of rocks leading out into the water. A line flew out. Then it was slowly, but expertly, pulled back in. It was a fisherman's line. And it was Anwa on the rocks.

His heart thumped in his chest, and his palms began to sweat. Interesting, Nath thought that he would have such a physical response to this woman.

He controlled his movements deliberately. He wanted to run over to her, hug her and say hi, but he knew that was inappropriate and would most probably scare her away. So, he slowed his footsteps and sauntered over very casually.

She turned her head and waved with a friendly nod, but her eyes looked deeply into his, just for the briefest of moments.

"Nath! Hi! Come, I can show you some fishing." She patted the seat beside her, a large flat rock. "Be careful; the rocks can be slippery."

Nathan walked onto the rocks, as she looked up and their eyes locked briefly once again. "Hi, Anwa," he said. "It is very nice meeting you again. I wanted to thank you for taking Carl to Winnipeg. With this loan, we can prosper."

"No problem at all, Nath. It was my pleasure. Now sit." She patted the rock again.

He took the offered seat and felt her warmth emanate from her. He caught a drift of that musky woman smell again. It made him smile.

"What are you smiling about?" Anwa laughed.

"Nothing, nothing," Nath replied. "Show me how to catch these elusive lake fish."

"The best fish here are called pickerel. We will try to catch some today." She stood and handed him the handmade rod. "Okay, you hold it like this." She gripped his hands around the rough handle. Her sensual electricity shot through his hands and sent warm sensations throughout his body. He wanted to hug her and pull her close. But he did nothing of the sort. He followed her hands and held the fishing rod as instructed. He watched her eyes light up as she spoke of where to catch the fish, which fish are the best tasting, what each one looks like, some roundish, some long, and what time of day is best.

"We usually use nets, but I have devised these rods that work well. Early morning is best around these rocks. The lake is so calm in the mornings and the fish venture closer to shore in the early dawn," she commented, motioning with her hands as if encompassing the entire lake.

"You love this," he stated simply.

"Yes, I do," she replied. "The lake is in my blood. I was born here on this land, and I feel part of the sea, too." Her brown eyes sparkled with knowledge and passion.

"I have a question," Nath asked. "What does your name mean? Anwaatin, right?"

"Yes, my full name is Anwaatin. It means *it is calm*."

"That is very sweet," he replied.

"And your name?" she asked.

"Nathanael means *he gave*," he replied.

"Interesting, so as in a giving person?"

"Yes."

She smiled sweetly.

He wanted to kiss her.

She immediately looked away shyly.

"Why do you do that?" he asked.

"Do what?"

"Run away, look away, when I want to kiss you," he replied.

She smiled and looked down nervously. "Because I have never kissed a man before," she replied. She darted a glance at him, then looked down again. "And I like you, Nath," she stammered.

Nathanael put the rod in his right hand and fluttered his fingers towards her chin. "You would be alright if I kissed you then," he politely suggested.

"Yes," she said, still looking down shyly.

He lifted her chin. "You have beautiful eyes," he said. "There's a smouldering passion buried deep within them. It's mesmerizing."

She looked up at him, her eyes locking onto his. And without another word, their lips met. She was moist and soft, her lips full and gentle. She instinctively opened her mouth, and Nath fluttered his tongue at her opening. He kissed her lips softly again, then darted his tongue into her mouth briefly, tasting her honey mouth. He felt his penis harden quickly and uncomfortably. He shifted to the side, trying to adjust himself.

She felt his uncomfortableness and broke the kiss. She looked down and saw the lump in his pants. "Does it hurt?" she asked.

He laughed, "No, it doesn't hurt, just uncomfortable."

"Why does it do this when you get close to me?"

"Because I have a gorgeous woman in my arms and my body notices," he replied, chuckling.

"Why does your body do this?"

He grinned, "Hmm, I'm not sure how to answer that in a gentlemanly way."

"Please answer. I won't be offended."

"Well, a man's penis hardens to get ready for sex. I believe it can't enter a woman otherwise. Although, I'm not 100% certain on that," Nath answered.

"Why are you not certain?" she asked.

"Because I have not experienced sex yet," he replied.

"Oh," she paused. "I have never had sex either," she said. Anwa gazed across the lake, thoughtfully. "Although, I've dreamed of having sex in the bushes many times."

His penis hardened fully. His head felt light. Then the fishing rod tugged in his right hand. He was momentarily stunned, not sure what was going on.

"Oh, you've caught a fish!" she shouted excitedly. "You reel it in this way. It's a very crude homemade rod." She showed him how to pull the line in as quickly as possible.

The water started splashing, and the fish appeared suddenly, struggling to escape. "Watch. You pick up the fish like this. Hook your thumb strongly in its mouth; it will stop fighting this way." She picked up the fish, took the hook out and handed it to him, showing him how to hook his thumb.

"Like this?" he asked, holding the fish out for her to inspect.

"Yes!" she smiled. "That's perfect. Now I will show you how to kill it and take the guts out."

"Oh, this I know, Anwa. I am from Iceland, remember!" He handled the fish until it was relatively still and then banged the small bludgeon tool, from her fishing box, onto its head. He then pulled a knife from his pocket and sliced down the fish's body, gutting it. "Will you eat it with me?"

"I would if we could make a fire right here." she smiled sadly. "But I don't think I can go to your camp home with you."

"Why?" he asked.

"Because many white men do not like native land people. Sometimes, they are very mean."

His eyes grew sad. "You may be right." He looked up briefly while he was gutting the fish. "I was hoping that I could convince you to spend more time with me. You could join me to eat this fish. I am good at cooking fish. My mamma taught me."

"I truly wish I could, Nath," she smiled sadly. "My mother taught me to be very careful around white men, especially fifty of them." Anwa started packing up her fishing box. She left the handmade fishing rod, pushing it slightly towards him. "A gift for you."

"Thank you, Anwa," Nath said, cleaning his hands in the lake water, then patting them on his pants. "Before you go, Anwa, I would like a hug. It's customary to hug people farewell in my country."

"Alright," she responded warmly, moving very close to him.

He smelled her musk again. It filled his head with a sensation he could not describe. Maybe, it was the lust sensation he had heard about from his friends. She moved her supple small body even closer until her large round breasts were touching his lower chest. She was almost a foot shorter than him, so he had to bend over to hug her. When he pulled her closer, his body lit up like it was on fire. Her breasts squished against his chest as his hands reached over her shoulders, enveloping her hair, her soft arms and head rested naturally on his chest, and his chin followed by resting on her head. Warmth spread rapidly throughout his body, energizing his emotions, his thoughts and his penis. It stiffened unbelievably hard, like steel.

She moved her face upwards and stared at his lips, amazed by their fullness. He kissed her sweet mouth again, tasting her. He darted his tongue inside again briefly, enjoying her honey sweetness. He held his hands across her shoulders still, keeping her body close to him. He was surprised when she began sucking on his lower lip. He groaned.

"Mmm, did that feel good?" she murmured.

"Yeah," he moaned.

"Okay, I will do that again," she grinned, then sucked on his bottom lip again, feeling his body shudder in her grasp. "Interesting," she smiled and then continued kissing him. She moved a small hand over his penis. "Can I feel it?"

"Yeah," Nath replied simply. He began to get a curious brain fog like he wasn't sure what words to say anymore.

Her small hand landed on his groin. Through his pants, she felt his penis, running her fingers curiously over the hard, long ridge. "Hmm, interesting," she commented. "Is it always this big?"

He chuckled, "No."

She curled her fingers around his penis and grabbed it lightly. Nath stiffened.

"Oh? Did I do something wrong?" she asked.

"No, you did nothing wrong," Nath said, as he pulled away a bit. "But I can't do that for very long. I will lose control."

"Oh? Okay, I won't grab it."

"Yeah," Nath chuckled. "No grabbing, not yet anyway."

"Alright," she replied, pulling away. She kissed his mouth again, briefly, pecking his mouth with little kisses. "I should go. You look hungry. Eat that fish and catch some more in the morning."

He released her from the embrace and felt a drift of cold air where her body was previously. She turned and bent over her fishing box, packing everything up.

She stood and turned to him. "I had a very wonderful time fishing with you, Nath. You are a very warm, gentle man."

"I would like to see you again, Anwa," he asked gently.

"Yes, I can show you where to hunt for deer next time," she smiled warmly.

"I would love that," Nath replied.

"Ok, well, see you later then," she smiled and picked up her fishing box, walking away briskly, with a little spring in her gate.

Nath watched her walk away into the forest. She turned back and waved happily. "Bye, Nathanael!"

He smiled broadly, waving back enthusiastically. "Bye, bye, Anwa!"

CHAPTER 6

Nath, Pabbi and Viktor ate fish for an entire week. They were all famished. Pabbi was quickly becoming impressed by his son's fishing and social skills. Nath began showing all the other fishermen what Anwa had taught him. Viktor, Gunnar and Kristjan learned how to make the fisherman's poles and string, assembling over thirty fishing rods in just a week.

Some settlers started building two larger boats for fishing as well. They found spots several areas farther out in the lake that had regular schools of fish. Pickerel, carp, whitefish and goldeye were plentiful. So much so, that some men began building a fishing hut closer to Gimli for trading and selling the fish. It was a promising business for the enterprising Icelanders.

The loan proceeds arrived on the following Monday in early November. The settlers were quite happy; everything was falling into place. Another large group decided to move to Gimli, leaving only twenty people at Willow Point. Kristjan and Viktor had travelled back to Gimli, collected the funds and paid Yuri in full. Aron was offered a permanent job at the farm, that he accepted happily, quite content to be fed daily, although he also had another reason to stay. There were rumours that Aron had been love bitten and was quite infatuated with Yuri's daughter, Julia. The men at Willow Point were not surprised. Many of the Gimli settlers were young, hardy, strong men, mostly under the age of twenty and single Icelandic females were scarce, so the men were eager to find mates.

The explorers were left with several thousand dollars from the loan proceeds. They devoted small amounts to develop the fishing industry and housing. The settlers began to break up into groups of fishermen and farmers. It was a promising start. The remaining funds were held in a community account for future use.

Nathanael stared at the fire, late at night, his tummy full after a large fish dinner. He drank weak beer with Viktor and sat beside his weary father. Pabbi had been busy building the boats and was showing his age. His beard had begun to grey, and his shoulders slumped forward.

"Pabbi," Nath said. "You should rest early tonight. You look tired."

"I think I will," Pabbi replied, running his hands through his long hair.

"We should cut your hair tomorrow. You are looking like a bushman without Mamma," Nath chuckled.

"That might be a good idea," Viktor replied, laughing.

Pabbi nodded grimly, "Yes, that will be fine." A dark look clouded his face.

"What's wrong?" Nath asked.

"Nothing wrong, son," Pabbi said seriously. "Just concerned about this Anwa woman you talk about so often to the other men. Have you seen her since the fishing lesson?"

"No, I haven't, Pabbi," Nathanael replied, his brow furrowing. "But, I am seeing her tomorrow to learn how to catch the deer."

"We can catch the deer with bullets, now that we have the funds," Pabbi argued.

Viktor agreed. "He's right. We will be getting a few guns in the next week for hunting."

"I would like to learn with arrows instead," Nath replied, stubbornly.

"You just want to spend time with this woman, that's all. You could care less about the deer and arrows," Pabbi argued.

"Yes, you're right," Nath stated. "I do want to see Anwa again. But I also want to learn how arrows work. She was an immense help with the fishing. You cannot deny that."

"True about the fishing," Pabbi replied stonily.

A heavy silence grew around the firepit.

After several minutes, Pabbi stood. "I'm going to bed," he said. He pointed a sharp finger at Nath. "I don't want you seeing Anwa anymore. She is Indian. She is not our kind. Stay away from her."

Nath locked eyes with Pabbi. "I'm not a child."

"You are Icelandic! Not Indian!" Pabbi shouted. "Don't be a fool! End of discussion!" With that, Pabbi turned and retired to the family cabin they shared.

Nath was furious. His blood rose into his head, and his temples throbbed.

Viktor stood. "I'm going to go to bed also. I like Anwa, but as Pabbi said, she's not our kind. It might be better to choose a different mate, if not just for the elders."

"What?" Nath shouted. "I can't believe that I hear this from you as well!"

"Hey, hey," Viktor replied, his hands up in surrender. "I was just saying, that's all. In the end, you will do what you want. Calm down." Viktor stood, putting his hand on Nath's shoulder. "Goodnight, Nath."

Nathanael seethed. He wanted to hit something, how dare Pabbi tell him whom he can see and whom he can't see. Anwa was right; there was a strong racist streak within the older Icelanders.

He drank the rest of his beer and grabbed another. No one will stop him from hunting with Anwa tomorrow, he thought. Not his friends and not Pabbi, either. He stomped to the lake, too angry to fall asleep in the same cabin as Pabbi.

The winds were blowing strong from the north, and light snow was beginning to fall, carpeting the sandy beach with a light blanket of white. He gulped the second beer down and threw it in the bushes angrily.

He heard a rustle.

It was dark. He squinted his eyes, straining to see the figure in the bushes. Was it the Indian boy again? He did not care! "Who is it?" Nathanael shouted at the bushes. "Make yourself known!"

Another rustle sounded farther away.

Nathanael rushed into the bushes, still reeling from the angry discussion with Pabbi. He crashed into the branches blindly, ripping his light coat and scratching his arms. He didn't catch anyone in the bush; the boy had gone already, probably far away in the shrubs now. He cursed and rushed back out onto the sand, frustrated and unsteady. Whoever it was in the bushes, he will find out who it was and scare the boy into never spying again. Nath lost his balance and fell back, kneeling in the brush. He felt frustrated and oddly defeated. He would not be told what to do by anyone. He crawled out of the bushes and brushed himself off. He felt a bit unsteady.

Nathanael stumbled. Slightly drunk with alcohol, he found his way back to the cabin. He disrobed, laid down in bed and masturbated himself to sleep.

❧ ··· ❧

Morning came early, the men all shouting orders to each other. Doors were slamming, the horses whinnying, and teams of men were grabbing shovels.

Kristjan rose angrily. "What is all the commotion about?" he shouted back, pulling on his pants and coat, then banging the door open.

The entire camp was covered in a thick blanket of snow. The wind howled throughout the settlement, throwing gusts of snow into the men's eyes. It was a chaotic scene as several men were trying to shovel snow with garden shovels, making paths and clearing the roads.

"What the heck in God's name?" Kristjan mumbled.

"It's cold, Kristjan!" shouted Viktor. "The temperature dropped drastically overnight. Hurry, get dressed and start helping to clear this darn snow!"

"For Christ's sake!" Kristjan cursed, pulling on his gloves and hat, and shuffled into the almost knee-deep snow. "It must have snowed twelve inches!"

"Tell me about it!" Viktor shouted back. "Did anyone wake Nath?" He stomped towards Nath and Pabbi's cabin.

The door flung open, and a dishevelled Pabbi stood confused.

"Wake Nathanael!" Kristjan shouted. "We need help with this snow!"

"Ok, ok," Pabbi turned and shouted inside, muffled by the cabin walls. "Nathanael! It's the first snowfall of winter! The men need your help! Wake up!"

❧ ⋯ ❧

Nathanael, his cousins and twenty other village men shovelled the roads and paths for several hours that morning. It was the heaviest snowfall the villagers had ever seen, even in Iceland. The cold was something they had been expecting, but they were not prepared for the sudden heavy snowfall. Nathanael pondered constructing a snowplow. He put together pieces of wood that the horses would pull to help with any future snowfalls. They tested it briefly, and it worked. He was praised for his ingenuity by the group of men. They ate breakfast heartily, relaxed and drank beer until near noon.

He looked at the sun and suddenly realized that he had forgotten all about his hunting lesson with Anwa. He stood as the men relaxed around the fire. "I will be back soon, men."

He charged out towards the road, pulling his fur hat over his head and stomped through the snow. They had agreed to meet at the main highway road. He stood straight, looking around. Nothing. Silence.

Darn it, he thought. He had missed her. She must have thought he was not interested anymore and left.

"Anwa!" he shouted into the bushes.

His heart fell with disappointment. Damn snow! He was too late.

"Nathanael. I'm here. On the west side of the road," she shouted back from the forest.

His heart leapt. He ran across the road to the line of trees and met her on the west side. "Sorry, I am late! The first heavy snowfall! We had to shovel our way out! Does it always snow heavily like this?"

Anwa stood proudly in a large deerskin coat and a fur hat. "Yes, we usually get a lot of snow. Sometimes 60 inches on the ground in a bad winter."

Nathanael hugged her warmly. "You look beautiful. How have you been, Anwa?" he said in her ear while hugging her tight.

She turned her head into his shoulder. "Cold," she chuckled. She didn't move to break the embrace, choosing to cuddle closer into his chest. The warmth they created together wrapped around them, enveloping them both in a loving embrace. It was comfortable, serene and somehow necessary. Their bodies moulded into each other so easily, almost as if they fit so perfectly together, no questions asked, like a missing puzzle piece.

"I missed you," Nath mumbled.

Tingles ran up Anwa's spine, his words scurrying throughout her body, lifting her spirits. She melted in his arms as her nose buried into his chest. She had missed him too, although she debated whether to tell him. She didn't want to appear too eager.

"I was thinking that you weren't going to come," she said instead. "I was going to leave. I was feeling disappointed."

"I'm glad you waited," he replied. Nath pulled her chin up and looked into her eyes. "Thank you." He kissed her lips slowly, relishing in her softness. She opened her mouth and let his tongue explore her. Her body responded instantly. "Mmm," she murmured.

Nathanael instinctively continued the tongue dances inside her mouth. She murmured again. His hands reached around her, trailing lightly over her lower back. He pressed into her lower back, holding her tighter, wishing he could feel her buttocks, but knowing that it was not a gentlemanly thing to do. She groaned.

His penis hardened fully, yearning to enter her. His head felt dizzy.

She broke the kiss.

They both looked at each other, up close and intimate. Her lips were swollen and red. She was panting lightly. Nath's lips were full and wet. "We are here to hunt deer," she stated breathlessly.

"Yes," Nath replied, his breathing heavy. "Just one more kiss, then we will hunt deer with arrows."

"Alright," she relented easily.

Nath cupped her chin and leaned forward. "I love kissing your lips, feels like heaven," he said.

Her body tingled with electric impulses as his lips joined hers again. His hot tongue explored her mouth. Anwa felt like she was melting away in his arms. She sucked on his lower lip, and he groaned. His lips were hot and hungry, and his urgent hands were moving all over her back. Her hunting pants were growing moist in between her legs.

Anwa broke the kiss again.

"We must hunt now," she stated but making no move to come out of his embrace.

Nath looked down at her, then kissed her on the top of her head. "Alright, alright," he relented. "We will hunt. Where are the arrows?"

She motioned towards the treeline. "They are in the bag. Over there."

"Okay, let's go get them," Nath released one arm and kept the other around her waist, holding her close.

Anwa felt so wonderful, almost as if this handsome Icelander protected her. A small possession that felt so absolutely warming and comforting. She left her hand along his waist as well, and they both walked waist-to-waist back to the treeline.

When they arrived, he released her. An immediate cold rush of air assaulted his torso. Strange effect that this woman has on me, Nath thought.

She ruffled through the bag and pulled out a long-arced wood item with a strong elastic-like string that was attaching the two ends. She pulled the string back with a long white-feathered arrow. She showed him how to draw the arrow into the bow, then she aimed it towards a nearby tree and released the arrow. It shot through the crisp winter air with a whistle and banged solidly into the trunk of the tree. She handed him the bow and a different arrow. She moved his hands into the correct positions and stood back, allowing him to shoot. She explained to him the arc of an arrow and how to aim at a target. Nathanael pulled back, aimed, and the arrow whistled into the same tree trunk. They both ran to the tree.

"Very impressive," Nath exclaimed, as he pulled the arrow out. He inspected the pointed end. It was sharp, very sharp. "Do you sharpen the ends?"

"Yes, we do," she replied. "We have sharpening tools in our tribe for this purpose."

"You are very resourceful," he commented.

"We have no choice. It is our way of life. To continue to live, we must do certain things," she replied. "As a settler, you must understand this. No?"

"Yes, I understand this greatly, Anwa," Nath replied. "Our group had to go through many hardships to get here. And we wouldn't even be here if our Iceland didn't erupt in ashes."

"Ashes?" she inquired.

"Mt Askja is a volcano," he replied. "It erupted in January of this year, ruining many crops and herds of animals. It continued to erupt and forced many of our people to flee. My mamma is still in Iceland. Pabbi says he will return to get her and my sisters when we are settled, next summer."

"You must miss your family," she said.

"Yes, I do. My Pabbi's here, but I miss my mamma and the women. The food is better, the houses are cleaner, and the hugs are warmer with women in my life."

She tiptoed up, reached and kissed him on the lips suddenly.

She stepped back, looking at him. "You are a sweetheart, Nathanael." She turned and started hiking through the snow. "Come, I will show you where the deer gather."

He followed her with a grin on his face and a spring in his step. They hiked through the heavy snow until they came up to a slight clearing. She turned back and pressed her two fingers against her lips. "Shhh."

He was silent.

She pointed.

A herd of deer huddled quietly near the clearing. One adolescent buck, four does, and two fawns gathered together to keep warm. It was eerily silent. The wind was calm in the small meadow, sheltered on all sides by trees.

Anwa bent towards his ear and whispered. "We only hunt males in the winter; the females need to stay nourished to get pregnant in the spring. Some might be pregnant already."

She stretched the bow back with the arrow and motioned to Nath, handing him the bow and arrow to shoot. She whispered, "Aim for the young male deer. Aim for just behind his front hip joint; there is his heart."

"I might miss," Nath whispered back.

"No, you won't, Nath," Anwa smiled. "You have good aim. Shoot."

Nath lined up the sights of the arrow onto the deer and adjusted for the arc; then let go of the arrow. It whistled and sliced through the air, alarming the fawns. The does noticed their fawns panic, then it rippled through the herd, but the male was the last to respond. The arrow sliced into the adolescent male, slightly lower than his heart, piercing the lung instead. The deer bolted and then stumbled. The rest of the herd, shocked and panicky, bolted into the trees, scattering in all directions. The injured deer hobbled away, obviously wounded, but still alive.

Suddenly, Anwa jumped out of the bushes, running full speed towards the deer. The deer turned to notice the Indian girl; his eyes looked panicky. Then he jumped in the opposite direction to flee. His front leg weakened, and he stumbled again, almost falling. Nath stood mesmerized, watching this play enact before him, quite momentarily stunned. He wasn't sure what was happening; his mind hadn't entirely caught up with his physical body. Anwa closed the distance quickly, jumping on the back of the deer. Nath instinctively ran full speed towards the buck and Anwa.

Anwa gripped the antlers of the buck and pulled out a sharp hunting knife from her coat. She sliced the animal's neck expertly and then immediately jumped off the animal, running back towards their shooting spot. Nath continued running towards her, he reached her and lifted her, grabbing her arm as they rushed back into the treeline. The animal turned to charge them, it stood, blood spreading on its neck and looked eerily at Nath's back. Anwa and Nath reached the treeline, and both instinctively knew what to do, climbing up the tree within seconds. Once they reached the highest heaviest branch, they both finally looked back.

The buck had charged a few feet, stood eerily, staring at them. Anwa and Nath panted heavily, waiting. Then it fell.

Nath grabbed her face and kissed her roughly. He pulled her away briefly, "Oh, my Lord, you are something else, Anwa. You are an amazing woman. You astonish me. Seriously."

She beamed, "Let's go field dress this animal."

"I know how to do this part, Anwa," Nath smiled. "The men will be delighted to have deer meat instead of fish for a while." He kissed her roughly. "Truly amazing." He kissed her again. "Ok, let's go do this."

CHAPTER 7

Nathanael, his friends and family had consumed deer until mid-week, then hunted for more. Pabbi was very proud of his son. His father was disappointed that Nath continued to see the Indian woman, but was thrilled that his son was becoming a leader in his community and learning to hunt and fish on the new land. Nathanael was genuinely becoming a principal figure within the Icelandic settlement, learning new skills, honing them and then spreading his knowledge among his companions. A large group of men began to consult with Nathanael about fishing, hunting, building and even politics. There were talks of forming an Icelandic government and that Nathanael would be an excellent candidate in council, possibly even hold the position of reeve.

Although, talks of government stalled when the weather grew frigid on the fourth day of the week. Snowfall continued every day, to everyone's dismay. There was an estimated seventeen inches on the ground already, with only small breaks in the harsh weather, and it was only the third week in

November. The snow was terrible, but the wind was wicked, it displaced the snow into drifts, sometimes right up to the front doors of their hastily built cabins.

The settlers became quite adept at snow clearing and shovelling. Nathanael's shoulders and chest began to grow muscular very quickly as a result of all the strenuous snow clearing. He could feel his pecs and deltoids burning. Every day, he shovelled first thing in the morning, stopping only briefly to see more snow clouds on the horizon. Nath cleared the horse roads and the paths, digging people out of their cabins. By afternoon, a thin sweat covered his skin under his clothes. His cousins and other men helped, but the older men were not fit for this task, so the majority of the cumbersome tasks fell to the young men. At six feet tall and now 165 pounds, Nath's previous thin body was shifting into a robust manly build.

At noon, he returned to his cabin, slamming the door open and breathing heavily. He had shovelled and cut meat for 3 hours this morning. He was irritable and feeling unsettled. He hadn't seen Anwa for two weeks. She didn't stop by, fearing racism. Nath didn't think to make any specific meeting times with her for anything else. He had learned from her all that was necessary for fishing and hunting. His comrades were now competent at keeping the community fed. They had even begun trading some fish and meat for warm clothing and vegetables.

Nathanael had been so busy with snow clearing, consulting with the settlers, teaching them, setting up community chats, that he had no time to go into Gimli himself, so he sent others to get supplies. As a result, he now realized, he had grown out of touch with Anwa, never really having opportunities to speak with her. Saddened with this knowledge, Nath disrobed, peeling the bottom layer of damp clothes from his body. He washed in the basin with plain soap and water, cleaning the sweat and grime from his body. It was a special treat; he only washed twice a week. Most people only washed once a week these days, but Nath was particularly diligent about his hygiene, sometimes he would wash three times a week in private.

Pabbi was gone to Gimli for the weekend, buying vegetables, bread, hay for the horses and more shovels. The cabin was quiet and peaceful. Nath enjoyed being by himself. It was rare, so he relished in these quiet moments.

His naked body glistened with water, and the soap bubbled on his chest. He rubbed a wet cloth over his skin, savouring the physical sensations. His pectoral muscles were very hard now; they formed solid rounded muscles on his chest. His shoulders were similarly hard and well defined. When he slipped the washcloth down his stomach, he noticed that his abdominal muscles were also hard and rippling, forming ridges along his entire stomach area. He was pleased with the changes in his body. He felt very masculine. His birthday was not for another month, but he felt like a fully-grown man now.

Even his genitals had grown, his penis, his pubic hair, it all looked very manly.

His penis twitched as he washed his genital area.

He immediately thought of Anwa.

He couldn't get her out of his thoughts. Every time he thought of a woman, it was Anwa that came to his mind. No one else.

Soap bubbled on his scrotum and at the base of his penis. He watched his penis harden, as he grasped it and thought of Anwa. Her hair, her supple body and her smell. His hand moved higher, to the tip of his penis, then slid down, the soap providing excellent lubrication. Finally, he could take no more and sat on the chair, masturbating fully. He imagined Anwa sitting on top of his lap, right here in the middle of the room, both of them very naked and aroused. His hands ached to touch her bare buttocks and guide her up and down on his lap. His mind floated to a sensual dream of a naked and aroused Anwa.

The spell broke when a sudden knocking thundered on his front door.

"Nath!" Viktor shouted outside of the door. "We need your help."

"Leave me alone for a bit," he responded grouchily. "I'm washing."

"The plow broke again," Viktor shouted through the door. "Come when you are done."

"I will come when I am ready!" Nath shouted. "Go, get out of here. Do your best until I get there."

Nath heard boots crunching into the snow, down the path, retreating from the cabin. He never gets a moment's peace around here, Nath thought. He was beginning to get irritable. He would have to be more aware of his behaviour, keep his spirits up. Maybe he should go into Gimli next time and make an excuse to see Anwa.

He continued touching himself until finally, he orgasmed forcefully. He grunted audibly, unable to contain his passion. He exhaled and laid back briefly, waiting for the intense sensations to mellow. Nath grabbed a small towel. Good thing Pabbi wasn't here, he thought. Nath chuckled. He lazily rinsed the cloth, then reclined naked on the chair for a while, just relaxing in his own space, his body satisfied.

He closed his eyes briefly and imagined Anwa as his wife; how they would have frequent sex in the cabin, every morning or the middle of the night, whenever they chose to. Her hair would flow underneath her as he mounted her and pushed himself inside her. She would gasp similar to her groans when they kissed.

He opened his eyes and looked at the ceiling. He would need to talk to her again and kiss her again. He wasn't sure how to progress things towards sex, but he was beginning to think that he would want her as his wife. Maybe he should ask some of his cousins for advice. No, he thought chuckling, they would be jeering him on every time Anwa was near him.

He will just go with the flow and see what happens.

Nath pulled on a dry pair of pants and made his way to the door. He grabbed his boots and coat, then left the cabin to help with the snowplow. He looked back towards the empty cottage. This could be their home together, he thought, as he stomped through the snow.

❦ · · · ❦

Nathanael and Viktor worked all day fixing the snowplow. It was a very long cold day. More snow had fallen, and they were reduced to hand shovelling all day.

The plow, constructed from wood and steel, was wide, approximately six feet in width and three feet in length. It attached to the horse's harness. When it worked, it was highly efficient, clearing the roads quickly and effectively. But there was a problem with the design. The wood did not withstand the constant grinding on the dirt road. It would chip and splinter, then fully crack in half.

Viktor had suggested that they attach a line of steel onto the bottom part, protecting the wood from the abuse. It was exhausting work. They had to heat the steel, mould it and then let it cool. They tested it, and several times it failed until finally, they knew what to do.

"We need to drill holes in the steel and fasten the steel to the wood with screws," Nath exclaimed. "Then it will stop falling off. And we need to sharpen the steel, so it cuts into the snow better."

"That's a good idea, Nath," Viktor replied. "Let's try it."

Viktor grabbed the bow drill, tied a cord to a long thick nail and then attached the ends of the string to the ends of the bow. He spun the line and watched it only make a small dent in the steel. "It's not working," he replied.

They tried again and again, but it simply would not go through the steel.

Nath heated the steel scraper over the fire again, waiting for it to glow red, then he hammered it with the large nail. A small chip appeared. "Let's try it again while the steel is softer."

"It is very hot!" Viktor exclaimed.

"Of course it's hot, cousin. Be careful," Nath replied.

Nath held the cool edges while Viktor again tried the modified bow drill on the heated metal. The radiating hot steel ground off. "Yes," Viktor announced as he continued with the holes, concentrating as he went along.

He finished the first holes, then Nath reheated the steel for the opposite side. Viktor again drilled another two holes. They repeated the process until they had bored twelve holes, six on the top and six on the bottom. Each side had now two holes on the far-left side, two in the middle and two on the far-right side.

"Now, we have to measure and drill the exact holes into the wood plow," Nathan instructed.

Viktor looked up at Nath, exasperated, "My hands are finished. Let's trade jobs for a bit. You drill, I will hold the wood."

"Ok, no problem," Nath replied, as they changed positions and continued with measuring and drilling the required holes.

"Let's measure again, just to be sure," Viktor commented.

So, they measured again, then nodded to each other and began drilling. Nathanael drilled effortlessly through the thick wood, yielding much easier than the metal, although he exchanged the nail for a traditional stick to heat the wood. The first two holes drilled fine on the far-left side, but as they began drilling the middle holes, the bow drill began to heat the wood so much that it started a small fire. Viktor threw snow on it immediately. The wood sizzled and steamed. They both laughed heartily.

"The last thing we need is a fire!" Nath chuckled.

Nath replaced the charred stick with another drill stick and continued boring holes in the middle. They finished the two middle holes and then measured again for the last holes. Viktor stabilized the wood as Nath bow drilled the last two far-right holes. Another fire started, again Viktor threw snow at it, and they replaced the drill stick with a new one and continued.

Finally, they finished all six holes. The moment of reckoning came when Nath and Viktor positioned the steel onto the wooden plow. It fit perfectly in the holes! They hooted and hollered.

"We did it!" Viktor shouted.

"Yes!" Nath shouted in reply.

"We need to get Kristjan and Gunnar to help steady the plow and steel plate," Viktor said, "So we can turn the screws into the holes accurately."

"Kristjan!" Nath shouted in a booming voice. "We need your help! Gunnar too! If he is available."

Another villager ran to get Kristjan and Gunnar. Several minutes later, the two men arrived hastily.

"We almost have this bastardly snowplow fixed for good!" Nath announced. "We just need you two to steady the two pieces while me and Viktor fix the screws in."

"Alright," Kristjan replied. Gunnar grabbed the right and Kristjan was securing the left. The screws were handed simultaneously to both Nath and Viktor as they worked at opposite ends, fastening the screws in. They stood back, admiring their work, nodded to each other and then continued with the second screws. After they had the four screws secured, Nath finished the job himself by fastening the last two middle screws.

They hooted and hollered again, amazed at their ingenuity.

"You are a smart man, Nath!" Kristjan said as he slapped Nath's back.

"Not so smart, but more tired of fixing this damn thing over and over again!" Nath laughed. "Let's get some beer!"

It was already nighttime. The whole plow repair had taken all day, they had taken breaks for lunch and dinner but still had many failures before the successes. It was a long day, but a productive one.

Nath was happy. "Let's drink to New Iceland. This snow will not stop us!" Nath exclaimed cheerily.

The men all clinked their beer-filled cups, as they gathered around the fire. They discussed the bow drill, the plow, the steel, the problems, and how they had overcome each obstacle.

Viktor and Nath were very proud. Nath felt gratified, and one would think he should be tired, but instead, he felt invigored, just as the other men retreated quickly to bed.

Viktor was the last to leave. "It was a good day, Nath," he said. "I'm glad we have you here in the village. You are a precious asset to New Iceland."

"Thank you, Viktor," Nath replied, hugging the smaller cousin.

"Well, I'm off to bed. Have a good night!" Viktor said as he left for his cabin.

"Goodnight!" Nath shouted back.

Nathanael stood by himself, watching the dying red embers in the firepit, feeling the cold surround him as the fire died down. He wrapped the fur coat tighter around his chest and stared at the last flickering flames. He was alert and didn't feel tired enough to sleep yet, so he stared out into the night sky, watching the dark clouds wash over the half-moon. The trees slowly swayed with the cold November wind, and the lake churned waves in the distance. The steady wash of the waves and the slight wind continued rhythmically until he finally took a step to the cabin.

A rustle moved the trees.

It wasn't the wind this time, Nath thought.

The rustle was very close.

Nath's senses screamed onto high alert. He could feel someone's presence behind him. Fear and something else, he could not quite describe, made him react instantly.

Nath twirled around and lurched into the bushes, grabbing the arm of someone. He jolted the person. Surprising himself, Nath pulled the light body towards the fire, throwing the boy down onto the ground, instantly jumping onto him with one knee on his small chest. A whimper escaped the boy's mouth.

"What are you doing here? Why do you spy? What do you want?" Nath growled at the boy.

Another whimper.

"Speak!" Nathan shouted angrily.

"Ah," the small stranger said.

Nathan gripped the boy's arm, pulled him up and removed his Indian headdress.

It was Anwa!

The shock of seeing her instead of a small Indian boy startled him so much that he couldn't make sense of it right away. He felt the surge of testosterone speed crazily through his veins.

Originally anger energy, now transforming into sexual energy, all combined to inhibit rational thought from his brain. He could not comprehend what was going on. He just acted. It was as if his mind stopped working.

"Nathan. It's me, Anwa," she breathed, her voice raspy and heavy.

His eyes glowed in the firelight. He immediately kissed her roughly, meshing his lips into hers. His penis hardened instantly. He ground his hard groin against her tummy, while his urgent tongue pushed inside her mouth.

She groaned. "Mmm, Nath," she breathed.

His whole body was on fire. Testosterone lit up his nerves, his veins, his groin and overtook his brain. He felt slightly light-headed and animalistic, as he clawed at her clothes.

She groaned deeply. Anwa opened her mouth to his, biting his bottom lip.

Shards of electricity shot through his body as he felt the pain in his lip, but it only spurred on his efforts. He pulled back and looked into her wild eyes. She stared back at him, with a yearning so intense that it hit him in the head like a sledgehammer.

She was breathing roughly now, groaning, and her eyes were half-closed.

Nath grabbed at her shirt, clawing at it until he exposed her breasts. He marvelled at their magnificence, briefly. Then he immediately sucked on the right nipple, pulling it all into his mouth. She squirmed, pushing her breast into his face, murmured something in her native language and groaned.

He gripped her left breast and squeezed it, the plumpness of it barely fit in his hand. He had never seen such breasts before. He sucked on the left nipple, then alternated back to the right. Anwa was squirming and groaning, beyond intelligible words, only murmurs and groans escaped from her mouth. The cold air blew over her bare chest, raising her hard nipples even further. Nath covered his head with his fur coat to keep her warm while he worshipped her ample breasts.

Anwa yelped with desire as Nath massaged and sucked her breasts as she lay at his mercy on the ground by the fire. She had never experienced any such pleasure before; it washed over her and took all her resistance away completely. She was his woman at this moment. She knew this.

Nathanael's penis strained against his pants, urging to get out. Anwa's hand somehow was down there now, grappling with his belt. This woman was his. He knew this in the depths of his soul. It hit him so hard again, that he felt light-headed, not quite able to comprehend the series of events, all he could do was ride the wave.

She suddenly had her hand inside his pants, her fingers wrapping around his penis.

He couldn't take it anymore. He wrestled Anwa's pants off roughly, stuffing them underneath her buttocks, adjusting her deerskin coat underneath her warm body to serve as a blanket on the rough ground. Her eyes gleamed back at him in the black night. Her breath came out in rapid heavy gusts.

"Yes," she murmured.

That's all he needed.

He pulled his pants down to his knees and grasped his penis. Momentarily confused, he let go and wandered his fingers into the spot between her legs, searching.

Anwa moaned loudly and ground her hips into the air.

Nath danced his urgent fingers over her groin and found the spot he was looking for; it was wet and slippery. He touched her vagina.

She gasped and moaned, her head stretching back in ecstasy. He marvelled at her response. She enjoyed what he was doing immensely.

He grasped his penis again and positioned his hips higher until he was level with that marvellous wet and slippery spot. He fingered her wet spot blindly again, then repositioned, making sure his penis was at the moist entrance.

His penis nudged into her vulva.

It was so wet and very, very hot. The heat threatened to take his orgasm right away, so he pulled away slightly and fingered her vulva again. He slipped his whole finger in; she gasped and whimpered.

This is hurting her, he thought. I need to be gentle; he knew this.

He rolled his finger around the tight entrance, opening it to allow his penis in. She whimpered again.

"It hurts?" he asked.

"Yes and no," she answered. "It is pain and pleasure at once."

"I will go slow," Nath stated.

He positioned his very hard penis at her entrance and nudged her wetness again. There was a steady resistance. He was confused; it was as if he could not enter her. He felt so overwhelmed with desire, but his penis was not going in.

"Push harder," Anwa breathed.

"But it will hurt," Nath groaned.

"You must get past my virginity," Anwa huffed. "There is no other way."

Nath pushed his penis harder into her.

Anwa yelped.

He felt something give way inside her. It was so incredibly tight, more than he had imagined it would be. His penis slipped in a bit farther. The tightness was so extreme that his penis felt a strange kind of pain from the tight walls surrounding him. He surged forward again and then dipped slightly back. She inhaled sharply. He gently slid all the way forward, filling her tiny vagina with every inch of his penis.

Anwa gasped and bit his shoulder. Her teeth sunk into his skin, she sucked this one spot hard, her lips pursing into his shoulder as if to counteract the pain of her broken hymen.

Her vagina continued to grip him fiercely, milking away his control. Nath felt his semen flooding into his penis. "It's too tight. I can't hold out much longer," he groaned.

"Nath, I want you inside me. No one else, just you," Anwa proclaimed.

"I love you, Anwa," Nath breathed into her ear as he slid his penis out again, then forward all the way back in.

"Oh, my, sweet Nathan," Anwa moaned.

His penis throbbed and twitched inside her excitedly. "I am going to come inside you," he stated simply.

"Yes," Anwa murmured.

Nath felt a surge of liquid rush through the length of his penis and breech the tip, exploding with a force both of them felt, flooding her womb with his semen. He groaned involuntarily. The blood left his head entirely, and he felt very dizzy and weak. His penis twitched again inside her, releasing another surge of semen, and then another, shooting inside her womb forcefully. His heart pumped crazily, and he closed his eyes, breathing heavily.

His arms suddenly felt very rubbery and weak, so he laid his weight on top of her. His penis throbbed and twitched crazily inside her vagina walls and remained semi-hard.

Anwa breathed out deeply, "I think I love you, Nath." She gazed drowsily over his shoulder, up into the dark, night sky.

"You are the most beautiful woman in the world to me, Anwa," Nath mumbled as he kissed her shoulder. "We should go inside the cabin. Pabbi is in Gimli for the weekend. You can stay here with me."

"That would be lovely," Anwa said, tears welling in her eyes. He moved to look at her face. He placed his hands along her cheeks, and then he gently kissed her moist mouth, with his penis still inside her womb. It was the most delightful feeling being physically connected with this woman, Nath thought. It was as if he was made just for her.

Nath shifted his weight and kissed her mouth lazily as he slowly began to pull out of her. A release of liquid gushed out and left Anwa's legs feeling quite shaky and weak. Nath somehow knew this, so he lifted her into his arms effortlessly and carried her to his cabin.

He kicked the door easily open, carried her across the cabin and laid her down on his bed, kissing her on the forehead before releasing her to close the door.

He hung the coats and laid the clothes down on the chair that remained where he left it earlier in the middle of the room. Anwa watched him breathlessly, examining his movements, the way his strong arms twitched when the muscles contract, the way his controlled movements glided along with everything he did, smoothly, never clumsily. He was an attractive man, with a strong jaw and a sexiness that she couldn't quite understand. She had never met such a man in her life.

He caught her staring. His blue eyes searched for answers, it seemed. "I've been waiting a long time to spend a weekend alone with you in my home," he said. "I must have thought about it every night since I met you on the beach."

She laughed, "I have done the same. My thoughts kept going back to you every night and every day."

He sat down on the bed beside her and gazed into her large brown eyes.

"So, Anwa," he commented seriously. "You have been the person in the bushes all along?"

She gazed down demurely. "Yes," she replied simply.

"You drove me nuts," Nath laughed. "You know, I thought it was a young boy, playing with me. I was intent on catching him and shaking him so scared that he would never spy on me again."

Anwa giggled, "I'm sorry. I didn't think you had noticed me."

"It's alright," he replied. "Good thing, I took your headdress off first!"

They both laughed.

"Why were you spying? Why didn't you just say hello?" Nath asked.

"I was scared of all the men," she replied. After a moment of silence, she added, "And I was fascinated about you. I wanted to learn as much as I could about you. I don't know why. I just felt," she paused, trying to find the right word, "compelled." She grasped his hand, and they gazed into each other's eyes. "Your culture, your bravery, your strength, your people, everything, it is all fascinating to me."

"Thank you," he replied. Nath smiled, then leaned forward and kissed her soft lips. Her honey tongue licked at his lips. He kissed her deeply and lovingly. His hands brushed against her bare breasts and slid down to her naked buttocks. Her skin was velvety soft and supple, with lovely curves everywhere. Nath had never felt this enchanted with a woman before. It consumed him, almost controlled him. It scared him a bit too.

He broke the kiss and undressed her completely, removing the last bits of clothing, socks and boots. When he was finished, he straightened and pulled the wool shirt over his head, revealing a hard, muscular chest and abs. He removed his socks and boots as well, then opened up the heavy blankets, snuggling into the space beside her, wrapping his arms around her warm body.

Anwa murmured, happily accepting his warmth into hers. She laid her head on his strong chest and snuggled into the crook of his arm while he enveloped her into his embrace, so fully and completely, it almost brought tears of joy to her eyes.

"I have never felt this way about a man before," she said.

He chuckled, "I was about to say the same thing. You fascinate me as well, Anwa. I don't want any other woman except you."

A tear slipped out of her eye as her heart thumped crazily inside her chest. Her feelings exploded into an unexplained stream. She began to cry.

"What's wrong?" he asked, smoothing her hair gently.

"Nothing's wrong; I'm just very happy. I know it sounds strange. But I feel very centred with you like I have somehow been waiting for you. Everything you say and do is also so similar to what I am thinking and doing. It feels I don't know, like coming home."

He kissed the top of her head softly and continued smoothing her hair. "You are so beautiful, Anwa. In every way possible."

She snuggled into his arms further, as he returned the embrace, inching impossibly closer, entwining his legs around and between hers. They laid together silently for several moments; he wasn't quite sure for how long since time seemed to have gotten a bit away from them. Her smell, her soft skin, her warmth against his, her touch, it was all heavenly, and it felt like they were floating on this cloud together, enjoying each other's intimate nakedness.

The cabin creaked in the cold night as the winter winds howled outside, blowing snow onto the roof and under the door. It was an extremely frigid night, but they were both incredibly warm, enveloped into each other, so much so, that the cold winter night didn't even exist to them. The heated embrace between them was the only thing that mattered at this moment.

Her breathing changed, he sensed. It became heavier and more rhythmic. He looked down. Her eyes were closed, and she had fallen asleep. He relished in the knowledge that the love of his life was sleeping on his chest. It was such an overwhelmingly warm feeling that a single tear escaped from his eye. Now he knew what it felt like to experience intimate happiness. He wondered, was this feeling love? Or was this how everyone felt when they had just had sex? He didn't know, but what he did know was that he didn't want it to end. He wanted her in his life more and more. He wanted to share his life with her. He would build himself a home for just the two of them.

After a while, Nath also drifted off to sleep, dreaming about homes and Anwa naked in his bed every night. The freezing night howled crazily over the cabin, as they both slept soundly, wrapped in each other's nakedness.

The snow had drifted underneath the door into the cabin overnight. By early morning there was a small amount of snow inside the cabin. Anwa's eyes fluttered open. At first, she was disorientated, not quite understanding where she was. Then she smelled his manly scent, spicy and woody. Then she felt his arms and legs still wrapped around her as if they hadn't moved all night, just falling asleep peacefully in each other's warmth.

His bottom leg was very hard, poking at her thigh. She shifted a bit to ease the space, so it was not uncomfortable for her, but he wouldn't budge. She gave up and laid within his grasp.

It was cold out, she knew. She could hear the wind howling, and her nose was cool. She could see Nath's breath as he continued sleeping. She wondered what this meant for them both. She felt a little bit afraid. He had released his sperm inside her last night. It was what she wanted in the moment; she didn't even think about having it done any other way, nor did she think of any consequences. It was as if he had high-jacked her thoughts; only the passion consumed them at the time. Everything had felt so right. But now, in the early frigid morning, she remembered what her mother had taught her about her monthly bleeding. It was to prepare her womb for a man's sperm so that a baby could be born inside her.

Anwa stared up at the ceiling. So, did that mean that she could be with child now, she wondered? How quickly does it happen? Would Nath be ready to build a family? How much did she love this man?

So many unanswered questions swirled in her mind. Her feelings for Nath were overpowering. She didn't want any other man in her vagina. But was she ready for this?

The sheets rustled as Nath moved slightly as if he knew what she was thinking. His breathing changed quickly, and the breaths came out shorter and more uneven.

"Good morning, beautiful," he murmured.

"Good morning, my handsome man," she replied.

His arms smoothed along her shoulders, down her back and then up again. His touch made her skin tingle and her heart sing happily along. She kissed him on his chest, little pecks that travelled from his shoulder to his nipples. She murmured while she kissed him, loving the feel of his skin. Along her leg, the hardness she felt earlier, wedged into her now. She realized that it wasn't his leg; it was his penis. His genitals fascinated her. She had never before held a penis. It was so smooth and rigid, but last night, it had changed, becoming very soft and flaccid after sex. It was like a chameleon, she thought curiously.

His morning penis poked eagerly at her thighs. She moved her hand down covertly, searching for that hard, beautiful piece of his body. Her fingers floated over his buttocks, hips and thighs. He groaned. As she did this, his penis jumped excitedly. Anwa was enraptured by the way his penis reacted to her as if it was talking to her. And it was; because her vagina was very wet at the moment! Amazing! Their bodies were holding a silent conversation, she thought, giggling.

"What are you laughing at?" Nath asked.

"Just how our bodies seem to talk to each other," Anwa replied.

Her hands finally rested on his groin, his rigid penis poking at her fingers. "Is it always this hard in the morning?" she asked.

"Always! Ever since I was about twelve years old," he answered, laughing.

She giggled, "I love this part of your body."

Nath smiled, "It's yours."

Her fingers gently wrapped around his hard penis. Nath let out a gasp, almost holding his breath. Then a few short breaths came out as she slid her hand up and then down.

He stopped breathing again.

His hand covered hers and stopped her hand abruptly.

"Am I doing something wrong?" she asked.

He chuckled, "No, sweetheart. You are doing everything too correctly. I will come in your hand if you continue doing that. And I don't want to do that. I want to please you first."

"Oh," she replied simply.

Nath removed her hand from his penis and took over, sliding his hand slowly along the curve of her waist. He danced his fingers along her skin up the side of her breast, over her shoulder and then deep into her long hair. His fingers splayed into her hair, dancing along her roots, sending tingles through her body. Then his hand slid back down her curves again, fluttering briefly along her breast, ever so slightly brushing the edges of her ample breast mound, sending electric sexual pulses throughout her body.

"Oh, Nath," she moaned.

Nath smiled, secretly rejoicing in her responses to his touch. He continued sliding his hand down her curves, smoothing along her slim waist, then her fuller hip and buttock. His large hand encompassed most of her left buttock. She whimpered. He took that as a cue and squeezed her buttock firmly, grasping as much of it in his hand as he could, pulsing it back and forth, squeezing and then letting go.

Anwa began to writhe inside the sheets; her hips began to move involuntarily against his leg. She could feel all the sensual energy coursing throughout her body like a rushing river, filling her vagina with a moistness that felt so overwhelmingly urgent, like a need, something necessary, something that needed to be filled.

Nath kissed her mouth as his hand fluttered down to the apex of her thighs, searching for that beautiful wet spot again. He found it quickly. His finger slid effortlessly inside her. It was still extremely tight, so he circled his finger again, trying to ease it open.

Anwa groaned and gasped at the same time. She was entirely lost in his touch, his embrace, his loving. She was his woman in this moment, completely and devotedly. She was his violin; all he needed to do was play the instrument in his hands.

And that he did, so naturally and effortlessly, as if the forces of nature were guiding his hands where to go next. Nath never felt so wholly relaxed with any other woman before. He felt so in tune with this woman like she knew what he was thinking, almost as if she knew him better than he knew himself. Nath just followed his instincts, and somehow understood what he needed to do next. He felt so utterly masculine, like every vein in his body pumped with testosterone. His heart thumped in his chest, warmly. His emotions were raw towards this woman in his arms. He truly believed that he loved her quite a lot. His attraction to her was so powerful it rendered him powerless to control it. He melted from her scent, her groans, her words. His penis was fully hard again, poking towards her thighs, eagerly pointing him in the direction that he needed to go. He slid her onto her back and mounted her. She moaned again. He felt so enraptured by their combined sexual energy that all he could do was just simply follow the tide. His penis found her wet spot effortlessly this time, nudging her entrance. The head of his penis entered her slightly.

"Ah," Anwa gasped.

It was tight, but his penis slid inside her a bit more comfortably this time. He slipped inside farther and farther, rocking gently, until he was fully inside her, his penis filling up every inch of space in her vagina. She gasped and stiffened. It felt painful again; her vaginal walls were gripping him snugly. He stopped rocking and just stayed still, his penis resting in her vagina, throbbing from the tightness.

"It hurts again?" he asked, his voice sensually smooth.

"Yes," Anwa breathed.

"I will go slow," he replied. "It fits a bit better this time, though."

"I know," she whispered.

He kissed her luscious lips and smoothed her hair with his penis inside her vagina. The connection felt so absolute as if this was a puzzle that had just been completed. His tongue inside her mouth and his penis inside her vagina felt like another dimension, similar to what heaven must be like, he thought.

He kissed her so deeply and lovingly. She kissed him back, her tongue seeking his tongue. Her back arched, and her vagina loosened a tiny bit. A surge of wet heat flowed along his penis and emptied onto his scrotum. This must be normal, he thought, as he fought the urge to orgasm inside her already. Her vagina milked his penis so wonderfully that he had to take it slow for his own sake as well, not just hers.

"You feel so amazing, Anwa," he mumbled. "I've never met a girl like you before."

"Oh, Nath," she moaned. "It's just like you know what to do when we are together like this. I have never experienced any of this before. It feels so amazing, Nathanael."

"I was thinking the same thing," Nath moaned. He smiled and looked into her large brown eyes, while his penis still filled her. The connection felt so strong. "I think I want my penis inside you all the time," he said chuckling.

Anwa smiled, "I agree."

He raised himself up on his elbows as he gazed into her eyes. Then he slowly moved his penis slightly back, sliding more and more, until he was gliding out halfway. Her eyelids fluttered, and her head pushed back into the pillow. She groaned.

Her face was in such a state of ecstasy, just looking at her, writhing and groaning, sent him into a spiral of orgasmic energy. It felt like he would lose control again, so he wrestled with it, closing his eyes and imagined building houses. He moved slightly out farther and then surged back into her wet vagina, hearing her groans of passion. He thought of placing pieces of wood onto the roofs of the cabins, trying to block the sensations from overcoming him.

It worked! The flow of semen stopped filling his penis.

He opened his eyes.

Anwa's hair was all over the place, swirling half over her face, the rest flowing all around the pillow, surrounding her face like a beautiful angel. Her eyes were half-closed, her mouth was slightly open, and her breasts squashed between their sweaty bodies.

"You are the most beautiful woman I have ever set eyes upon, Anwa," Nath murmured.

She moaned again, completely lost in ecstasy. She mumbled something back, then groaned his name.

The semen began to fill his penis again. He again closed his eyes, concentrating on his movements. He pulled out slowly inch by inch, then when he was almost all the way out, only his tip still inside her; he glided back into her, filling her vagina to the very end. He stopped, feeling his penis filling her, throbbing. He slowly repeated these movements over and over again, finding a luscious rhythm. He maintained this pace, pulling almost all the way out, then gliding back in. He could feel her desire increasing. Her vagina began tightening, then releasing, as if it was pulsating. He felt so controlled and empowered. He was determined to satisfy this wonderfully beautiful woman beneath him. This was his sole objective now. Firmly and physically, he needed to relieve this woman that he loved, of this sexual tension. Her back arched, and she began to breathe rapidly. She grasped his back with her arms and bit into his shoulder again, this time with a strong passion. She writhed fervently against him, meeting every stroke, as his luscious pace intensified. He somehow instinctively knew that he should not break that pace, no matter what she did.

Finally, as if she had just reached some pinnacle, some imaginary cliff, she shouted his name, her body stiffening and her back arching firmly. Her vaginal muscles contracted all around his penis suddenly. He was taken by surprise. It was something he knew he could not control at this point. The semen rushed into his penis, responding to the steel grip from her vagina. There was no controlling his orgasm this time, he realized. But he also knew that he had somehow brought his lovely woman to orgasm.

Her juices suddenly washed over his penis, like a hot shower; even his scrotum was wet, the liquid coating everything. He bit his lip. The feeling was so intense.

Anwa mumbled incoherently in her native language.

Then she shouted his name, "Nath!"

That was it; his control vanished. The semen burst from his penis, spraying into her vagina forcefully. He could feel everything so entirely, so deliciously. He released load after load of sperm into her vagina, filling her womb impossibly full. He felt powerless to stop, an animalistic urge taking over. He jutted his hips farther into her instinctively, his penis ejaculating more semen into her womb.

She gasped and groaned, accepting his loads of sperm, so willingly, so eagerly, that it made his head spin.

"I love you," she breathed passionately as her body began to vibrate.

Nath felt the energy from his body drain entirely. His arms went limp and rubbery; his head swam, his buttocks shook, and his chest was sweaty with exertion. He laid fully onto her, letting his body recuperate. With his head buried into her shoulder, he kissed her neck, then her ear. "I love you, my sweetness," he murmured in her ear.

Tingly sensations travelled up her body upon hearing his heartfelt words. She loved this man so thoroughly, and he loved her back the same. She must be the luckiest woman in the world, Anwa thought.

Nath kissed her shoulder again. "I mean it, Anwa. I love you, and I want to marry you."

Anwa's head swam. She felt dizzy and light-headed. "I want to marry you, too," she breathed.

"Good," he replied. "I'm glad we both think the same. I don't ever want another woman. I only want you, Anwa. Just you." He gently kissed her shoulder again, as if sealing the agreement.

Anwa kissed his head in agreement. No words were needed. Their bodies moulded into each other, slid apart briefly, then cuddling so effortlessly and lovingly, as if in one smooth movement, with her lying on top of him now. They lay together like this for several minutes, maybe an hour, they did not know, for they both drifted off to sleep again, so utterly satisfied and content. They slept like babies, within each other's arms, for another few hours in the early snowy morning, while the cold wind blew wildly over the cabin.

CHAPTER 8

Nath awoke with Anwa still cuddled on top of him. Her scent filled his nostrils and his heart. He felt so wonderfully happy with this woman. He smiled and kissed her on the head. She mumbled and shifted her weight.

"Anwa, babe," Nath gently nudged her.

"Mmm," Anwa mumbled.

"Babe," Nath urged. "I have to urinate."

She chuckled and slid her body to the side. Nath gently removed himself from the warm bed, covering her up warmly.

He rushed out the back door to relieve himself. The blast of cold air was expected, but his foggy mind didn't quite register the enormous amounts of snow yet. His only urgent thought was to urinate. His bladder was extremely full. He urinated for a very long time, then finally shook his penis and felt a wet slippery substance on his penis. He looked down at his hands. There was blood. Not a lot, just a pinkish show of blood, but enough to worry him.

He closed the door. The cabin was very cold. He had forgotten to refill the wood stove with firewood last night. He reached over, threw two logs in, lit a match and closed the small iron door. They had purchased a few of the wood stoves last week when the weather began to get too cold. He was glad they had one. Pabbi was supposed to return with another few wood stoves from Gimli.

Nath grabbed a moist rag from the kitchen area, cleaning himself quietly, then hurried back to the warm bed. He snuggled into her warm body and kissed her head. "Babe," he prodded her gently.

"Yes," she responded, sleepily.

"There is some blood on my penis," he stated, concerned. "Should I be worried? Did I hurt you that much?"

She smiled lovingly, staring into his blue eyes, "It's normal, Nath. My mamma told me that when a hymen breaks, it bleeds a bit. It is the sign of a virgin. You didn't hurt me, babe."

"Oh," he replied dumbfoundedly. "So many things happen to women's bodies. It's bewildering."

"Yes," she answered. "It is. I agree."

They cuddled for several minutes, enjoying each other's warmth until finally, it was Anwa that spoke. "Can I really stay here all weekend?" she asked.

"Yes, definitely," he replied. "My friends and cousins all know you. They know I have felt strongly about you for some time. It will be alright, Anwa. Please stay."

"You talked about me to your friends?" she asked inquiringly.

"Yes," he responded confidently. "You are the woman I want. I am not too good at hiding my feelings."

She kissed him on the shoulder. "Yes, I will stay until your father returns then."

"Perfect," he replied. Nath squeezed her tightly, hugging her warmly one last time, then released her. "I must go shovel snow again, my sweetness. When I was urinating, I think I noticed a large amount of snow that must have fallen while we were sleeping."

"Alright then," she stated. "I will stay inside and clean up. Do you have any warm water?"

"I will put a pot of water on the woodstove for you," Nath said. "If you need to urinate, there is an outhouse in the back. I can walk you to it if you like."

"That would be lovely," she replied.

Nath got up, slipped on pants and a coat and began to boil water. He watched as Anwa dressed, pulling her long wool pants on and wrapping herself in the deerskin coat.

"You ready?" he asked politely.

She nodded, and he walked with her to the outhouse, holding her hand. The snowfall was considerable. Another 24 inches overnight. It was difficult making their way to the toilet. Luckily, it wasn't too far.

He waited as she entered the outhouse, surveying the snowy landscape. He estimated over 40 inches had accumulated on the ground now. He couldn't believe it. That was a lot of snow in such a short time. And to make matters worse, it was bitterly cold. He estimated it was probably -40°F already, maybe colder. This was not the kind of weather that the settlers needed. They were simply not prepared for this. They had brought a few wood stoves with them from Iceland but not nearly enough. They would need those extra wood stoves from Gimli in a hurry.

Anwa came out, and Nath walked her back to the cabin, then kissed her on the forehead before leaving to get the new snowplow. "I will be back in a few hours," he said. "Clean yourself up, have some tea and keep the wood stove burning. There is some dried food if you wish to put together a breakfast."

She hugged him warmly. "Be safe out there," she said. "It is a very cold day. Winters here can be brutal. The cold has killed many people. Don't underestimate the dangers of this land."

Nath nodded and kissed her lips, "Thank you. I will heed your warning. I will come back inside periodically to warm up."

He pulled his fur hat on and grabbed the doorknob, stopping briefly. "Anwa," he mumbled nervously.

She looked up at him, her large brown innocent eyes burning into his heart.

"I love you," he said humbly.

She rushed over to him, hugged him fiercely and mumbled into his chest. "I love you, Nathanael." She released him, and he walked out into the frigid air, closing the door behind him.

The wind blasted in his face, freezing his exposed nose and chin instantly, it seemed. He trudged through the snow with his head down to shield his face from the blowing snow. Finally, he arrived at the horse stable. He opened the door and checked on the horses. They were cold, but okay. The heavy furs they had laid on top of them had kept the animals warm enough overnight. He was glad they had started doing that every night.

Nath grabbed the snowplow and pulled the horse's reins until the animal stood up. He talked gently to the horse and pet the strong animal's neck. The stud neighed and nudged him playfully. He harnessed the horse and guided it outside, as Viktor approached.

"Good morning, Nath!" Viktor shouted.

"Good morning, Viktor! A lot of snow fell overnight!" Nath replied.

"Yes, it is a lot of snow! Too much!" Viktor exclaimed. "Hey, Nath, was that Anwa I saw going to the outhouse with you this morning?"

Nath blushed. "Yes, it is Anwa."

Viktor grinned, mischievously.

"Not a negative word from you," Nath stated confidently. "I want this woman to be my wife."

Viktor laughed, "Alright! No problem."

Nath stood facing Viktor, sincerely. "I mean it, Viktor. I love her," Nath said gently.

"Alright, alright!" Viktor replied. "You will be the one to tell your Pabbi, not me!"

"That's right," Nath chuckled. "And I will. But we have more serious things to worry about today. This cold is worrisome. Anwa said that the winter's here could be fatal for some. So, let's get some of this snow plowed and then check on the cabins that don't have the wood stoves yet."

"I agree," Viktor said, as he hooked the snowplow onto the horse. "We will clear just the main road for now.

Nath pulled a shovel from the horse stable and started shovelling a walkway towards his house. "You lead the horse," Nath instructed. "I will try to get as many pathways cleared as I can."

The two cousins worked tirelessly for over an hour, clearing and shovelling roads and walkways, while some settlers began to emerge from their cabins. Looking about bewilderingly, they were shocked at the cold and massive amounts of snow. The horse was tiring quickly and needed to be warmed up and fed. Nath led the horse back to the stable, covering the animal with the fur and leading him to the hay.

A shout sounded throughout the settlement.

Nath rushed outside, as a crowd had gathered at one of the farther cabins. It was closer to the lake, more exposed to the wind than the others. Someone was crying.

"What is going on?" Nath shouted.

"He's dead," a young man shouted. "Sweet Jesus. Pray for us."

"Who?" Viktor shouted worriedly.

"Gunnar," Kristjan replied despondently. "Our young friend."

"Sweet Jesus," Nath shouted. "Let me see." He pushed his way into the cabin at the lakefront. He found two other men in the cabin, shivering, blue lips and ashen white skin. "Move these men to a cabin that has heat! Right now!"

Several men rushed about, picking up the two shivering men, bundling them and carrying them to Viktor's cabin. A few other men stayed. The younger man was still crying. Nath approached the bed and found Gunnar's body. He was blue. All his skin was blue, his face, hands, everything. Nath felt for a pulse in his neck, his wrist, he even put his ear to the boy's chest. Nothing. The boy was dead, frozen to death. Nath fought off tears and shouted orders to everyone. They needed to prepare a burial.

"Gunnar was my closest friend," the young man stated.

"What's your name, young man?" Nath asked, sympathetically.

"Alexander," he stated simply. "My father is Olafur."

"How old are you?" Nath asked.

"Fourteen," Alexander answered.

"Okay, Alexander," Nath instructed. "We need to make sure this doesn't happen again. To anyone. Okay? Do you understand? This is something we could not have foreseen. We will begin installing more wood stoves, but in the meantime, I need you to gather the other men, awaken everyone and get the youngest ones into the few cabins with the stoves. Viktor's, my cabin, Kristjan's and a few others are the ones with the heat.

And you will also need to start the large firepit in the communal area. The rest of the men can keep warm there. Can you do that, Alexander?"

"Yes," Alexander answered, clearing his eyes.

Nath hugged the boy and patted him on the back. "You're tough, like us," Nath said. "You will survive. We will all survive. We will learn never to let this happen again. Now go."

Alexander rushed away, calling to the other men, knocking on doors.

Nath looked down at the body of Gunnar and, fighting tears, he slowly began to wrap the boy in the sheets until he was fully covered, head to toe. He turned to ask for help and was surprised to find Anwa at his side.

"Could you help me remove the body?" Nath asked her and several others.

"Yes, of course," she replied.

Nath, Anwa and two other men ceremoniously lifted the light body of Gunnar up and out of the cabin. They laid him in the field, while Nath hurriedly shovelled a shallow hole in the snow. Anwa gathered large sticks and tied them in a cross. The group laid Gunnar down in the snow. Anwa pushed the cross into the snow at the top of the makeshift grave.

"We will call the others after they have gathered everyone, and we will have a small service for Gunnar," Nath announced.

Another shout sounded a few cabins away, as dread filled Nath's heart. Anwa looked at him with tears in her eyes. "I'm sorry, I should have told you earlier about the winters here."

"It is not your fault," Nath replied. "Let's face this with courage, not blame."

He grabbed her waist and walked with her solemnly, a few cabins down.

Another crowd had gathered. Nath made his way through the men into the cabin. Another young boy and an older man, presumably his father. Both dead.

Nath started shouting instructions. Men hurried about, wrapping the victims in the sheets and lifting them to the same gravesite where Gunnar lay. Nath paused outside the cabin, shielded from the crowd momentarily. He hugged Anwa and nuzzled his head in her shoulder, trying to shield his tears. He began to cry in her furry hat. She clutched him strongly, protectively. "You are strong, my dear," she whispered in his ear. "These people depend on you. You will persevere. Just rest your head on me for a moment. The grief will pass."

Anwa hugged him strongly, propped up against the outside of the cabin, while men hurried about, building fires and removing bodies. Nath cried into her hat and released the weight of grief and responsibility onto her, letting it go. She murmured and then started singing softly, very quietly, so only Nath could hear. It was a wistful mourning song in her native language. He could not understand any of the words, but he could understand the meaning. It was a song of grief, hardship and loss. Her voice flowed into him, through his mind, his heart and his blood. It soothed him and balanced his emotions. The hard day melted behind him as he sought solace in her arms.

"I'll take care of you," Anwa sang lightly at the end of the song. "You won't ever have to worry. I'll be there for you."

Anwa kissed his head and squeezed him tight for a few moments, frozen in time, while chaos erupted around them.

It was as if the world had stopped.

Five people in total perished from the first cold winter storm; two were older men and three were the youngest boys. The community of Willow Point held a mass funeral in the gravesite near the lake. It was a hard lesson to be learned. They needed heat in each and every cabin to survive the brutal winters here. The heavy snowfalls had made travel difficult, so the arrival of the stoves was delayed. Pabbi finally returned to the village five days later. Thankfully, he had arrived with five wood stoves in the trailer as well as food and more rations.

Anwa had stayed with Nath for the entire week, always helping with everything, never content to be hidden in the cabin. She was fearless, helpful and loving. Nath felt genuinely gifted to have her in his life. They made love every night and every morning. Each time it felt better and more comfortable. He looked forward to touching her naked skin every night under the warm blankets.

Pabbi was not happy about Nathan's choice of a woman; they argued as he made his opinion known loudly. Nath did not agree with his racist remarks.

"I don't want that Indian in our house," Pabbi shouted angrily.

Nath felt his blood boil and took two breaths to calm himself before speaking. "Then, I will build another house for just me and Anwa."

"What?" Pabbi shouted. "How are you going to build a new house in this bastardly cold weather?"

"Then we will have to wait until the spring," Nath shouted back. "You would keep us apart until spring for your own idealistic bigotry!"

"Damn right, I am!" Pabbi shouted, his face turning red. "Maybe by then, you will have come to your senses and find a white woman."

Nath felt his control slipping away from him. His anger boiled up to the surface and threatened to rob him of his sanity. He stared angrily at his Pabbi, the man he had looked up to his entire life. He was only now seeing him in such a strange, different light, that even Nath couldn't believe it. Nath's emotions were so jumbled in his brain that he couldn't process words to his thoughts anymore. His physical impulses took over instead. Nath's fists were clenched, and he took one large step towards Pabbi.

Pabbi took a hesitant step back and sneered, "You can do better than an Indian woman."

Fueled by testosterone, Nath's arm shot out so quickly he didn't have time to even think about what he was doing. With his fist still rolled up, his knuckles connected hard with his father's jaw. The impact jarred both of them. Nath took another step forward as his father stumbled backwards. Pabbi teetered from the force of the hit and lost his balance, falling back onto a pile of logs.

Nath quickly went to his father's aid, trying to help him from falling further. The wrathful fog in his head dissipated quickly, leaving Nath instantly remorseful. Pabbi's lip had split open; red blood started oozing out from the injury.

"I'm sorry, Pabbi," Nath bent down, grabbing his father's arm and threw it over his shoulder, lifting Pabbi from the log pile. "Let's get you in the house, clean you up."

Pabbi was disoriented, and his head swam. "What have you done?"

"Pabbi, let's not talk for a while," Nath responded. "Let's just deal with the cut on your face."

Nath walked with his father to the cabin. He kicked open the door and laid Pabbi down on the other bed. Anwa stared with shock, as she watched Nath nurse his father. Nath grabbed a cloth, wetted it and held it firmly against Pabbi's lip and jaw. "Anwa, please get me something hard and cold from outside, ice if you can find some."

She asked no questions and just ran outside. She returned several minutes later with a small block of crusted ice snow. She handed it to Nathanael. As he reached for it, she gasped. "Nath, look at your hand!" she exclaimed. "What happened?"

Nath looked at his throbbing fist, crusted with red blood and quickly swelling on the middle knuckle. "Oh, I didn't notice that."

"I will get you a cold cloth for your knuckles," she responded, urgently. Anwa grabbed a large wet cloth, running outside again. She immersed it in the snow, scrunched it repeatedly until small icicles started forming on the fabric and snow stuck to it everywhere.

She ran back in and tended to his right hand. "You fought," she stated simply.

"Yes," Nath replied, feeling guilty.

Anwa didn't speak further, just began examining his knuckles, feeling the bones, then she pushed on one bone hard. Nath yelped. "Sorry, sorry, babe, just bite your lip, almost finished," Anwa whispered. She flexed his fingers straight, felt the bones again, following them in a straight line, then finished by wrapping his hand and knuckles securely.

When she looked up at Nath, his face was shockingly white. "Babe, come here, lie down. I will take care of Pabbi," Anwa said worriedly.

"No," Nath argued, fearing that Pabbi would retaliate.

"Nath, listen to me, babe, please," Anwa said, smartly. "You broke one of your knuckles. I set it and wrapped it. I will get you some alcohol to ease the pain. Please, Nath, you need to lie down."

Nath stared at her, feeling numb. "Alright," he said. Anwa guided him to their bed and tucked the blankets around him. "Just rest for a bit." She ran her fingers over his brow. "You silly fighting men."

Anwa then hurried back to Pabbi and inspected his lip. It was quite bloody, and his jaw was also quickly swelling. She pressed on the gash firmly with the cloth. Pabbi groaned. She held it firmly for three minutes, counting in her head. Then she peeked under the cloth and was happy to see that the blood was beginning to congeal. "Hold this firmly, Pabbi," she instructed.

Pabbi nodded and followed her instructions.

Anwa rummaged in the cupboards until she found some spirits. She poured two ounces, one in each small cup. She took the first one to Nath, instructing him to gulp the shot down. He grabbed the cup and downed the liquid quickly. He grimaced as the alcohol seared his throat.

"Good," she stated. "That will help with the pain."

Next, she grabbed the other cup of alcohol and took it to Pabbi. He swallowed the harsh liquid as well. She rechecked Pabbi's lip; it was slowly starting to crust up.

Then she went over to Nath and sat down beside him. She was happy to see that the colour was returning to his face. "How are you feeling?" she asked.

"Better," he replied. "Thank you, Anwa." His eyes searched hers.

"I love you, Nath," Anwa stated. "I don't want to see you hurt. What did you fight about?"

Pabbi shuffled in the bed, overhearing their conversation. The words, I love you, floated in the air. Maybe his son was indeed in love, he thought.

The room grew quiet.

Nath looked into her brown eyes, feeling ashamed. "I don't want to talk about it right now, sweetheart. Another time and I will tell you everything."

"Alright then," she said thoughtfully. "You should both rest."

She threw some more wood in the stove, then snuggled with Nath. She breathed in his being, the feel of his skin, his aroma, his touch, it was almost as if she was a part of him. She didn't want to leave, but she knew that she must. She felt Nath's breathing slow, and his muscles slowly went slack as he fell into a deep sleep.

She had overheard the shouting earlier when Pabbi and Nath had fought. The words seared through her heart. I am an Indian, she thought. Pabbi is right. She has no right to be here with Nath. It had been so wonderful to live with Nath for an entire week, though. It felt like heaven, she thought. Everything felt so easy with him like she was doing exactly what she should be, almost like the stars had somehow aligned to allow Nath and Anwa to be together. Everything felt so right.

But Pabbi was never going to allow her into his family because she was an Indian. She began to cry softly, feeling sorry for herself. All of the past week came rushing back to her, making love every night and every morning, the deaths, the funerals, and saving the men that had barely survived the winter storm. And now a fight that had left Pabbi with a bruised jaw, a split lip and Nath with a broken knuckle.

The tears flowed freely down her face as she relived all the love, death and hurt.

She quietly sobbed for what seemed like an eternity, until finally, she wiped her eyes, intent on her decision.

She would stay until dawn, just to make sure that both men were okay, then she would leave. She was Indian, and Nath was Icelandic. The community would not tolerate the union.

She would rather die than have Nath physically argue with his father again. Family meant so much to her. She lost her own father to the sea, and she wished that she had treated him better in the ten years that he was with her. She could never break the bond that Nath and Pabbi had. Even if they did manage to work it out somehow, Pabbi would never accept her into the family. It was just how things were. She couldn't change that she was native, nor would she ever want to.

Anwa soon fell into a disturbed, broken sleep, awakening several times to check on both men. She tossed and turned, crying in her sleep, her eyes swelling from the constant tears. She dreamt fitfully of Nath's broken hand, Pabbi's concussion and a life without her dear Nathanael.

CHAPTER 9

Nath's eyes blinked open from the bright sun filtering into the bedroom. He squinted and moaned. His hand felt the bed beside him. The sheets were cold. He threw the blankets off and looked around. His heart jumped into his throat. He intuitively knew that something was wrong. "Anwa," he called out.

No response.

He got up hurriedly and checked the cabin. The house was warm; she had been feeding the fire during the night. Maybe she was in the outhouse, he thought.

Nath hurriedly put his boots on, running outside, forgetting his fur coat, he arrived at the outhouse, knocking on the door. "Anwa," he called again.

Nothing.

He opened the outhouse door. It was empty. There were footprints in the snow that led into the forest. Nath stared at the footprints as his eyes filled with tears.

Anwa had left him.

His heart jumped and flipped as his eyes swelled with emotion. His thoughts became all jumbled, and his heart fell into his stomach. He felt dizzy and started to cough. Tears flooded from his eyes, making everything blurry. He thrashed into the forest, hugging himself; he had forgotten to put a shirt on, and he suddenly felt the cold seeping into his bare chest.

"Anwa!" he shouted at the trees. "What have you done? Where are you?"

She was not here; he could feel it in his blood. She had left hours ago; he had been too injured to notice. He looked down at his bandaged hand and cried even harder. She had nursed him expertly; she even set his bone! He hadn't known that she had such medical knowledge.

"Why?" he cried at the trees. He fell to his knees in the snow and wept. His emotions flowed out of his body in a torrent. His eyes were flooding with tears, and the forest looked surreal. "Come back," he whispered to himself. "Come back, Anwa."

The cabin door slammed open. It was Pabbi. "Nath!" his father shouted. "Get back in here! At least put a coat on!"

Nath looked up and couldn't even see Pabbi. The tears were flooding his eyes so badly that his vision was obscured. His throat constricted as he sobbed. A few moments later, a hand laid on his shoulder. It was Viktor.

"Come inside, Nath," Viktor said, soothingly.

Nath looked at Viktor, then looked at his bandaged knuckles, then down at his freezing knees in the snow, and then his eyes rested at the cabin.

Viktor helped Nath up, and they stumbled back into the cottage.

"Are you alright, Nath?" Viktor asked.

"She's gone," Nath stated simply. "Anwa is gone."

Pabbi watched as his robust grown son crumpled into bed, curling up and sobbing heavily.

"Maybe we should leave him be," Viktor said. "Come with us, Pabbi. We need help installing those wood stoves."

"Alright," Pabbi said, letting his arms fall to his sides, dejectedly. He reached for his jacket. "You know," Pabbi said quietly. "It's my fault that she's gone."

Viktor patted his back. "It will be alright."

"It's my fault," Pabbi repeated. "All my fault."

❧ ⋯ ❧

The next day Nath opened his eyes and stared at the ceiling. His heart was crushed. As quickly as all the love and happiness had flooded his life, it drained out of him like a rushing river, leaving nothing but an aching loss behind. He couldn't even get out of bed. Everything seemed dull and lifeless. His mind was so overcome by emotion that he couldn't even comprehend why she would have left. He had to urinate, but part of him didn't even want to move. He was barely functioning. It felt like there was an actual physical pain in his chest. He hugged his chest and rocked silently.

He felt ill and lethargic like someone had sucked all the energy out of him, taking his appetite as well. Last night, he didn't even eat. His stomach was raw and hurting, food smelled awful, and he felt like vomiting in his plate.

How was he supposed to move on without her? It didn't seem possible.

Nath turned his head to the side and felt a stray tear escaping down his cheek. He touched his eyes; they were swollen and raw. Nath exhaled heavily and swung his legs over the bed, pulling on his pants and coat. He trudged outside like a zombie. After relieving himself in the outhouse, he shuffled back, his shoulders slumped, and his energy gone. He opened the door to the cabin, looked around and it hit him with an extreme vividness again.

Anwa was gone.

Why?

The realization dawned on him with such clarity that his head hurt.

She must have overheard the argument with his dad. She heard the mean racist words that had come from Pabbi's mouth. She knew why Nath punched his father.

But he didn't tell her.

He was too scared that she would leave, that she would be hurt, offended. Nath wanted to protect her from the racism; he tried to keep her safe from the vicious views of his comrades. He intended to keep her in a bubble away from everyone.

Instead, he lost her.

Nath rubbed his hands over his face; nobody wanted them to be together. Icelanders were supposed to marry white folk; natives were supposed to marry natives. The cultural differences were too stark, too different.

He didn't know what to do; he felt numb and so terribly hurt. She had asked him; she had prodded him to talk about it, and he had refused.

He was a stupid man. Now he had lost the only woman that had meant anything to him.

Nath removed his coat, walked towards the bed, crawled in and curled up, hugging his knees. Love hurt so much in this moment.

The door creaked open.

"Nath?" Pabbi said.

Nath could hear him, but he didn't respond. Anger bubbled into his throat. It was his father's fault; it was Viktor's fault. It was everybody's fault for sneering at them as a couple.

"Hey, son," Pabbi said quietly.

Nath didn't respond.

Pabbi sat down at the table, thoughtfully. "I know you hear me," Pabbi said. "And I know what you're thinking." He paused, looking down at the table. "I just want you to know that I'm sorry. It's my fault that Anwa left. I didn't know how much you loved her, Nath. I didn't know. I'm sorry."

Pabbi stood up, with tears welling in his eyes.

The silence of the room answered back with an emptiness he could feel. Pabbi turned and left the house, closing the door gently behind him.

Nath heard the click and felt like screaming at the door, throwing rocks at it, yelling with a ferocious anger, but the energy had left his body. All he could feel was remorse and pain. Maybe everyone was right; Anwa and Nath could never be together. It was an impossible romance.

He closed his eyes and let the dreams overtake him.

❧ ⋯ ❧

Anwa felt her limbs go numb again. She was in her bed at Mamma's house. Her arms felt so weak, and her legs refused to support her, it seemed. Although, it was all just in her head. She moved gently and sat up. Her mamma had left with Garth briefly, to help with bringing in the boats. Anwa was too exhausted to do the work. She was left alone in the house with her thoughts. She felt like vomiting. It had been so hard to leave Nath. She had thought in the moment that it was the right thing to do. She loved him so strongly that she never wanted to be the one that splintered his family, the bond he had with his father and his comrades, this was special for him, she knew. Family meant everything to Nath. She was just a woman, an Indian woman, who would never be accepted in his life.

She curled her knees into her chest. Tears fell silently onto her knees as she hugged herself.

Had she made a mistake? She loved Nath so much. She had never met anyone like him before. The bond between them was so incredibly strong. The attraction visceral.

But nobody would accept them being together.

She climbed out of bed and felt dizzy. She had hardly eaten the last two days. She grabbed a cup and boiled some water for tea. She smelled the warm soup on the stove. Her mother must have left it for her. She looked at the soup, staring at it as if it was something important. She needed to eat, she told herself.

Anwa grabbed a bowl and scooped some soup into it. She sat down and hovered over the steaming liquid, lost in her thoughts. She stared into the deer soup, stirring it absentmindedly.

She left the only man she had ever loved.

She felt sick.

She had to eat, though.

Anwa brought the spoon up to her lips. It was warm. She felt the meat on her tongue and forced herself to chew it. She almost gagged when she swallowed it. She looked down at the bowl and pushed it away. She sipped the tea instead.

She hadn't brushed her hair or even changed clothes since leaving Nath's cabin. Her heart felt like someone had stuck a knife in it. Pabbi said she was an Indian, not good enough for his son. Maybe it was true.

She started crying heavily; she felt lost and helpless to change anything. Her body heaved and began to absorb all the loss physically. Nobody would accept an Indian wife with a handsome, strong Icelander man; Nath deserved better.

Anwa stood and grabbed the table, unsteady. She truly was feeling ill. It wasn't just in her head. She felt the bile creeping up into her throat. Her stomach lurched, and she ran out of the house urgently, trying to get to the outhouse.

But she didn't make it.

She fell on her knees halfway down the path, vomiting the acidic contents of her stomach into the snow. She heaved again and again, bewildered. Finally, the sickness feeling settled, and she could straighten.

She looked up at the sky, breathing in the crisp air in a deep inhale.

Love makes you feel sick, she thought. Anwa stood gingerly and walked the rest of the way to the outhouse and closed the door, feeling another surge of sickness erupt from her mouth. She heaved again, the bile coating her mouth. She spit and then just slumped onto the dirty floor. She hugged her knees, shivering.

"Anwa!" Bea yelled into the backyard. "Where are you?"

She could hear her mamma, but her voice was hoarse.

"Anwa!" Bea's voice hollered, becoming a high-pitched worried shriek.

Anwa straightened and opened the outhouse door, walking gingerly to the cabin.

Bea was standing by the cottage door. "Anwa, oh my God!" Bea shrieked as she rushed over to her weak daughter. Bea held her shoulders and walked with her back to the cabin, closing the door. "You need to rest. You haven't eaten much. I made soup. My poor baby, are you alright?"

"No," Anwa answered feebly. "I feel sick."

"Let's get you in bed, my sweetie," Bea said worriedly. "Did you try the soup?"

"Yes," Anwa answered. "I got sick."

"Oh my," Bea fretted. "I will get you some tea with honey."

Bea folded her daughter's small body into bed, covering her with several blankets. She smoothed her hair and kissed her forehead. "I'm sorry, sweetie," Bea said softly. "I know how much you loved him. Sometimes love just isn't enough."

Anwa burst into tears, curling over onto her side, hugging the blankets.

Bea busied herself, making her daughter a medicinal tea for stomach upset. "This will help," she said, bringing the cup to Anwa. Bea sat down on the bed beside her. "Drink," she said.

Anwa took the cup and sipped the warm, soothing liquid. It warmed her insides, but her heart was still broken and beating so painful inside her chest. Then something occurred to her, a light of hope, a ray of reasoning. She glanced up at her mamma. "You know what everyone doesn't understand?" she asked.

Bea smoothed her hair again, "What is that?"

"No matter what people think about Nath and me, what they really don't understand is how strongly we feel for each other. It's beyond love; it's beyond comprehension. I feel Nath in my gut, in my body, in my heart. That's what people don't understand. They only see what is on the outside. They just want to make sense of everything around them. They don't truly know about how we both feel inside."

❧ ···· ❧

In two weeks, he had lost almost ten pounds. His head swam with thoughts of Anwa consistently throughout every single day. He remembered her smell, the softness of her skin, her laugh, the way she moved against him, her kisses. Sometimes, he even thought that he could actually smell her on his sheets. But it was only his mind playing tricks on him.

He felt numb. Everything he did was dull, seemingly without purpose.

Nath was miserable; every day had just blended into the next, seemingly without purpose, without clear reason.

Pabbi had apologized, but it meant nothing now. She was gone. There was nothing he could do now to repair the hurt he had caused. He had lost the only woman in the world that meant anything to him. He now knew that he had lost the love of his life.

The pain in his chest hurt so terribly, every day and every night. Nothing made him smile anymore; he felt gloomy and dismal.

"Nath, get out of bed," Pabbi said, sympathetically. "We need your help outside again to plow."

"I feel exhausted, Pabbi," Nath answered. "I don't know if I can."

"Enough of this, Nath," Pabbi said, his eyes pleading. "You have to do something to get back to being yourself again. You hardly eat. You hardly do anything but sleep. Come on, Nath, I have apologized many times. I've installed all the wood stoves. Me and Viktor have been plowing every snowfall for two weeks. It's time you started helping." An empty silence filled the room. "We miss you, Nath."

Nath looked up; his eyes were red and swollen. His face was becoming gaunt and pale. Pabbi was worried about his son.

"What would it take to get my son back?" Pabbi asked.

Nath just looked back, with an empty stare.

"Okay, you are going to come with me," Pabbi announced, removing the blankets from Nath's legs. "We're going for a walk along the frozen lake. Me and Viktor have cleared a path. Let's go. You are getting up."

Pabbi grabbed Nath's pants and laid them on his bed. "Get dressed," Pabbi instructed.

Nath nodded and pulled the pants on. "Alright," he answered indifferently.

A few minutes later, Viktor was at the door, and they started trekking towards the ice lake. It was a rare beautiful winter day. The sun was out, and the wind was light, but it was still very cold. Nath stopped suddenly and gazed across the lake. The horizon was amazing, the frozen lake was whiteish, and the sky was bright blue in contrast. Icicles hung from the trees along the shoreline, like ice ghosts somehow holding out their white fingers to the lake.

Viktor and Pabbi silently stopped, gazing out across the vastness of the frozen landscape.

"I have to talk to her," Nath said to the lake.

The lake responded with a gust of wind. It blew into all three men's faces.

Nath looked at his father. "I'm going to Gimli tomorrow. I have to see her. I have to talk to her."

"Alright," Pabbi said, solemnly.

Nath's brow furrowed. He would walk to Gimli tomorrow; he would find her and talk to her. His heart both jumped and recoiled at the same time. The fear of rejection was so heavy in his heart; he felt like not taking on such a bold action. But something was telling him to go. He must. There was no other way that he could move forward. He had to see her again, even if it meant that she would possibly reject him.

Nath turned and walked back to the cabin, as Viktor and Pabbi followed. They trudged along the cleared path, past the lake cabins, until they arrived at the horse's barn. Nath stopped abruptly as if he just had an epiphany.

Nath turned and stared at both men with his icy blue eyes. "If you ever call her an Indian one more time, you will never see me again," he said. "Her name is Anwa. You will address her as such." Then he shuffled into the barn to check on the horses.

❦ · · · ❦

Anwa's mother, Bea, brought a cup of steaming hot tea to her place at the table. Anwa stubbornly waved it away. She was feeling nauseous again.

"You have to drink," her mother stated. "You have hardly eaten for the past two weeks. Please at least drink something."

Anwa pursed her lips in response and drank the tea. She had not slept well; actually, every night, she didn't sleep well. Her dreams were filled with images of Nath, their lovemaking, the life they had shared for that blissful week together and the fight that ended it all. She was disappointed and terribly sad. Her heart felt heavy and painful like it somehow had been physically harmed. Food continued to make her sick to her stomach. Mamma was after her to eat more. Anwa nibbled here and there, but her appetite was simply gone.

"Mamma," Anwa said softly. "I have to ask you something."

"Yes, my dear, anything," Bea answered.

"Promise not to be mad with me," Anwa insisted.

Bea squinted her eyes, curiously. "Why would I be angry? I know how much you loved Nath. It's obvious."

"But it's more than that, Mamma," Anwa looked down awkwardly.

"Ok, what is it?" Bea asked, curiously.

Anwa sipped at the tea, then looked up briefly. "What happens if your monthly cycle is late by a few days?"

"How many days?"

"Just two days so far," Anwa replied.

"It might be nothing," Bea replied. "A full week without bleeding. That is when you might have something to worry about."

"Thank you, mamma, for not getting mad," Anwa said softly.

Bea put down the pot of boiling water, crossed the hut and hugged her daughter warmly. "My dear, I love you more than anything in this world," Bea said. "But you are a woman now. You will be eighteen-years-old next month, and I am grateful that you were able to experience true love. I know you feel despaired and distraught that he's not in your life, but things are not always clear to us in the moment. The path of the future is not always something we understand when looking ahead, but it is always clear when we look back. If the love you felt with Nath is meant to be, it will come back. If it wasn't, then you will move on. And we will deal with any consequences as they arise. I will always be here for you, my sweetie."

Anwa sniffled the tears back. "Thank you, mamma," she mumbled, as she hugged into the warmth of her mother. "I love you."

Nath packed his bag with dried meat and water. To keep warm, he dressed in a wool sweater and pants, a large fur coat and wrapped his feet in his Icelandic sheepskin boots. He set off for Gimli at first light.

Viktor and Kristjan ran to catch up to Nath.

"We need a few more furs and blankets," Kristjan said, as he ran up to Nath.

All three men trudged through the snow towards the road. The snow was soft and yielded to their footsteps. It was sunny but cold.

"What are you going to say to her?" Viktor asked.

"Funny," Nath replied. "I've been asking myself the same thing. I really don't know. I guess I'm just going to ask to talk to her, apologize and tell her that I love her."

"That's a good start," Kristjan replied.

Time passed slowly as silence descended upon the group. With only the sound of snow crunching below their feet, the group continued travelling for two hours before finally arriving in Gimli. They walked towards the snow-crusted marina.

No one was there. It was deserted, so they continued on towards Aron's home. Nath had not seen Aron for a month, mostly due to the cold weather. He had heard from Viktor that Aron had built a homestead next to Yuri's farm. He had purchased the 160 acres from the Dominion for ten dollars. In agreement with the Dominion contract, he promised to live on the land for three years and cultivate it. Yuri, Julia's father, had gifted some of the money, and the remaining amount was paid directly from Aron's savings. He had worked steadily at the farm, stashing away most of his hard-earned wages. Aron and Julia were getting married next weekend. The town of Gimli had a happy vibe; everyone the group encountered smiled and waved. But of course, everyone knew that a wedding was imminent. Gimli was undoubtedly beginning to have a homey feel.

They finally arrived at Aron's property. It was a vast farmland, mostly with trees and shrubs still. Aron had erected a crude log cabin, complete with all four walls; no tent materials were used in the construction. The group chatted about the structure of the cabin.

Viktor spoke first. "I was thinking of moving the settlement closer to Gimli and build similar cabins. We could bring the materials from our old cabins with us and construct more permanent homes. What do you think, Nath?"

"That's something to think about," Nath said. "We would need to get a break in the weather. At least a few days. It would be nice to be closer to everyone else and build more permanent homes, so we don't have any more deaths."

Kristjan knocked on Aron's door.

They heard footsteps and then Aron appeared at the door. "Holy Jesus! My brother and cousins!" Aron exclaimed happily. "Come in, come in." Aron hugged them heartily. When he hugged Nath, he felt his slim arms and his gaunt face. "Nath, what have you been up to? You look sick. Are you okay?"

"I'm fine. Just tired," Nath replied.

Viktor interrupted, "He's not fine at all, Aron. We are looking for Anwa. They broke up. He wants to just talk to her. That's why we are here."

Nath lifted his eyelids tiredly. "Viktor's right. I need to talk to her, Aron. Do you know where she is?"

At that moment, Julia walked in the front door. "Oh, hi!"

"Julia," Aron said happily, smiling. "My brother, Kristjan and my cousins are here to visit." Aron turned to the men, addressing them all. "You are all coming to our wedding? We are celebrating it at Yuri's house."

"Yes, yes, of course," Viktor replied, smiling. Kristjan and Nath nodded in agreement.

"They are here to find Anwa, my dear," Aron said to Julia.

"Oh!" Julia replied excitedly. "Well, you are in luck then, because she is living at her mother's house with Garth, which is the next property beside us to the east."

Nath's eyes lit up. "Oh? That's great to hear. Have you heard from her?"

'Yes," Julia said. "We have been chatting here and there over the past couple of weeks."

"You are friends?" Nath asked.

"Sort of," Julia said. "Me and Aron just moved in, so we are beginning to form the start of a nice friendship."

"Oh," Nath replied. "That's good."

Silence descended on the group, abruptly.

Julia broke the silence. "She is quite distraught, Nath."

"She is?" Nath replied, with a glimmer of hope in his voice.

Julia wrapped her arms around Nath, hugging him warmly. She then pulled him away, looking him in the eyes. "Looks like you have been distraught too, Nath. You need to talk to that woman. You know that she loves you deeply."

Nath's eyes welled with tears. "I hope so."

"She does," Julia confirmed.

Aron interrupted loudly. "I have an announcement to make, especially for my brothers and kin." He grabbed Julia by the waist and hugged her to his side. She smiled with a glow only the lovesick can show. "We are with child! Julia is pregnant with my first child. She is the love of my life. A good wife too!" Aron smiled happily and grabbed some cups, pouring some weak beer and handing them to the group. "Toast to our marriage and our future children!"

The men clinked the cups and chatted loudly for several minutes. Julia watched as Nath grew quiet.

Nath was so happy for Aron and Julia. He wished that he was marrying Anwa. That was what he always wanted, even from the beginning. Nath thought about having children; a family was something he would love to share with Anwa. He accepted this. The thought of her having his child spread a warm feeling throughout his body; he would love that. She was the only woman in the entire world he would even think of having children with and raising a family together. She was special to him. So much so that he couldn't function without her. Nath's eyes glossed over, with a faraway look.

Julia noticed. "Nath," she said. "Go to Anwa. The others can stay here while we celebrate the good news. Talk to her. Tell her you love her, and you will never let her go again."

Nath smiled warmly. "Thank you, Julia," he replied. "Hey, brothers! I will be back! I'm going to find Anwa. Celebrate, and I will rejoin you, men, later."

They all agreed in unison, nodding and happily chatting. Nath waved goodbye and closed the door behind him.

He walked along the packed snow on the road, heading east towards the small cottage. The little home stood boldly in the wind with a trail of smoke billowing out the top from the stove. He could feel her presence already. He knew she was there. His emotions began to flood over him. His heart banged wildly in his chest. He rehearsed what he would say, talking out loud. Then erased everything and restarted. Everything sounded so stupid. Now he wasn't sure what he would say at all!

Before he knew it, he was at the front door, knocking. He must have been running again because he was out of breath. The effect this woman has on me is out of this world, he thought.

The door opened abruptly.

It was Anwa.

Nath was in shock; he hadn't seen her in two weeks. She was such a wonderfully warm woman. He could feel her energy emanating throughout the room. They locked eyes; he was dumbstruck. Her long thick black hair flowed freely down her shoulders. Nath was absolutely astonished by her beauty. His foot felt like it was in his mouth as her large brown eyes stared right through his soul.

"Anwa," Nath said foolishly, stumbling over his words. "I rehearsed a thousand things to say to you, and now that you're standing in front of me, I have completely forgotten every one of them."

"Nath," she laughed softly.

Nath took a step towards her, closing the distance between them. The magnetism was so strong; he could feel it's physical pull. "I miss you," Nath quietly stated. He opened his arms, bringing her into his chest, wrapping himself around her.

Anwa melted into his body, glancing up at him, her brown eyes welling with tears. "Oh my, Nath, I have missed you so terribly," she replied, hugging him fiercely, burying her face in his fur collar. "I'm so sorry."

Nath's heart exploded. His pent-up emotions released into a torrent of misery and happiness. She started sobbing into his neck. Tears dropped from Nath's eyes onto her head. He had no control over his emotions with this woman. Sometimes, it just felt like he was going with the tide, always floating along with Anwa, never even aware of the sequence of events until afterwards, just enjoying every moment so thoroughly and joyfully.

They stood there at the door, crying on each other, so happy to just be in each other's embrace again. Her smell wafted into his nostrils, filling him with her pheromones until he felt high and giddy. Her softness made his heart melt instantly. He forgot every single thing he had rehearsed and just said the next thing that came to his mind.

"Marry me, Anwa," Nath said, kissing the top of her head. "I don't want to be with any other woman than you.

Pabbi apologized. No more racism. Not from my family, anyways. I will never hide stuff from you again. I will involve you and treat you like the special woman that you are. I don't want to live without you, babe." Nath cried, tears silently dropping onto her head. He gripped her body tightly, like if he was to release her that she might leave again.

She looked up at him. Her eyes glowed with joy. "Yes, Nath, yes," she replied, laughing through her tears. The sobs of joy were swelling her eyes and wetting her cheeks.

It was the most beautiful thing in the world to him; Anwa crying and laughing at the same time. They both laughed together.

"Close the door!" Bea's voice boomed through the cottage. "It's the middle of winter! Geez!"

Nath scooped Anwa's legs up and carried her into the cottage, kicking the door behind him.

"Nath!" Bea cried in surprise.

"I am marrying your daughter, Bea," Nath said. "Do I have your permission? Garth, is he here?"

Bea beamed happily. "No, Garth is not here," she said. "But it doesn't matter because after what we had to go through with Anwa for the past two weeks, everyone in the town of Gimli knows how much you both love each other!" Bea smiled.

Nath beamed in joyful delight. "Oh!" he said, laughing, as he carried Anwa throughout the house.

"Nath!" Anwa giggled. "You are so silly!"

"Oh, my sweetheart," Nath said. "No, far from it. I never want to live without you again, in this life or the next. It was the most terrible feeling of despair that I have ever endured. Even the arduous journey travelling from Iceland cannot compare. My Anwa, dear, you are the one for me."

"You can put me down now," Anwa said, giggling.

"No, Mrs. Anwa Olason, I will not," Nath laughed. "You might run away again! I might have to strap you to my body permanently!"

Bea and Anwa burst into laughter, simultaneously.

"I'm not joking," Nath said, laughing along with them. "Grab your clothes; you are coming to live with me. We are going to be married, and we are going to have children together. I will build a home in Gimli, right across the street, if I can. We will start moving building materials tomorrow. Most of the settlers are moving here anyway. I will convince Pabbi to come too. We will be living together close to both our families. Then we can raise our children with support. I want to have a child with you, Anwa."

Anwa glanced at Mamma, briefly and knowingly.

Nath caught the glance. "What?"

"It's nothing, Nath," Anwa said. "Mamma said I need to wait a week."

"What?" Nath said. "No, I am not waiting a week. You are coming with me right now. Grab your stuff."

"No, no, it's not that, Nath," Anwa replied. "You misunderstand. It's my period. It is late. But I need to wait a week before I can be sure."

Nath suddenly felt light-headed. He laid Anwa on the bed, sat down beside her and was at a loss for words. His heart thumped crazily in his chest, and his thoughts were all jumbled, so he just kissed her. His lips met hers, and his mind floated in a maze of happiness. She was going to have my baby, he thought. He slipped his tongue into her mouth and tasted her wonderful sweetness, everything he missed so dearly for what seemed like an eternity. And now she was back! He would never lose her again.

She broke the kiss and smiled. "Okay, Nath," she said. "I'm going to pack my things now. We will leave the right way together."

"Ok, sweetheart," Nath replied, smiling, as he watched her rush around the cabin, snatching clothing and personal items.

"Anwa," he said suddenly.

She stopped and looked at him.

"I love you," Nath said softly, a tear streaming down his cheek. "I love you so much, Anwa."

She hugged him fiercely. "I love you too, Nath."

CHAPTER 10

The next day, the weather calmed down, allowing Nath and a few others to begin the move to Gimli. They packed up the trailer, their belongings, dismantled the cabins, along with the half tents and moved everything to Gimli. It took several trips, but they were able to complete the move in two days.

Nath had found a parcel of land to build upon, close to the lake. He bought it from the previous owner, a small fisherman. It was perfect, close to the beach and the boats. Nath and Aron constructed their cabin in one day, working tirelessly. Pabbi stayed at Willow Point for the time being. He said he would join the group later when the homes were built, and everyone was settled. There were already 25 solidly constructed homes built from the first big move from Willow Point, Nath was one of the last. The cabins were built with log walls, no tent material, complete with windows and a door in the middle of the east wall. The homes were approximately twelve feet square, with the wood stove in the middle. The rafters were topped with withered grass rubbish and plastered with clay. Nath built his cabin similarly. He placed one bed along each side-wall, one for Pabbi and his larger bed for Anwa and himself. They both loved their delightful new home!

By the end of the week, Nath and Anwa spread the news that they were expecting a baby. The period never did come, so they both took that as the confirmed sign of pregnancy. Just knowing that his baby was developing in Anwa's tummy filled Nath with so much warmth and tenderness, he was overfilled with joy. They had chosen to get married along with Aron and Julia this weekend in a large family gathering.

Anwa felt so deliriously happy. "What will we do for trade?" she asked, as she boiled water for hot tea.

"Fishing, of course," Nath replied.

"Oh!" Anwa smiled. "That would be perfect."

"I know," Nath said, turning to close the space between them. He hugged her and ran his hands along her thighs, feeling her curves through her clothes. "It's exactly what we should be doing together."

Anwa looked up and kissed his lips gently.

Nath responded immediately, moving his hands up to her ample breasts. She moaned and arched her back, pressing her tummy into him. During the move and building, they had few opportunities for lovemaking; but they quickly did it anyway, sometimes in the forest, sometimes in the tool shed hastily, tearing at each other's clothes, but it was always hurried with imminent interruptions. This was the first day they were left entirely alone. "We have been so busy moving and building," Nath stated, his eyes hooded a sexy invitation.

"Yes, we have," Anwa agreed, sucking gently on his lower lip. "Too busy."

Nath groaned and pressed his erection into her tummy. "I want you," he murmured into her ear.

Anwa grabbed his stiff penis and rubbed it through his clothes, running her hands along it repeatedly, until he could take no more. He gently laid her back onto the bed, pulling his pants down and entering her smoothly, sliding into her vagina effortlessly. Anwa lifted her dress higher and fumbled to remove her blouse. The heat increased ten folds suddenly. Her vagina trickled moisture all over his penis, flooding him with her honey. It was almost too much for him to maintain control. He stopped abruptly and looked at her face.

Anwa's face was sweaty and flushed. She was still fumbling with her blouse, trying to untie the brassiere. Nath helped her, and they both removed the offending garment. He laid fully onto her bare breasts. A hot electric current raced throughout his system, making his penis almost painfully hard. He slid out of her slowly, hearing her whimper for more. Just the sound of her whimper almost made him lose control.

He took a deep breath and slid slowly back inside her wetness. She gasped, her mouth opening wide, and her neck stretched up in ecstasy.

He had to close his eyes and think of building cabins. He squinted his eyes and concentrated on thinking about log walls until he could feel his penis soften slightly inside her.

When he opened his eyes, she was still in the throes of ecstasy, her mouth open. He kissed her mouth, darting his tongue inside her. She moaned and opened her mouth further, encouraging him. He was intensely focused on her lovely mouth.

"I have an idea that I would like to try," Nath said.

Anwa opened her eyes halfway in the sexiest way. "Mmm, yes. Put it in my mouth. I want to taste it," she replied, reading his mind.

Nath's heart rate doubled. He slid out of her entirely and placed his penis in her eager mouth. She accepted it lovingly, licking, kissing, then finally swallowing his penis inside her mouth. It was the most exquisite naughty feeling for them both. Nath could feel her sweet tongue and lips caressing his penis.

Anwa felt immersed in his scent. It was all over her, in her vagina, in her mouth, and his groin was completely in her face. She felt light-headed now. She simply loved the way he smelled. It was her favourite smell in the entire world! And he tasted heavenly. She had never done such a thing, but she loved it. All her senses were alive and vibrating. She licked and sucked, alternately, then grabbed her favourite body part in her hands, licking the tip.

Nath groaned heavily.

It spurred her on, and she felt compelled to continue ravishing his penis.

Suddenly, he stiffened and pulled away, breathing heavily.

Anwa looked up at him, questioningly. The moonlight streamed through the window, showing his sweaty naked body to her, all covered with her saliva and wetness.

Then he did something odd. He turned around, laying above her, with his head at her vagina and his penis in her face.

"Mmm," she moaned, happily licking at his penis again.

Suddenly, it was her that stiffened. His tongue licked at her vagina, tasting the delicacy. She gasped loudly and jerked. He grabbed her buttocks firmly. "It's okay, sweetheart. Relax. Let me taste you," he said lovingly.

"But," she weakly protested.

"Just relax," he murmured.

He flicked his tongue at her clitoris and felt her shudder. He tried licking other parts of her, waiting for the right responses. Finally, he just plunged his tongue into her vagina.

Anwa gasped loudly. She mumbled in her native language, momentarily lost. Nath licked her honey into his mouth, savouring the hot liquid. She tasted so luscious that he thought he could do this all night. Her vagina was so soft and spongy; her smell very pleasant and slightly sweet.

Anwa tried licking at his penis at the same time, trying to focus on him, but quickly lost her control. The sensations grabbed her, and she felt like she was coming towards a cliff, a pinnacle. Her whole body began to quiver. Nath held firmly onto her buttocks as she began to squirm. Instinct told him to hold onto her as she reached her orgasm.

Finally, the tension was too much for Anwa to take. She shouted and ground her hips up into his face as a gush of fluid released onto his beard, soaking his chin thoroughly. He held onto her firmly, licking up the watery mess as her body shuddered in his grasp. She moaned loudly, sending shards of electricity throughout his body. He was immensely pleased with himself for producing such an intense response from her. He felt like someone had just crowned him king!

Nath giggled.

Anwa giggled in return, sweaty and exhausted. "What are you laughing about?" she breathed.

"Nothing," Nath responded. "It's just that I feel immensely proud of that."

Anwa laughed.

Nath turned his body around and smiled up at her. Anwa's face and chest glowed with a gleam of sweat. Her hair flowed all over the place, alongside the pillow, the bed, some above her pillow. It was a lovely disarray of sexual bliss.

He moved up and kissed her lips, then smiled at her. "You are so beautiful, Anwa," he said, smoothing her hair.

"I love you, Nath," Anwa said softly.

"I love you too, Anwa," he replied slowly. Nath moved his hips, then grabbed his penis and positioned himself.

He entered her vagina smoothly, sliding into her extreme wetness. She moaned and relaxed her hips as he slid in and then out of her. Her vagina was incredibly tight and pulsating against his penis, oddly. It must be an aftermath physical response from tasting her, he thought; it felt deliciously different like her vagina was throbbing around his penis.

His control vanished within seconds, and he could feel his orgasm gripping his mind in a tunnel of no return. He increased his rhythm until all he could hear was Anwa's groans and gasps. His blood pumped into his groin. His head swam in a light-headed sensual fog as all his senses collided into this one sexual moment in time.

His semen burst from his penis deep into her vagina. Anwa gasped, feeling the force of the ejaculation inside her. Another burst of semen released from his penis and then another, emptying him entirely.

He felt weak and unstable. He laid fully on top, kissing her shoulder as his body shuddered and trembled. His heartbeat pumped crazily in his chest, and his breathing was heavy. Anwa smoothed the back of his head as he lay still fully inserted in her vagina, his penis slowly softening.

His sweat was all over her. They both lay depleted and exhausted; their breath finally slowing. Her hair was sticky with her own sweat, but he loved every imperfection of her. He loved her curvy hips, her large legs, her large breasts, her small waist and, most of all, her lovely vagina.

But it was her that spoke first. "I love everything about you, Nath," she breathed.

"You must have been reading my mind," Nath replied. "I was thinking the exact same thing about you, my sweetheart."

Nath changed position, sliding to the side and pulling Anwa towards his chest. He was amazed at how perfectly she fit into his grasp. Anwa let out a sigh of love, and they cuddled into each other's arms. They murmured in soft conversation until they both fell asleep enveloped in each others warmth.

They had married on the weekend and were officially husband and wife now. This filled both of them with a pleasant feeling of fulfillment. Nath loved his wife immensely, and Anwa loved him back every chance she had.

But there were other problems, specifically the weather. During the following week, the weather grew terribly cold. They were running out of dried meat and rations. Fishing, while the lake was frozen, was not impossible, but something they had to learn. They would try ice fishing as soon as the winds calmed down. But the immediate concern was food. They had to get some food into the village. There were many people sick and weak from the dwindling rations and the cold. Several people had died from scurvy and Nath was afraid there would be many more deaths if they didn't get enough food. They had to do something.

"We need to get some more dried meat and vegetables," Nath said. "Many townsfolk are sick. I am scared that we will lose more people."

Anwa poured some hot tea into a cup. Her pregnancy nausea had started again. Her mother told her to keep nibbling and drinking lots of fluids. "We can travel to see my big brother, Mikom, in the Sandy Bar village," she said. "Typically, the village stores enough dried meat to last them the winter.

I'm sure my brother will trade some. Maybe we can give him some Hudson Bay blankets; I love those."

"How far is Sandy Bar?"

"It is a full day walk on a nice summer day, but during the winter, it could take two days," she said.

"Maybe we could take the horses," Nath replied.

"Yes, we could," she said. "Mikom has horses as well. He could feed them upon arrival. The journey would be hard on the horses. We would have to take it slow and keep them warm when we rest."

"How long do you think it would take with horses?" Nath asked.

"Probably two to four hours," Anwa replied. "Depending on the road conditions and the wind. Horses don't like cold wind."

"Hmm," Nath said, nodding in agreement. "I think it's worth the risk. The weather will just get colder. It will be January soon."

"My birthday's in January," Anwa mentioned.

Nath smiled broadly.

"What?" Anwa giggled.

"My birthday is in January also," Nath said. "January tenth."

"Mine is January fourteenth," Anwa laughed.

He kissed her forehead. "I love you," he said. "We will celebrate it as one birthday. Ours together."

Anwa's face broke into a huge grin. She smiled happily.

"I love seeing your happy face," Nath said, smiling.

"I love you, Nath," Anwa replied, pecking him with kisses along his chest.

They hugged in the cabin, silently, for several minutes, enjoying the solitude.

Nath spoke first. "We will leave in the morning," he said. "I will check on the horses and make sure they are kept warm and well-fed tonight."

"Alright, babe," Anwa agreed.

The morning sun shone brightly against the white snow, almost blindingly, as they packed up the horses and prepared for the journey north. They tried to pack light but also took some emergency items just in case they faltered on their journey. It was risky taking horses on a winter journey. It was risky just a human going on a trip in this cold weather. Anwa packed the meagre rations they had left, as well as the blankets for the horses and the rifle Nath insisted upon, just in case they came across any deer.

The roads were rough, snow-packed, and the journey was painstakingly slow. The snow on the ground had reached almost 50 inches, more in the drifts. They decided to take the lakeside path instead of the road. The route was more direct, and along the lake, the snow was evenly packed. Although the lake could become very windy and the gusts worried Anwa, she knew horses were sensitive to extreme wind. Nath and Anwa discussed the risks and drawbacks, deciding on the lakeside path over the weathered horse road. It could save them time, and they could arrive an hour earlier if everything went well. They decided if the wind became fierce in spots, they would alter their route and travel closer to the treeline.

Nath shielded his eyes from the blinding sunlight and mounted the horse, as Anwa did the same. The horse's hooves clambered and crunched on the snow as they set off to Swampy Cree village.

The wind was light so far.

Anwa's horse pulled a small sleigh behind them, enough room for the rations that they would be hauling back. It was empty except for the blankets and a few emergency camping items. Nath shifted his body to find a comfortable position on the saddle and glanced behind him to check on Anwa. She looked more comfortable than him; he chuckled to himself.

The weather was cold but passable as travelling weather. How long the horses would be able to journey without resting would be the determining factor in the travel time. They trudged on, hopeful that the journey would be quick.

The landscape blended into a frigid white tundra that continued on forever, it seemed, and they both began to get weary. As they neared the more northern areas of the lake, the wind started to pick up. Here the lake widened so much that you could no longer see the other side. It looked like an ocean and sometimes acted like it, with snow squalls, wicked winds and lake tides.

The horses started neighing and hanging their heads down.

Anwa shouted to be heard over the winds, "Let's move into the treeline! The horses won't last long in this wind!"

Nath veered the reins to the left and guided his horse closer to the treeline. The wind was still fierce here. The horses stopped completely. He turned around, "What do we do?" he asked. "The horses don't want to continue in this wind."

"We will have to enter the forest then," Anwa replied. "It's not ideal, but we have no other choice. We should have just taken the main road."

"There would have been just as much wind there too," Nath answered. "The road only goes so far north; then it disappears into a snow-packed wilderness. At least this way, we know where we are going, and the snow is crusted. We are making good time. Don't worry."

Anwa nodded skeptically, "You're right, I guess. I was hoping not to put the horses in any danger, either way."

"We are putting ourselves in danger too," Nath pointed out. His short beard was forming icicles, and his face was reddening from the wind. He tucked his chin into the scarf around his neck as he guided the horse into the forest. Reluctantly, the horse moved slowly and cautiously into the treeline. Anwa's horse followed.

"Maybe we should stop and give the animals a rest," Nathan mentioned, shouting behind him.

"Good idea," Anwa answered back. "We could boil some snow and give them the water while covering them with blankets."

"Okay," Nath replied. "Let's stop when we see a good area to take a rest."

The trees gathered overcrowdedly in the lakeside forest, mostly oaks and aspens, although there was the occasional evergreen. Nath loved how the forest beckoned you but, at the same time, repelled you. The small branches stuck out everywhere, breaking with the impact of the horses and his legs. The horses were tiring, so Nath halted his horse and disembarked, walking with the reins as he searched for a suitable resting spot.

Several yards away, he caught sight of a small clearing, approximately 10 feet by 10 feet. The snow was packed, and there was enough room for a little fire, even some ground was showing.

He led the horses to the small clearing as Anwa followed, jumping off her horse too. They finally arrived at the clearing and Anwa began digging in the sleigh, pulling out the blankets. Suddenly, the horses started backing up. She grabbed the reins and began pulling back the horse to the clearing, tying the reins to a tree. The horses continued pulling away.

Nath was confused. Why were the horses pulling back? He grabbed his horse's reins and guided the animal to another tree. His horse was almost fighting him as he finally tied the animal's reins.

That was when he sensed something might be wrong.

Horses don't do that unless they are frightened, he thought. Nath looked at Anwa; he could tell that she was thinking the same thing. She dug in the sleigh bag and handed him the rifle.

Nathan nodded and grabbed the barrel, quietly surveying the area. At first, he didn't see anything. The horses grew very quiet. It was daylight, but the forest was dimmer, and shadows played with his sight. Anwa was scanning intently too, but they both failed to see anything. Nath's eyes searched the area, falling to the clearing itself. He noticed the snow was packed quite hard like something had been living here.

Then his peripheral vision caught some movement to their right. It was a large animal, greyish with lots of fur. It was in the shadows. Nath slowly turned his head as the wolf's eyes met his. Nath's instincts went to high alarm. Immediately, he wondered where the rest of the pack was, but he would not take his eyes from the wolf's position.

"Anwa," he whispered. "It's a grey wolf. I want to know if he's alone or in a pack."

Anwa surveyed the rest of the bushes. "I see two other wolves, both to our left, one slightly behind us and one directly left of us," she answered.

"Then he's probably the alpha wolf," Nath said. "And we just walked right into their lair."

Nath raised the barrel slowly, inch by inch, as to not startle the wolves. When he had the rifle on his shoulder, looking through the sights, he noticed the male wolf stand. It was a huge wolf, almost 3 feet high, with dark grey colouring, mixed in with white. The animal moved stealthily towards their position one paw in front of the other, crouching very slowly, assessing the threat. Nath noticed that the alpha wolf was not growling, although the fur at the back of his neck was standing.

Nath cocked the rifle. The large click sounded throughout the forest with an echo.

The wolf stopped in his tracks. It seemed like the animal had heard this ominous sound before. The area was being heavily hunted by farmers to protect their livestock, resulting in the almost extinction of the Manitoba Wolf, a smaller reddish breed. Maybe this wolf had encountered humans before and knew the risks or worse he didn't care.

Nath aimed, looking down the sights. He heard Anwa breathing beside him.

The bushes crackled as the wolf moved ever so slowly, creeping towards them again.

"The two others are moving closer, too," Anwa whispered.

Nath cleared his throat and shouted at the animals sharply. "Make your move, Alpha!" he yelled.

"It's a young pack," Anwa said softly. "Inexperienced and hungry. That's not good. They are toying with us." Anwa pulled out her bow and arrow stealthily, aiming it at the wolf behind them, another big male.

Branches snapped as the lead alpha wolf crept towards Nath, quicker this time.

Nath clicked his tongue. "Now," he shouted to Anwa.

He pulled the trigger. The rifle recoiled as Nath pushed his shoulder firmly back, steadying the impact. The bullet whizzed through the air just as the lead wolf reacted, leaping towards them. The bullet stopped him in mid-air. The wolf yelped and fell to the snow-covered ground, just as Anwa's arrow whistled through the air towards the other male wolf. The arrow hit the beta wolf in the chest, stopping his momentum and bringing him down to a pile on the snow.

Nath swerved his gun to the remaining wolf, but she was already gone, the branches snapping as the female wolf escaped into the thick forest.

He moved cautiously to the limp wolves, pointing his rifle at it. He gently nudged them with his foot until he was confident they were both dead. "Let's start a fire," Nath said. "The horses are jittery and need water. I'm hungry, and even though I don't care for wolf meat, I will eat just about anything. We can cook it over the fire."

Anwa prepared the fire as the adrenaline eased out of her blood. She grabbed a pot and threw mounds of snow into it. The snow began to heat, melting into water for the horses. It thawed quickly over the fire, while Nath field-dressed the alpha male with his hunting knife. When he was done, he dragged the carcass closer, slicing strips of meat off, impaling the bits on sharp branches and holding them over the fire. The meat sizzled as Nath and Anwa blanketed the horses, talking calmly to them. Anwa fed the horses hay and water as Nath continued roasting the wolf-meat. The horses soon settled down, feeling safer and warm. They wouldn't stay long, just to rest, warm up by the fire and eat.

Nath pulled the wolf-meat kabobs from the fire, handing one to Anwa. "Does your culture eat wolf?" he asked.

"Not often," she answered. "Only when they become a danger and food is scarce."

"Like now," Nath said, chewing on the meat.

"Exactly," Anwa answered. "I remember a time when I was younger and living at the Swampy Cree village with Mamma.

There was a pack of wolves that had stalked the village, seemingly interested in our food stores and our horses. We would scare them off with shouting and throwing rocks, but they were persistent."

"What happened?" Nath asked, guzzling water to wash down the tough meat.

Anwa chewed thoughtfully and swallowed. "Well, finally, one morning, we realized that the wolves had gotten one of the horses. She was a smaller horse but a much-loved loyal animal. The village was outraged. So the elders decided it was time to fight back. We stationed two sentries near the horses and another two near the food stores. They switched every four hours, so nobody felt too tired. Well, only two days later, the wolves were back."

Nath listened intently, enthralled with her story. "How big of a pack was it?"

"It was a large pack," she answered. "Probably eight wolves or more. Some days only five showed up, but other days it was all eight. I remembered as a little child that the nighttime howling was frightening."

"You must have been scared," he commented thoughtfully, wiping his mouth with his sleeve.

"Yes," she replied. "I was quite scared, but I felt safe within the village too. There were many skilled hunters in our village, women and men. Actually, that's how we were all raised to hunt for our food. It was essential for our survival."

"So, go on," Nath said. "What happened with the wolves?"

"Okay," Anwa continued. "Well, one evening after dusk, one of the good-sized packs, approximately seven wolves, showed up at the horse shelter again. Since it was evening, the entire village was still awake. A call was yelled out, alerting the elders. Approximately five hunters came out to the sentry position, ready with bow and arrows. They walked casually to the sentry positions, one by one. The wolves were skittish around humans, but they were also becoming more confident. After all, they had successfully eaten one of our horses. Another should be easy. All seven wolves began surrounding the horse stable. Then the hunters sprung, yelling and hollering, slinging arrows into the wolves." Anwa paused, placing a mouthful of meat into her mouth, chewing it and then swallowing. She wiped her mouth delicately with her hand and continued. "All seven wolves were killed. The horses were all very startled but settled down quite quickly when they realized the village had come together to protect them once and for all. The wolves never came back. We ate wolf meat for a few weeks afterwards."

Nath smiled. He loved her so much. Finding out about her history just gave him this fuzzy feeling in the depths of his heart. It made him love her so much more. A surge of affection spread warmly throughout his body. His eyes gleamed as he smiled at her. "I love you," he said. "I hope you know that."

She chuckled, "You say the most endearing things at the most unexpected times."

He laughed heartily, "Yes, I guess I do." He reached over and kissed her. She kissed him back as they embraced warmly, cuddling in front of the fire. "You know," he said. "I have never meant a woman before that I truly felt had my back like you. I feel like you would kill for me as I would also do the same. But, you, Anwa, are like this pillar of strength in my life that I can't quite explain. You are full of spirit, inner strength and this lovely femininity as well. You are beyond special."

Anwa smiled with tears forming in her eyes. "I love you, Nath," she said. "You are better than the best man that I have ever hoped for." She kissed him again and melted in his manly arms. They sat together by the fire for a few more minutes, just enjoying their full tummies, the love they both shared and the warmth of the fire.

Finally, after several minutes, Nath spoke, "We should continue our journey. Let's pack up and go, sweetheart."

Anwa nodded, and they both packed everything up, including the extra wolf meat and carcasses. The fur could be used for warm coats at Swampy Cree, a good trade for rations.

They mounted the horses and continued the journey throughout the frozen wilderness.

❧ ⋯ ☙

After two hours, the wind began to pick up again, swirling snow into the forest. They rode on as the cold temperatures started to play with their sense of direction. They kept close to the lake, always keeping an eye on where it was. The freezing humid temperatures had formed small icicles on Nath's beard, and white ice stuck on Anwa's eyelashes and brows.

"It is getting too cold," Nath shouted back towards Anwa.

"We are almost there," Anwa shouted back. "Let's just keep going. It should be just a little while longer."

The horses were tired, but they kept trotting. Anwa and Nath spoke gently to them, warming them with their own body heat. It seemed like an eternity in the snow-covered wilderness, step after step in the crunchy snow, leading nowhere.

Then finally, Nath saw a large plume of smoke in the distance. "Is that your hometown?' he yelled optimistically.

"Yes!" Anwa shouted back. "I think I have never seen another sight as welcoming before!" She laughed. "After this wicked journey, hot tea would be like heaven! My relatives will be most welcoming. You'll like Mikom!"

Nath laughed, the icicles on his beard jiggling as he spoke, "I think I will too!"

The horses trotted on until they arrived within 100 feet of the village. A few people mulled about, and a small boy ran out to greet them. Anwa spoke to him in Ojibwe, telling him to retrieve Mikom, that his sister had come to visit.

The small boy ran back energetically, yelling to the others happily.

Nath and Anwa laughed as the horses neared closer and closer to the village. As they approached, Anwa realized that her fingers were frozen, and Nath's nose looked like it was frostbitten.

A tall, husky man opened the flap to the teepee and trudged through the snow towards them. Anwa jumped off her horse and ran towards him. The man grabbed her into his arms and swung her about warmly. She walked back to Nath with the man, introducing them. Mikom was a very tall, confident man. He had rough skin and was prone to acne outbreaks, so it gave him the appearance of a tough guy, but he wasn't. Mikom was rough when he needed to be, but generally, he was gentle and calm. But today, he was wary. He eyed Nath suspiciously.

"Mikom," Anwa said, proudly. "This is my husband, Nathanael Olason."

Mikom's face instantly changed into a broad smile. "Ahh," he said happily. "You have married! Already? This is great news!"

"We are expecting a child too," Anwa said. "So, we thought it was best to marry quickly."

Mikom grabbed her shoulders and hugged her warmly. "I am very happy for you, my sister," he said. "Come in, come in!" He gestured to the large tent with smoke billowing from the top.

Anwa grabbed Nath's hand and led him to the tent. All over the reserve, tents dotted the close-knit native community. Nath spotted a rough barn in the trees, sheltered with felled logs for a roof and a few blankets, serving as a warm area for the horses.

"Can we take the horses to be fed, Mikom?" Nath asked. "They are tired and cold."

"Oh, yes, yes!" Mikom answered, grabbing the reins from Anwa and leading them to a young man in the center of the community. He spoke briefly to the boy in Ojibwe. The boy nodded and then grabbed both reins, leading the horses to the barn.

"They will be well fed and given warm blankets," Mikom announced, sincerely. "Let's go have some hot native tea to warm you both up."

"We have brought some wolf meat too," Anwa said. "Please take it to your stores. It's a gift for you."

"Wonderful!" Mikom said excitedly. "Had some trouble with wolves again?"

"Some, yes," she laughed.

Another younger man took the wolf carcasses to the food storage area. Nath and Anwa smiled as Mikom lead them to the central teepee.

Nath entered the tent and sat down, graciously accepting the offered hot tea, made of roots, leaves and berries. It tasted sweet, with a maple syrup flavour. It was a delicious hot drink.

Anwa cuddled close to him, curling her frozen fingers around the hot cup. "We have been making teas for a long time," she whispered to Nath. "We always boil our water because we believe that un-boiled water is unhealthy and will give you illness. This tea is similar to the one I make at home, but it has roots and maple syrup in it." She looked up at Mikom, addressing him directly. "Thank you, my brother, it's delicious, as always."

"You are welcome!" Mikom replied, noticing their visibly frost-bitten faces. "Come closer to the heat; you look absolutely frozen. Are you both okay? It is quite a journey in the midst of winter to come here to Sandy Bar."

Nath curled his fingers around his warm cup as well. "We are frozen for sure, but we will be okay. Your hot tea and warm tents will soon melt away the cold."

Mikom nodded, then turned his eyes to his sister. "Anwa. I love you and am thrilled to see you again, but I must ask. What brings you here in such dangerous frigid conditions?"

Anwa looked up at Mikom, blowing on the tea. "We are here to ask for your help, Mikom," she said. "The community of Gimli has just started. We have built almost 25 homes, but the winter and the unfortunate timing of the settlement has depleted our meat and food stores." She paused for effect. "People are dying, Mikom. It's an emergency. We need your help."

Mikom sipped the tea thoughtfully and stood. "What can we help with?"

"We brought some Hudson Bay blankets to trade for dried meat and vegetables for the village," Anwa bargained. "It's all yours, including the wolf fur, if you have any rations to spare for the growing Gimli community. Please help us."

"Hmm," Mikom scratched his head. "I believe we have some extra dried meat in storage. But vegetables are scarce. I will give you what I can." He nodded gravely, looking into his cup. "This is not good news for the Gimli settlers."

"I agree," Nath spoke. "As Anwa has said, the timing of the arrival in October meant that winter was upon us quicker than we could have imagined, and since we had already been travelling for six months previously, our storage of food was already low. Anwa helped us to learn how to catch the fish and where the deer gather. But now the weather has immobilized everything. We would greatly appreciate any food you could give to the community. If the blankets are not enough of a trade, would you consider a trade of money?"

"Money?" Mikom asked. "Currency means little to us. The blankets and wolf furs will be enough. If we need more, I trust you will get more blankets or whatever personal items once the weather warms up. We can consider it a loan."

"Yes, yes, of course," Nath replied.

"It's a deal then," Mikom stated, shaking hands with Nath. "We will load up the horses with sacks of food in the morning. In the meantime, I will feed you a nice dinner of dried deer and salted fish." Mikom put his arm around Nath and welcomed him to the family, warmly. "You are a good man. I am glad Anwa chose wisely. You are welcome here anytime."

The next day Anwa and Nath awoke to the winds wailing against the tent walls. They rushed out of bed and looked out. A severe blizzard was blowing in, obscuring the roads and reducing visibility to zero. The snow was falling steadily as the winds swept it into drifts, creating an almost impenetrable barrier around the village of Swampy Cree.

"You won't be able to travel today," Mikom said as he watched their anxious frowns. "You will need to stay until the winter storm passes."

Anwa and Nath nodded in agreement but glanced worryingly at each other. They silently agonized about the people in their town of Gimli. Nath swallowed hard. The forces of nature were against them. There was nothing they could do.

So they silently ate breakfast with the people of Swampy Cree, praying for the weather to break.

❦ ··· ❦

The return trip was delayed by still another day. After the blizzard had passed, the drifts and heavy snowfall had made the small horse roads inaccessible. The Swampy Cree village was wholly surrounded by drifts, and the recent snowfall was in excess of 30 inches. Anwa and Nath grew anxious. The food was loaded and ready to go, but the roads were impassable. The native community eventually came together and cleared the paths for their safe passage out of the reserve, but it was still slow and arduous. Nath and Anwa grabbed shovels, helping to dig themselves out of the snow and clear the way.

Finally, on the third day, Anwa and Nath left, arriving at Arnes, approximately halfway on their journey. They stopped to warm the horses and feed them before continuing on their trip. The weather was still dangerously frigid, but they had decided to take the main road this time. They left the horses with the stable hand and stopped at an emerging postal station he had heard about in the town. He wanted to mail some letters back to his mother in Iceland, informing her of the pregnancy and marriage to Anwa. He scribbled hastily to his Mamma, telling her to organize their things for travel. They would be joining the next group of settlers soon, bringing his sisters as well. Preparations were already underway for a very large group of Icelanders, sometime in the summer of 1876. A man named Sigurour in Arnes was arranging for letters to be sent back home to Iceland. He was a kind man. Nath liked him. Sigurour informed him that it might take weeks, but his letter would get there. Content with this, Nath nodded his approval, paid him with some coins and left to retrieve the horses.

When they returned, a farmhand was covering the horses with blankets and feeding them quietly. He was a friendly man, but something was disturbing him. He seemed quite shaken. He mentioned that he had just heard of the stories coming in from Gimli this morning. There was a major tragedy.

"What happened?" Nath said as shivers ran up his spine, lifting the hairs up on his head. "We are travelling back to Gimli with food rations today."

"Oh," the farmhand replied, sadly. "You didn't hear then. It's awful, the cold weather. It is terrible in Gimli right now. I'm so sorry."

"Oh my God," Anwa said, knowing the answer already.

"Lots of deaths in the last two days," the farmhand stated. "Many more than expected. Please, hurry. I will warm the horses and feed them for a few more minutes; then, you must go. Save your people, Nathanael."

Nath's skin goose-bumped all along his arms and the back of his head felt tingly, the hair all standing on end. He was too late, he thought, too late.

⁕ ··· ⁕

Nath and Anwa arrived in Gimli two and a half hours later. They distributed rations to each and every household in written loans for blankets, personal items, anything they could offer in exchange. They would travel back to see Mikom again and give him the items as agreed upon in late spring.

Thirty-four people had perished from the elements and scurvy. It was a sombre day. The town of Gimli organized a mass funeral and burial. Nath felt like his efforts were wasted. He had not arrived back in time to save all those people. He had failed.

"You did not fail, Nath," Anwa stared deeply into his blue eyes. "You have saved the people that were left, that barely survived. It could have been worse."

"But, Anwa," Nath said, soberly. "Thirty settlers died. I could have done more. I could have thought about leaving earlier, like a week before, maybe. My judgement was wrong. It's my fault."

"Nobody is blaming this on you, except yourself," Anwa said, lightly touching his cheek. "You are a smart, resilient, hard-working man. But you are just one man. You cannot save the world, Nath."

She kissed his lips gently, and he returned the kiss. Her hands wrapped around his muscular body, and she hugged him as they kissed.

"Thank you," Nath said.

The funeral procession led straight down Main Street to the fields outside the town. It was a sunny day, but frigidly cold. Many of the dead were young children, mostly under the age of sixteen and the elderly. Alexander, Gunnar's best friend, died, along with his younger brother and his father, Olafur. Many people were crying, their faces covered with veils.

The snow crunched under their feet as they walked somberly with the crowd. No one spoke; silence filled the entire congregation. Only the sound of weeping and sniffling could be heard. Nath walked along with his hand in Anwa's tight grip. She was his rock, he thought. Anwa was always there for him. She helped him during the first round of deaths at Willow Point and now at Gimli. She helped heal him and nursed Pabbi. She showed him where to catch the fish and deer. And now, she had been instrumental in obtaining winter food rations for the survivors. Without her, who knows, he could have been one of the dead. He owed this woman his life, he thought.

And she was having his baby!

"Are you okay, babe?" Anwa asked, looking sideways at Nath.

Nath smiled. "Now that we are together again. Yes," Nath replied. "Don't ever leave again, please. And," Nath squeezed her hand. "I thank you for everything you've done for my people, from the bottom of my heart. You are an amazing woman in so many different ways. I cannot imagine living another day without you. I love you so much."

Anwa squeezed his hand back. "I love you, Nath. It will get better from now on. Think positively."

"I hope so. I'm not sure how much more hardship we can handle," Nath said.

The crowd's pace started slowing down; they had arrived at the cemetery field. Thirty-four holes were dug, most very small, some larger. The priest conducted the ceremony. He reminded us that God teaches us lessons through hardship, that we must learn from our mistakes and always strive to be better people. When tragedy strikes, we need to believe that God will always be there for us.

The ceremony lasted only an hour, with each body being named and buried, the relatives crying whilst throwing dirt onto the graves. The weather was bitterly cold, so the ceremony was rushed, people left once they had buried their loved ones. Nath and Anwa departed with a group of relatives after Alexander's family was buried.

Pabbi was with them. He hugged Anwa. "Thank you for obtaining the food rations from your brother in Sandy Bar. It was a very nice thing to do. You have saved many lives."

"You are welcome, Pabbi," Anwa said. "We are family now. I would do anything for family."

"Yes," Pabbi said, nodding. "Yes, we are."

Nath squeezed her shoulder and kissed her hair. "We're in this together, babe."

CHAPTER 11

The next few months seemed like things were getting better, but then the food started dwindling again. The weather was still cold, but warming slightly. The winter rations had lasted three months, but even Nath's supply was disappearing now. Several more deaths occurred back in January and February from the cold, although, now, some townsfolk were dying from starvation again. Nath was sure that this was something they had the power to do something about within the community.

Nath and Anwa had celebrated their birthdays back in January, both turning 18. It was a milestone. They were adults with their own cabin, their own decisions and their own lives. It was March, and they were preparing to go ice fishing today. Nath was not going to starve to death. Anwa had suggested they revisit Mikom, but Nath had enough of this. He felt compelled to fix the problem.

"So, is this all we need?" Nath asked.

Anwa nodded. "Axe, long slim tree trunk for measuring, a tent and, of course, the nets," she answered.

"Okay, let's go," Nath urged.

Anwa and Nath walked out onto the frozen lake dragging a sleigh full of supplies. They travelled out quite a distance. The wind was fierce here. Anwa pointed at a spot, and they settled there, putting up the tent to protect against the wind. Nath hammered the tent pegs into the ice, while Anwa pulled the tent tight. They both worked together until the tent was erected. Then they both went inside. Nath started chipping the ice with the axe, starting with a square to minimize splashing. It took an incredibly long time, almost an hour before he had broken the hole right through the ice. He went outside and axed another hole in the ice.

Anwa, meanwhile, measured the first hole with the tree trunk. She estimated that the ice was 4 feet thick, and the nets needed to be in the water another 5 feet deep, so they needed to measure a total of 9 feet with the long slim deadwood. Nath returned and gripped the tree trunk as well, helping her lower it. Once they had it submerged, they both tugged it back out satisfied with the measurement. The depth was perfect, 9 feet, 4 inches measured.

They lowered the nets, secured them through the two holes and then retreated into the tent, warming each other with their body heat. Nath's hands were freezing. Anwa pulled him in closer to her, and they cuddled, sitting on a flat piece of wood, in silence, breathing in the stillness of the afternoon. There was only the sound of the wind flapping against the tents. It was rhythmic and somehow calming. They snuggled tightly, wrapped in each other's embrace. Nath loved spending these solitary moments with Anwa. He wrapped his arms around her, while she held both his hands, blowing warm breath onto them. It was so special to share silent moments with another human being, especially someone he loved deeply. He felt like he was the luckiest man on earth. It was spiritual. The world felt like it just stopped in time; nothing existed except this.

Anwa moved his cold hands inside her shirt to her bare breasts. They were hot! He chuckled. She giggled.

It soon worked, though. His hands grew warmer and warmer. He kissed the top of her head and began rocking her. The movement was lovely, almost as if they were tangibly bonding. His entire body felt like it was becoming one with hers and the baby's like they were all merging into one. It was the most exquisite feeling in the world.

The wind continued blowing against the tent. Nath had no idea how much time had passed, but the sun was setting, and it was growing dark. Finally, they kissed each other lightly and broke the embrace.

"We need to go back," Nath said.

"Yes," Anwa agreed. "We will come back tomorrow to check the nets. Maybe we will have fresh fish for dinner tomorrow."

"That is the plan," Nath said, smiling.

❧ ··· ❧

The next afternoon, they returned to the ice fishing holes. They peered in and pulled at one end, then continued pulling and pulling the long nets. It was heavy! Finally, the netting surfaced with seven whitefish! Nath pulled them onto the ice. They were aggressive fish, full of muscle, squirming and making a commotion.

Nath laughed heartily and hugged Anwa.

They did it! They were going to survive after all!

❧ ··· ❧

During March and April, Nath and Anwa took out many fishermen onto the lake, showing them how to dig holes and ice fish. People looked up to Nath and believed in him. They learned much about ice fishing as a group. During April, though, the weather began warming more and more every day, so they needed to be extra careful about thinning ice. Near the beginning of May, they stopped ice fishing altogether and started using the hardiest boats to break up the remaining ice and set nets out in the water. Since Nath and Anwa's home was built so close to the lake, they had easy access to fishing. They fished together every morning.

But Anwa's tummy was starting to grow large. She had nausea for the first several months but was feeling much better now. She would be six months pregnant in the middle of the month. Her round tummy showed through her clothes, but not through her coat. She felt immensely proud to be carrying Nath's baby.

Julia was also showing a round tummy. She was seven months pregnant so the babies would be born within a month of each other. It was an exhilarating time, but Anwa also felt apprehensive. She had never had a baby before. She had heard of some women dying during childbirth, so she was afraid of this.

But Nath reassured her that everything would be alright. He would be her rock.

She smiled.

They were lying on the bed together after a long day of fishing. They were building two more boats and preparing to employ several fishermen to set nets, bring them in and dry the netting on the beach. It was tiring work and Anwa was beginning to lose some of her energy, due to the pregnancy.

"Did I tell you how beautiful you are today?" Nath asked.

Anwa giggled. "No, I don't believe you have," she replied teasingly.

"Well," he smiled, his eyes crinkling with joy. "Then, babe, you are incredibly beautiful, Anwa, my sweetheart, and I love you so very much."

Anwa laughed, "How did you get so sweet?"

"You bring it out of me," Nath replied.

"You're silly," Anwa giggled. She jumped up to get a hot tea, wriggling out of his grasp.

Nath pulled her back into the bed playfully. "Where do you think you're going?" he asked, tickling her hips.

She squealed in delight and tried wrestling out of his firm grasp.

"You will not win!" Nath shouted with glee. "Surrender now or face punishment!"

Anwa laughed heartily, then collapsed in his arms, her round tummy pointing up towards his nose. Nath looked down and kissed her belly.

"Are there any windows in there?" Nath asked, jokingly. "Please, I would like to see my child. So curious."

"Windows?" Anwa laughed. "Silly man!"

"Boy or girl," Nath said. "I don't care which, I just want to meet this new life we created together." Nath lifted her shirt and ran his hands all around her naked belly, smoothing her round tummy. "No kicking today?"

"Not much, no," Anwa replied. "Although this morning, she was kicking up a storm."

"Do you think it's a girl?" Nath asked.

"I don't know or care either," Anwa replied. "I just don't want to call our baby it! So, it's a she for now, until our baby arrives, then we can be sure."

Nath continued running his right hand in a circular pattern over her round tummy. "Your skin is so soft." He bent and kissed her tummy again, putting his ear to her belly. "I think I can hear her heartbeat," he said. "It's very fast!"

Anwa ran her fingers through Nath's hair, playing with the thick wavy mess. He looked up at her and noticed her hooded eyes beckoning him. He moved up to kiss her lips. Her mouth opened effortlessly. Her pregnant belly was protruding in between them, so Nath slid behind her, spooning her and kissing her neck.

"This spot," Nath murmured. "Right between your ear and your shoulder. I love that spot. It makes you melt in my arms." He kissed the spot lovingly and caressed her belly, his arms reaching around her.

"Yes, I love it when you do that," she replied, her voice soft and sexy.

Nath pursed his lips and began sucking the spot on her neckline, softly at first, then gradually sucking harder and harder. He felt her body melt into his.

Anwa groaned. "Yes."

Her body was his. He felt that he owned a part of her somehow like she was partially his. His penis fit so lovely inside her vagina now, so much so that they often had sex several times a week, even throughout the growing pregnancy. He was always very gentle and aware of the baby's position. As her tummy grew, he loved Anwa even more it seemed. He thought the pregnancy made her more attractive. Her hair was thicker and longer. Her body was even curvier, her hips and buttocks forming delicious mounds, and her breasts were heaven on earth. They were so plumper and perkier than before. He worshipped her breasts often, sometimes just playfully with no intention of having intercourse. But often it developed into that anyways. He could not keep his hands off of her. He wanted to touch her, kiss her, smell her, be inside her all the time. He could not, of course, this was impossible. He had to fish, hunt and help the others in the community. Although he always tried to be with her as much as possible. She meant so much to him. Sometimes he would cry silent tears of happiness at night when no one was watching. He felt so gifted to be with Mrs. Anwa Olason. It was as if his prayers were answered. She was everything he had ever dreamed of and more.

Nath ran his hand along her round belly. He smoothed the naked skin and hugged her while his penis hardened. He slid his hand on her tummy, lowering his touch until he brushed over her vagina. She groaned as he searched with his fingers, feeling for that distinct area of her lady parts that excited her so much. He loved exploring her body, the things that aroused her, trying many things, sometimes finding out what she didn't like it, sometimes hitting a gold mine. He felt like her body talked to him when she was in his arms. Even when it was just a typical day, and they were fully clothed, she would sway her hips and stick out her buttocks when she sat down; he always noticed these little clues. Then he would be all over her, his hands finding all the places that drove her crazy with lust. He loved pleasing her, but he also felt the yearning, so strongly, that the more he aroused her, it had a boomerang effect on him, stimulating his own body, building up the sexual tension like a volcano, preparing to explode. He had become quite good at controlling his orgasm now. He felt good about this. He could last for a while now. It allowed so much more time for her to achieve pleasure. He was so delighted about this.

He felt so content and comfortable with her now; everything fit so well. She was his, and he was hers.

His arms wrapped around her tightly from behind, his hands finding her vagina. His index finger rubbed her clitoris lightly, then circled it swiftly, just how she liked it. Her body shook, and he continued with the swift circles until he could hear her moans filling the room. He sucked on her neck roughly while eliciting another groan of ecstasy as he continued spooning her sexually.

"Nath," she moaned.

He grasped his fully erect penis and positioned himself by her entrance from behind. It was so wet that he could feel the moisture leaking onto her buttocks. He lay his penis between her thighs and continued his assault on her clitoris; his arm wrapped tightly around her. She moaned and then her legs started vibrating. He could not hold off any longer. His penis needed to be inside her.

He thrust his hips, and with one movement, his penis entered her vagina from behind, sliding into heaven. He thrust again. His bottom arm held her hips tight, and his other arm continued rubbing that sensitive spot at the front of her vagina. Her legs began vibrating with more intensity. Anwa gripped his arm tightly and started mumbling words. That drove him crazy when she did that!

He slid out and then thrust back in, gently, slowly, but rhythmically, never stopping. He could feel her vagina squeezing him tighter and tighter. He bit his lip to hold his semen back as her orgasm released all over him. He slowed down and bit her shoulder, breathing heavily. Nath could feel the snug contractions of her vaginal muscles squeezing him and the warmth flooding over his penis. He stopped moving and just laid still, his penis resting inside her.

He breathed and closed his eyes briefly, trying to allow time for her orgasm to lose intensity.

He kissed her neck gently. "Baby," Nath murmured. "You're so beautiful." Nath ran his hand along her head, smoothing her gorgeous hair.

Anwa took a sharp breath in and then let a deep cleansing breath out. "You are such a wonderful husband. I love you so much, my handsome man." She grabbed his fingers and started kissing them. They were still wet with her fluid, but she didn't care, she thought it was kind of sexy. So she continued kissing his fingers, then licking and sucking on the longer finger, bringing it all the way into her mouth then out.

Nath watched her intensely as she sucked on his finger. She was the sexiest woman alive, he thought. She could make him fully erect in less than 2 seconds. He grasped his penis and slid carefully out of her vagina. He moved up to her face so she could taste his penis. She leaned up eagerly and licked up the wetness around his scrotum, his groin and at the base of his penis. She was enjoying this, he could tell.

Anwa liked savouring her taste combined with his. It tasted just fine actually, if anything, it had an aphrodisiac effect on her. The more she tasted their combined fluids, the more it excited her.

Nath was enthralled watching her do this. His eyes were glued onto her full lips, lovingly lapping and licking his groin. He was becoming a bit too excited. His penis was so incredibly hard that he thought it might start hurting her. So, he slowly eased himself away from her luscious lips.

She looked up at him with the sexiest eyes ever, begging him, her eyes talking to him.

Nath grabbed her hips, repositioning her to the center of the bed, so they were both sitting facing each other.

He leaned her back a bit, allowing space for her belly between them. Anwa naturally propped herself back onto her hands. She spread her legs for him beautifully. He was suddenly overcome with emotion. She looked so accepting and beautiful; it just took his breath away. He felt very odd, almost like he was tearing up. He looked down and willed the emotions not to get the better of him. He looked at her vagina, pink and wet. That did it. He had to enter her again.

Nath positioned himself closer, lifted her and slid his legs under hers, so she was sitting on him, her legs wrapped around him. Nath slipped his arms around her body, hugging her. He nuzzled his head in her breasts. She wrapped her arms around him and kissed his head, the baby snuggled in between them. He could stay like this forever and be totally happy. It felt so warm to all his senses; smell, taste, touch, sight, and even hearing her rhythmic breathing.

They may have stayed that way for some time because he noticed her breathing had changed; it slowed down and became lighter. He didn't even know how much time had passed, but he didn't care. These were the best moments of his life; he knew this. And their baby nuzzled in between them; a baby made out of pure genuine love, the kind of love people search for their entire lives and sometimes never find. The deep kind of love that touches your soul.

Nath kissed her breasts.

Then he grabbed one breast and kissed the other. Anwa breathed in quickly, her hand fluttering down to search for his penis. Her fingers slid over his groin, fluttering here and there until finally, she wrapped her hand around his hardness while he sucked on her nipple. They looked into each other's eyes, so many words exchanged through body language, but not uttering a single sound.

She leaned back to allow the baby room and Nath slid his penis into her again, reaching his arm around her and holding her lower back as she propped herself onto her hands. He watched as her vagina eagerly accepted his penis, and he glided effortlessly into her wetness. The image was too much for him. His control quickly vanished. He thrust gently into her over and over until she began to writhe and squirm again. He enjoyed making it his mission to please her.

He could feel her walls tightening again. Her breaths came out forcefully, and her moaning increased.

Anwa felt so incredibly in love with her man. He was part of her, inside her, outside, everywhere. She would give him everything he needed, always. She felt his hard penis caressing her interior walls, hitting that spot deep inside her, over and over. She didn't know what that spot was, but it felt exquisite. Her body began to quiver again, slowly at first, then picking up speed quickly, as if there was a sudden urgency. Anwa moved her hips in unison with his thrusts and felt him hit that deep spot again. She moaned deeply.

Nath watched his beautiful wife writhe on top of him as he met her movements and thrust back each time. His penis strained to let go of his sperm. He was close, but he had to wait for Anwa.

She ground her hips into his lap as he grabbed and squeezed her ample buttocks with his large hands. That did it. Anwa lost all control and gasped, mumbling how much she loved him and finally, yelping as her orgasm pulsated throughout her entire body, making her breasts bounce, and her legs tremble.

Nath could not hold back any longer. The view of Anwa's naked body writhing on top of him sent him out into the land of oblivion. By instinct, he thrust his penis in as far as it could go. His penis exploded inside of her in a kaleidoscope of emotions, so strongly that he felt tears might come to his eyes. His semen burst into her vagina, again and again, twitching inside her tight walls. He exhaled out a massive lungful of air.

"Babe," Nath said softly.

Nath felt so comfortable and happy. He was grateful for having such an amazing woman and was getting overtaken by emotion again. He tried to hide his eyes from hers. He didn't want her to see his sensitive response, so he pulled her close and hugged her, with the baby between them again. Anwa murmured something in his ear, and Nath hugged her tightly. Anwa wrapped her arms around her husband's muscular body and rocked him slowly and rhythmically. She could feel his emotion; she didn't need to see; it melted into her body as he talked silently to her of his profound love. She was his everything, and she was glad because she felt the same way. She would always be there for him, happiness, sorrow and even death. They would forever share this special bond, this she knew for certain, in the very depths of her soul. She would never leave his side.

CHAPTER 12

The spring snow thaw of April and May had raised the lake levels considerably, making the fishing lucrative in June but also washing away large portions of the beach. The area of the beach was now half the size it usually was.

A sudden storm surge in late May had destroyed many boats and cabins, grabbing the boats and flinging them out to sea, never to be seen again. The cabins were flooded, and walls and roofs swept into the sea. The spring storms created a sense of panic with the Icelanders. They hadn't realized the lake could whip up that high of waves. Everyone now kept their eyes to the skies, watching the clouds and wind patterns.

It was now late June, and the weather was turning on them again.

Nath and Anwa pulled the boats ashore quickly, as many other fishermen were doing the same. There were close to thirty people pulling the boats in hastily, hauling equipment into the sheds and securing down valuables with an impending sense of urgency before the approaching storm hit. The winds were picking up considerably, and they had learned from the last storm that the waves could turn on them with little notice.

The lightning flashed menacingly across the lake. Nath could see the approaching storm. It was a rare one, coming from the southeast, although dark clouds were also closing in from the north. A crack of thunder clapped loudly, making Anwa jump.

"We have to get out of here!" Nath shouted over the swirling wind. "Let's try to pull the boats a bit farther onto the shore, tie them to the nearby trees, and that's it. There's nothing more we can do."

Anwa nodded and helped pull the boats in with Garth and Bea. Viktor and Kristjan pulled the other boats, helping where needed. The winds swirled around the sand, throwing it up into their faces. Nath squinted, shielding his eyes from the sand and tied the last boat to a tree.

"Let's go!" Nath shouted, grabbing her hand as they ran to their cottage. He waved urgently to his extended family. "Get out of here!" Nath yelled. "We will all perish!"

Garth shouted back, hysterically, "Nath!" He pointed to the small dock. "We are missing one of the boats!"

Nath stopped, confused and looked back. "What? Which one?"

"The medium size boat we used for retrieving the evening nets," Garth replied. "It's not here."

Nath's eyes widened alarmingly, "I sent three fishermen out a few hours ago. They didn't come back?"

Garth asked the other fisherman if they had seen the missing men. Every answer that came back was no; nobody had seen them.

"Looks like they didn't come back," Garth said, panicking. "What should we do? Who were they?"

"Three young men offered to work for me a few days ago," Nath answered. "Just to help us catch up on the bounty of fish coming in. They seemed a little inexperienced but still capable. I think their names were Jon, Sig and Robert, all Icelanders."

"What should we do?" Garth asked, glancing at the growing waves.

A loud clap of thunder rumbled ominously closer to the shore this time. Then a lightning strike flashed down, hitting the lake. Everyone jumped and started running. The lake exploded in a large splash sending massive waves rolling towards the shore.

"Nothing we can do right now!" Nath yelled. "Everyone, seek shelter now!"

He ran as hard as he could back to the cabin, grabbing Anwa's arm along the way. They reached the cabin as a massive wave washed ashore. He banged open the door and pulled Anwa inside, closing the door securely. The cabin was farther from the sand, safe from the waves, he hoped.

"I haven't seen a summer storm this bad before," Anwa said, her voice cracking with fear. "Should we go to my mother's? Her house is farther away from the shoreline."

"Once the lightning passes, maybe," Nath answered. "It's right on top of us now."

The thunder clapped loudly overhead as the entire beach lit up in a bright white light. The lightning struck the dock, where they had all been standing. Nath and Anwa peered out the small window watching the lake destroy the pier. The lightning had cracked the dock in half, and the waves grabbed the pieces greedily, whisking it away into a sea of foam and waves.

"There goes the dock," Anwa said, dishearteningly.

"At least the boats are still tied to the trees," Nath replied, pointing to the rising shoreline.

The waves crashed onto the beach dangerously, pulling the sand out with the riptide. The waves were reaching almost ten feet growing by the minute.

"Nath," Anwa said. "I'm scared. We're too close to the shoreline."

"Let's wait another minute or so," Nath said calmly. "The lightning is moving fast. I don't want to go out into the streets with the lightning over our heads like this."

As if to validate his words, another lightning strike hit a nearby tree. The deafening clap, so close by, made Anwa shriek. She jumped, and Nath held onto her. "Baby," Nath reassured her. "We will leave in two more minutes. It'll be alright. It's the winds that are sending the water onto the beach, but the lightning right now will surely kill us."

Anwa stood shivering in his arms, her pregnant belly in front of them both. He wrapped his strong arms around her as the thunderclaps sounded a little farther away, moving to the west. "Keep steady," Nath said, calmly. "We will leave soon."

They stood entranced, watching the lake, winds and skies open up onto the shoreline. Rain began pelting down hard, obscuring everything. The waves grew even more, frighteningly high, mercilessly whisking several items out to sea. The boats remained tied to the trees, but they were now partially floating, the waves entirely obliterating the beach, the sand no longer even visible.

"Okay, now," Nath said urgently. "Run!"

He grasped Anwa's hand, and they ran out the back door, racing down the street towards Bea and Garth's house. The rain poured down upon them, urging them to run faster, to flee away from this destructive path.

Nath pulled her closer to him, trying to shelter her, but it was simply futile. They were both entirely soaked from head to toe as if they had gone swimming with their clothes on in the lake. Their shoes sloshed as they ran through puddles and small ponds forming on Main Street. A few other people ran away from the shoreline, also fleeing from the destructive surges.

Finally, they reached Bea's house. Anwa banged on the door. "Mamma!" Anwa shouted. "Open up! The lake is too close to our house! We had to flee!"

Bea flung the door open. "Come in! Hurry!"

Nath and Anwa rushed in as Bea slammed the door shut. They both stood there, dripping wet as if buckets of water had just been thrown at them.

"Oh, my God!" Bea shrieked. "What happened?"

"The waves took the dock away!" Anwa replied, her eyes wide with fright.

"The storm surge must have been twenty feet high!" Nath added. "We couldn't even see the beach anymore."

"Stay here for the night," Bea offered. "We can all go back in the morning to assess the damage."

"Thanks, Mamma," Anwa accepted.

"First, let's do something with your wet clothes," Bea said. "I can wring them out, and we can dry them by the stove. I will give you some old clothes for the time being."

❧ · · · ❧

The next morning, the town gathered along the shoreline. Nath, Bea, Garth and Anwa huddled in a circle surveying the damage.

The lake was beautifully calm today, the waves lapping gently at the small amount of sand the storm had left. The beach was pressed into a weather-beaten sand, making it look perfectly remodelled and packed. The clouds were high and thin, the sun shining warmly on their backs. Nath shook his head at the irony.

"It is always like this after a storm?" Nath asked.

Anwa nodded, "It often is. I have no idea why but the day after a wicked storm is usually calm and serene."

"That's ironic," he said as they all walk in a group towards the boats.

The two boats were still tied to the trees, moored onto the sand. They inspected the boats; one had some damage, and the other appeared okay. "Nothing we can't fix," Garth said, confidently.

The boats that weren't tied to something didn't fair as well. There were planks of boat bottoms littered all over the beach, bits and pieces everywhere. The dock was gone entirely, swallowed up into the lake somewhere. Everyone agreed to start rebuilding it as soon as possible.

They were sifting through the wreckage when Anwa tapped Nath's shoulder. "Look," Anwa said solemnly. "Our home." She pointed into the distance towards their log cabin.

Nath grabbed her hand. "Let's go take a look," he said.

They walked calmly hand in hand along the beach. As they neared the cottage, Nath noticed the sand was stuck to the bottom part of the outside walls, the entire cabin almost surrounded by sticky wet sand. The structure was still standing strong and intact, though, which surprised and elated Nath all at once. He had feared so much worse.

As they got closer, Nath noticed the bottom part of the house was wet, the wood much darker than the rest of the log cabin.

He opened the door and walked onto a moist floor. A few of their personal items were wet, but everything else was fine.

"Oh, thank heavens," Anwa said, gratefully.

A few wet boots and several other odd items that were strewn on the floor were soaked and stuck to the wood. The pots and cups lay haphazardly on the table, obviously left in a rush to vacate. They were intact. The water didn't reach anything above an inch of the floor. It looked like the floor had been washed by the rushing water but mercifully left everything else undamaged.

"Just the floor was affected," Nath noted. "The house is solid. We built it well. It is a strong structure. It looks like the roof, walls, windows, floors, furniture and doors are all undamaged."

Anwa looked down, picking up an old wet scarf. "I'm so grateful," she said.

Nath picked up a few items, placing them on the table. "We will need to go through everything. Clean up the floor and air out the cabin."

He noticed Anwa picking up several items thoughtfully and placing them on the table. Nath grasped her hand and pulled her to him. "Babe. We were spared. There is still a bit of work here, but I will do it, babe. You are too pregnant to have to deal with this." He glanced down at her, pulling her chin up. "Look at me," he said. She glanced up at him, her eyes happy.

"Things are getting better, aren't they?" she asked. "It seems like every time we think we've done it; we've triumphed, then another disaster happens. But this time we were spared."

"Yes, things are getting better, babe," Nath said, wrapping his arms around her. "It's our new lives right now. We don't have a lot of control over it. It is getting better, babe. Don't worry about this mess. I will get it all cleaned up in no time. We have each other. Our home's still standing. We are both alive, and our baby is too. That's what matters."

Anwa buried her head into his chest. "I love you," she said, mumbling into his chest. "You know something? I trust you with all my heart."

"So do I," Nath replied, hugging her tightly.

The floors were still moist and sticky. "We should let the floors dry," Nath said softly. "Let's go; I will come back with Pabbi and clean it up tomorrow."

They walked out the front door, hand in hand.

"Nath!" Garth shouted from the beach. "Come quickly!"

Alarm bells rang inside his head as Nath quickened his step towards the beach. "What is it?" Nath asked, his arm still curled around Anwa's shoulders.

"Those three fishermen are unaccounted for," Garth said sadly. "The boat is nowhere to be found."

Nath breathed slowly in, accepting the news. "We will go out this afternoon," Nath said. "Viktor, myself and you Garth, in one boat. We will get another boat to follow us. We will search for the vessel and the missing fisherman."

"Alright," Garth said. "I will join."

❧ · · · ☙

Later that afternoon, the search crew set sail. They travelled north and west but found nothing. They sailed for several hours, finally giving up. As they turned the boat around to head back, the men on the other boat shouted.

"Look! To the northwest!" a young man hollered, pointing into the distance.

Nath pulled the sails and turned the rudder, racing to the floating wreckage. As they neared, Nath realized it was a complete unsalvageable mess. Planks floated in the waves near a deserted shoreline. Pieces of the boat were littered across the waves, with the bow of the boat still partially intact. It was stuck into the sand, moored helplessly.

They scanned the area; there wasn't one human body to be found.

The lake had claimed them all.

Nath shook his head, solemnly, "Let's turn back. There's nothing for us to salvage here. The lake just claimed three young fishermen. Let this serve as a lesson for the future. We need to build a lighthouse. We need to watch the weather better. Let's go. There's nothing we can do but learn from our mistakes."

Nath turned the boat around and headed back, with the second boat behind them. Nobody said a word; there was nothing to say. The lake had won.

❦ ⋯ ❦

The next day Nath began the clean up of his cabin. It was already drying in the hot sun. Pabbi, Viktor and Aron all came by to help. They threw away all the mouldy items and emptied the entire cabin, pulling out all the furniture and beds. The mattresses were ruined, but the other furniture was fine. Aron offered to loan them a spare mattress until the new ones arrived. The entire town came together to help one another. The community was busy repairing and cleaning up.

Nath and his cousins had helped others as well. The entire town of Gimli worked to rebuild everything that was destroyed in the big storm. They learned many lessons. To listen to the wind, tie-down what they could and never let boats out in bad weather. Later that afternoon, several men began to build up the beach with sand walls and rocks, so the storm surge didn't flood everything. Several men were laying wood planks down, rebuilding the old wood dock with a similar one. There was talk of building a stronger, lengthier dock and a lighthouse when they had enough resources.

It was not as bad as Nath had thought. He had his family and friends, but most of all, he had his pregnant wife and his future was bright.

CHAPTER 13

By late July 1876, the early summer storms had settled down, and calm weather finally took its place. The warm summer breezes wafted in from the lake. Anwa loved the serenity, warmth and humidity of Lake Winnipeg. It was such a stark contrast to the storms of June.

Anwa waddled outside to watch the boats leave. Her belly was quite swollen now, although she still helped clean the nets and hung them out to dry every day. They had set up several wood drying racks on the beach for the netting. The other fisherman followed their example, and now the beach was littered with the drying racks.

Nath waved to her as he drifted away onto the lake. The boat went out every evening to set the nets and every morning to haul the fish to shore. Anwa and Nathanael were employing almost ten fishermen to help set nets, haul the fish, clean them and start packaging them for sale. Nath had built a fishing hut on the shoreline to organize and package the fish, alongside a few other fishing businesses that were starting up.

Pabbi, Viktor and Kristjan, as well as twenty other towns-folk, helped Nathanael build the first large fishing vessel in Gimli. They used some of the funds from the loan to import the materials to make it. Garth and Anwa provided their knowledge from the lake, fishing and the early boats to draw up a plan of the vessel.

It took one month, and it was now finished.

It was a two-masted sailboat called Hekla. This type of design was new and innovative since all boats were either small skiffs called byttu or the larger single-masted yawls called dallars. Nathanael was proud to have attempted and successfully finished such an ambitious project.

Hekla was 10 metres long and doubled ended, pointed at both bow and stern. It was a beautiful boat, and the community was quite proud of it, celebrating the completion as a large friendly group.

Nathanael and his employees would take it out in the morning to retrieve the nets. They could bring back so many more nets this way in less time. The boat was huge for a fishing vessel. He had never fished in such a large boat before. When it sailed smoothly into the water, Nath felt his stomach settle, and his nerves calmed. The project was stressful. He wasn't sure if he was qualified to build such a boat or if it would even be seaworthy. But it was!

Nath was proud and relieved at the same time. He steered the sails into the middle of the lake and headed north. The community had figured out that the fish were more plentiful in the more northern stretches of the lake, and this boat provided the means to get even farther than ever before.

The moist breeze hit his face as he leaned with the crew to one side, getting the speed of the boat to increase substantially.

They didn't want to waste time travelling to the northern reaches of the lake.

He thought of Anwa. She was eight months pregnant now. The baby could come at any day according to the elders of her tribe. Bea was with Anwa every day, helping her with cleaning and preparing for the birth of their baby. He felt such extreme adoration for his wife. He still teared up at night sometimes, wondering how he deserved such a wonderful woman.

He did not want to risk any harm to the baby, so he refused her admittance to fishing trips, even though she gallantly argued and walked away in a huff. He smiled. She was a stubborn wild woman, that was certain, but he loved her with all her flaws just the way she was. Her belly was huge, sticking straight out front and sitting low on her abdomen, so much that she had trouble walking sometimes. He laughed to himself; it was an endearing image.

The boat slowed down after 20 minutes of travelling. They chose the spot that Garth pointed out and released the nets. Their day would be finished soon. All the men aboard rejoiced when the last fishnet was set. The sun was going down, it was just after dinner time, and the beautiful round sun moved its way across the lake horizon until it seemed to touch the lake, spreading rays of sunlight through the clouds and all along the lakes shimmering surface. It was a calm day, and the boat swayed on the gentle waters. The lake was so unpredictable, some days it would whip up the wind and unleash high water, other days it was so incredibly calm as if God's finger came down and touched it into submission. These were the days that he loved the serenity of his New Iceland. He felt gifted to be living in its watery peaceful presence.

The stormy days were awful, though; he coped with it as everyone else had to in Gimli. Nath had finished cleaning up the cabin with his cousins' help, washing the walls, floors and replacing all the furniture. It didn't take nearly as long as he thought, two weeks at the most.

Nath stared out into the horizon and laid back with the other men, absorbing the beauty before them. No one spoke; they just all appreciated the sunset in silence. It was a challenging lake at times but also so serene and blissful at other times. The beauty of the lake was so hypnotizing at times that it gripped your soul and convinced you to stay.

Nathan was content and happy to be here. Things were improving. Soon, the rest of his family would arrive as well. He was looking forward to seeing his mamma and sisters again. It had been almost a year. Mamma had written a letter back informing him and Pabbi that there was a huge exodus of Icelanders being organized. They would soon be on one of those ships. The entire family would be together again.

❧ ⋯ ❧

Anwa waited patiently for the Hekla to return. She sat on the beach, warming her skin in the pleasant sun. She was upset that she wasn't allowed to go out with them. It was her pregnancy, and she had the choice of what she wanted to do, she thought. She was still somewhat angered by Nath's insistence that she stay behind, although she smiled at his fatherly care of their unborn child. Nathanael would be a good father; she knew this.

She ran her hands through the sand, filtering the granules over and over again, feeling the soft sand slipping through her fingers. She was reminded about the first time they had met, right here on this very beach. They sat in silence, awed by the beauty of the lake. She had known back then in her heart that he was the right man for her; she just didn't realize it fully at the time. She was so enraptured by Nathanael back then that she couldn't even help herself. She chuckled at the memory.

She was thrilled.

She felt like every piece was in its place now. Like she was somehow inexplicably complete.

The baby kicked hard suddenly as if on cue. Yes, and you too, my darling, she thought. She laid a hand on her belly as she gazed at the sun setting, falling below the lake, almost dropping out of sight. Then she saw the Hekla in the distance. She smiled. Her man was coming back home. She brushed the sand off her legs and stood, squinting into the distance.

The boat was coming back at high speed, the sails tight.

It would be time to give birth to this child soon, she knew. Her tummy felt heavier and heavier every day as if it would just drop out one day, she laughed. Of course, it would not, but it was funny to think that it might. She hoped that the baby didn't come out until Nath's mamma was here. Then the whole family could be included in the childbirth and the aftermath. The more help, the better, she thought. Anwa was still a very young eighteen-year-old woman. She was unsure how to be a mother, fearful of giving birth and somewhat insecure about motherhood. She felt that with more support, it would be easier. Both grandparents could help Anwa and Nath learn how to be excellent new parents. She crossed her fingers that everything would go smoothly.

The boat cruised closer and closer to shore. Anwa walked to the dock, spotting Nathanael at the helm. His brown hair was slicked back with the moisture, and it made him look so handsome and rugged. Her heart swelled as the boat came closer and closer. Then he waved at her. She beamed a huge smile back at him, waving. He was the most handsome man in the world!

CHAPTER 14

It was August 11, when the smaller boat finally made its way along Lake Winnipeg to the Gimli shoreline. Margret Olason was sore and irritable from the long journey to New Iceland. Emma, her eldest daughter, and Eva, the youngest, were equally irritated and weary from travelling. The trip had taken almost a month on a larger vessel called the Phoenician, starting in July 1876. Margret and her daughters boarded the Phoenician from their Icelandic homestead in the eastern district of South Mulasysla. This area, along with North Mulasysla, was one of the hardest-hit areas of the volcanic eruption from Mount Askja. They had nothing left of their land or their livestock. When Margret received the letters from Nathanael and Pabbi, she was eager to leave. She was going to be a grandparent!

The large Allan Line Steamship had 391 passengers. The Phoenician was a massive ship with a large round steam stack protruding from the middle of the boat. It left Iceland in mid-July, stopping in Scotland and then Quebec City. It was a crowded ship, and several people began to look ill by the end of the journey. Margret and her daughters felt fine, but some people were feverish and looking seriously ill. Everyone brushed it off as seasickness, but Margret still stayed far away from the sick passengers, just in case.

Finally, a boat arrived in Winnipeg on August 10. There were plenty of officials registering the settler's names in Winnipeg, dividing them up into groups that were to be employed in Winnipeg as servants, in farms outside Winnipeg and the remaining joining their Icelandic relatives in Gimli. Margret and her daughters met with a few aunts and had a wonderful dinner in Winnipeg. A beautiful older aunt named Anita promised to keep in touch and offered assistance if they ever needed it. Anita was married to a wonderful French man and had five children. Margret was so grateful for their support and warmly hugged them goodbye.

Margret, Emma and Eva boarded the smaller boat that morning, while the sun was growing warm. By late morning, the sun was scorching. They were sweating in their heavy dresses and petticoats. Emma was so happy when she saw the Gimli shoreline, and a warm breeze wafted over the boat. There was a vast crowd of Gimli residents waiting for them! Emma shrieked and rushed to the front of the ship, scanning the group of people trying to locate her younger brother, Nathanael. He was only one year younger, but he was actually much more mature than herself, she thought. She loved him so much and missed him dearly.

She could not spot him. Maybe he does not know the arrival time of the ship, she thought. Many of the people waving from the beach and dock were tall, very slim men with long beards. The crowd was large, approximately one hundred people. Emma squeezed her sister's hand.

"We are here finally," Eva said excitedly.

"Yes, we are," Emma agreed, happily. "But I can't see Nathanael! Where could he be?"

Eva scanned the crowd, squinting. "I don't see him either," she said. "I don't understand. The Gimli community was told about the Large Group that was coming. He should be here."

Margret smoothed Eva's hair. "Dear, he's here," Mamma corrected. "Right there." Margret pointed, knowingly able to spot her son's gait. A tall, distinguished gentleman approached the dock. He was in the lead of the group. His hair was slicked back, and he wore a black suit. He was a handsome, confident man with a short beard but with an air of authority.

"Oh, my Lord," Emma exclaimed, wondrously. "That is Nathanael! Look at the way he walks! So proud and manly."

"He is a man now, Emma," Margret stated proudly. "And a father soon. I heard he is also being groomed as the district's assistant reeve, serving in the emerging New Iceland government."

Emma and Eva clapped happily, waving energetically to their grown-up brother. Emma swelled with pride and admiration. She didn't even notice him; he had changed so much! He was no longer a teenaged boy, Emma thought.

The boat bumped softly into the dock as both sisters rushed through the crowd, excitedly. They bumped shoulders with others.

"Excuse me, miss," Emma politely pushed her way through. "Yes, thank you, make way, excuse us."

Eva followed her older sister as they wound their way to the front of the crowd, finally stepping off onto the dock.

A man grabbed Emma's hand. "Be careful, watch your step, miss," he said.

"Welcome to Gimli," another familiar man said.

They were crushed into a jolly crowd of well-wishers, some of them familiar, some not. It was all so overwhelming that it was all Emma and Eva could do to stay together, so they held each other's hands.

Then another man grabbed Emma's hand. "Welcome to New Iceland, sister," a deep voice said.

Emma shrieked, threw both arms up in the air and hugged her brother fiercely. "Nath!"

Nathanael's neck bowed down to accommodate his much shorter sister, but oh my, her energy threw him. She grasped his neck and shoulder's so tight that she was going to throw him off balance. Nath laughed heartily. "Emma! My energetic sister, as always," he said, chuckling happily.

Then Eva shrieked and ran at him hugging his waist fiercely. Then he did momentarily lose his balance, laughing and stumbling backwards. He regained his balance quickly and hugged them both back fiercely. They were all laughing.

"We missed you," another female voice smoothly stated.

Nath turned his head to see his mamma, standing there with their luggage. "Mamma," Nath said, tears welling up in his eyes. He wrapped his arms around her as well, his big frame squishing all three of them into a group hug.

Pabbi and Anwa pushed through the crowd until they found the group family hug and added themselves to it.

"Anwa! Pabbi!" Margret shouted. "We missed you all. Welcome to the family, my beautiful daughter in law."

The small family finally walked into the town, following a flow of celebrating people. There was food, drinks and musicians playing on the beach. People were dancing, laughing and cheering. The Olason family talked excitedly about the trip, the settlement, the marriage and the pregnancy. They had picked out names for the baby. If it were a girl, they would name her Annabella. If it were a boy, they would call him Mikom.

The entire town rejoiced all evening long, drinking and eating. Nath and his extended family sat around one of the many fires set up on the beach. They talked into the night until the sky began changing into the dawn. Everyone had so much to catch up on. The Olason family was together again after a long year of separation.

It was one of the best days of 1876.

CHAPTER 15

Anwa's back was hurting today. It was August 16th, and the family had settled into Pabbi's cabin. Anwa and Nath had been there all week, helping the relatives unpack and socializing with them since their arrival. Bea and Garth were there often as well, with some more blankets and sheets for the daughter's extra beds. Anwa suspected it must be the constant standing that was giving her the backache. She reached behind her and propped her bent arm on her lower back, the way only very pregnant women do. Nath immediately noticed and cuddled her into his arms.

"Are you feeling alright, babe?" he whispered gently in her ear.

"Yes, just my back is hurting a bit," Anwa answered softly.

"Do you want to sit down?" he asked.

"No, I'm alright for now," she responded. "Maybe later, though."

"Okay, babe," Nath said, smoothing her hair and kissing the top of her head. "I will just hold you." He wrapped his strong arm over her shoulder, pulling her into him so that she could rest some of her weight onto him.

Bea was chatting with Margret while the sisters were getting into a heated discussion with Pabbi about the sleeping arrangements. Nath agreed that the sisters should not have to sleep in one bed. They would move another bed into the cabin.

"There will be no room to move if another bed is in this home," Pabbi growled.

"We can accommodate a smaller bed for Eva then," Nath replied, trying to reason with his father.

Bea looked up suddenly. "Are you alright, my sweet?" Bea asked, alarmed, moving quickly towards her daughter.

Nath looked down and felt Anwa's weight crush onto him. "Babe, sit down," Nath said. "Someone, get her a chair!"

Emma jumped and rushed a chair over. Anwa slumped into it quickly.

"What's wrong, baby?" Nath said, kneeling in front of his wife.

"I don't know; my back just really started hurting all of a sudden," Anwa answered, breathlessly.

Bea sat down on the floor beside her daughter. "When did the backpain start?" she asked.

"This morning, a bit," Anwa answered. "Then it began hurting more and more as the day went on. Maybe too much standing?"

"Any contractions?" Bea asked.

"Some light ones, like normal," Anwa said. "I've been getting those often now."

"Have they been feeling stronger than usual?" Bea asked.

"Umm, maybe a bit," Anwa answered. "Do you think maybe it's time?"

"It's any day now, Anwa," Bea said, concerned.

"Alright," Anwa said. "I will just rest here for a while."

Nath stood back up but stayed very close to his wife. His leg was touching her shoulder, and his hand rested on her neck as he massaged her gently.

Emma and Eva resumed their fight with Pabbi.

"No more beds in here!" Pabbi shouted.

"Then I'm going to go live with Nath then or Viktor!" Emma shouted back.

Suddenly, Anwa shrieked and clutched her round tummy, bending forward.

"Babe!" Nath shouted, kneeling in front of her again.

Chaos erupted as Bea began shouting instructions to everyone for blankets, warm water and cloths.

Anwa grunted and shrieked again. "The baby, it's coming! I have to push!"

Nath grabbed his wife in one swift motion, lifting her under her arms and legs, up out of the chair and onto Emma's and Eva's bed, the closest one.

Anwa clutched at her husband's arms. "It hurts, babe!" she shrieked.

"It's alright, sweetheart," Nath said, calmly. "I'm here; we will do this together, babe. You're strong. Everything will be alright. Relax and breathe."

Anwa looked into Nath's eyes, hearing everything but in so much pain from the contractions, she couldn't quite understand.

"Breathe!" Nath shouted at her.

"Alright!" she shouted back, grimacing from the pain. She grunted again. "I have to push!"

Bea rushed over with a warm washbasin, placing it on the floor at the bottom of the bed. "Nath!" she said. "Move her body, so her legs are at the end of the bed. Now!"

Nath picked up his wife again and positioned her as instructed. Anwa gripped his arm fiercely. "It's alright, baby," he reassured her. "I'm here. Everything's going to be okay. Relax. Breathe."

Anwa's eyes darted around the room and then closed briefly as she tried to calm down her breathing. Nath smoothed her hair. He could feel her fingers relax a bit on his arm.

She opened her eyes and looked deep into his eyes. "Our baby's coming, isn't she?"

"Yes, I believe so, babe."

Anwa moved her head as Nath adjusted the pillow higher, then she laid back. Nath snaked his arm around her shoulders and placed his hand in hers. "Anytime it hurts, just squeeze my hand as hard as you must."

She kissed his shoulder.

"It will be alright, babe," he said. "Listen to me. It's all very natural, part of the process of the living. Our baby is going to be with us soon. It's wonderful. I love you so much, Anwa."

Anwa snuggled her face into his shoulder. "I know," she replied. "I love you, Nath. So very much. Some days, it feels like every piece of me has a piece of you in it. All connected."

He kissed the top of her head, smelling her clean hair. Nath looked down at the end of the bed. Anwa's legs were spread open with her knees bent, the end of the bed at her buttocks. There was a sheet over her knees, creating a little tent to cover her woman parts from everyone's eyes.

Bea brushed her hands along her daughter's ankles at the end of the bed. "Breathe Anwa," Bea said softly. "And when you get the urge to push, push hard, but keep breathing, even if you have to force it out."

"Alright, Mamma," Anwa said.

"How does it feel right now?" Bea asked.

"It is better," Anwa replied. "But, I'm starting to feel some cramping again."

Anwa exhaled long breaths forcefully out, while Nath held her shoulders. Then she grunted again.

"Push," Bea instructed. "I'm here. I will catch the baby. Don't worry, just push."

Anwa's forehead beaded in sweat as she crouched over and growled as she pushed with her internal muscles. "Ah," she cried.

Nath stiffened as she clawed his hand. She pushed again, grunting loudly.

"Keep pushing," Bea said, loudly. "Almost there. I can't see the head, but keep pushing, Anwa."

Anwa's breathing came out in heavy pants. Her hair was wet with exertion. Nath yelled at his cousin. "Get her some water!"

Viktor jumped up and rushed outside, returning in seconds with a cup of water. He handed it to Nath. Anwa gulped the water from the cup at her lips. He tipped it back, let her breathe and then tipped it forward again, letting her have another gulp. He handed the cup back to Viktor as she began to grip his hand firmly.

"Baby's coming," Anwa yelled. She crouched forward towards her large belly again, pushing with all her might. She screamed as the baby moved inside of her.

"I can see the head!" Bea announced. "Push hard!"

Anwa grunted forcefully as she pushed with everything her body could do. Nath gripped her shoulders, feeling like he was pushing with her. His whole body was extremely tense, and he felt himself gripping her so tight it felt as if he was having the baby himself! "Push, babe, push, you can do this," Nath encouraged her.

Anwa started panting and kept pushing.

"One more small push!" Bea yelled. "Baby is almost out. I'm here, sweetie."

Everyone in the room stood tautly gripped to their spot.

Anwa crouched again and pushed hard, just as she felt the baby slide out. The baby's head, arms and shoulders were in Bea's hands, as the last push slid the rest of the baby's body out into the air, breathing life into the newly born child. Bea quickly washed the infant and cut the cord. The baby cried briefly, gurgling. Then suddenly, the baby wailed louder than anyone in the room.

Everyone in the room cheered. Nath laughed.

"It's a girl!" Bea announced, cheerfully.

Anwa laughed as Nath hugged her and then kissed her on the lips. "You were wonderful, my beauty."

Bea finished washing the baby girl in the warm water, then Emma handed her a sheet to wrap up the screeching infant. Finally, Emma took the baby and gave her to Anwa.

Anwa clutched her screaming daughter. "Everyone, meet Annabella!" she hollered over the baby's cries. "She wants everyone to know loud and clear that she is here now!"

The entire room erupted in pent up laughter.

Nath kissed his daughter's head; it felt so surreal. This was his daughter! Anwa and Nath had made her! He felt light-headed and gushing with love; his heart felt like it might burst open and flood the place. Nath was so elated and full of love for his wife, his daughter and his family. He had never felt like this before in his life; it was like every motion, every action, had slowed down in time. He was so present in the moment, picking up on every detail, the smell of his newborn daughter, his sweaty wife in his arms, his family all in the room; it was all so dreamlike, almost as if someone had written a story and it was currently coming to life as they spoke. It was the most astounding feeling in the world. Nath was a father!

Anwa kissed Nath's lips as the baby started suckling her breast. Nath gazed at his baby daughter, running his hand along the back of her small head and smiled. "Annabella, you have the best mamma ever. Her name is Anwaatin. And I love her more than anything in this world right now."

CHAPTER 16

The past month went by so quickly, Nath thought. The baby cried every morning and several times during the night. Anwa fed her every time she cried. It seemed to settle her down. Sometimes, Nath felt so useless being a father. He held Annabella and rocked her when she was crying when Anwa wasn't available. But he felt so new and inexperienced. Nath honestly did not know what he was doing most of the time, but he loved every minute of it! Having a baby with Anwa was the best thing that had ever happened in his life.

Most of the nights were sleepless, so they both slept in during the day, sometimes until the afternoon. Bea, Mamma and his sisters would visit every day, helping with food and cleaning. They would hold the baby whenever they could and wash Annabella. This lucky little girl had lots of love from everyone.

Nath had hired his employees to continue with the fishing season for him. Stockpiles of fish were being salted and prepared for transport to Winnipeg. It was a bountiful summer for the fledging fishing industry. Nath was happy and excited about the future for his family; he couldn't ask for anything else. His life felt so complete.

Anwa was sleeping beside him, with Annabella in her arms. They had both fell asleep nursing. They often did this, Anwa said the suckling always lulled her to sleep. He cuddled them both, his arm across Anwa's shoulders and Annabella's small body in between them. Tears welled in his eyes as his heart gushed with love for them both. He never knew what it felt like to have a family, never really understood, until now. He knew how much his parents had loved him now; everything seemed to make more sense, in a very mature adult way. The world wasn't about him anymore; it was about all the people that he loved in his life, every single soul.

Anwa murmured and turned away. At that moment, the baby rolled onto her side and snuggled into Nath's chest; a little hand fluttered onto his bare chest, the tiny fingers entwined in his chest hair. Nath felt his eyes moisten with emotion. Happy tears of love and joy flooded out from him uncontrollably. He didn't want to move or disrupt anything because he didn't want this moment to end. Wet tears dropped from his eyes onto Annabella's head. Nath had no control over his overwhelming emotions. He loved his little baby girl so much, and she loved him back.

The time must have passed because when Nath awoke, Anwa was not in bed at all, it was only Annabella and him. He opened his eyes and looked down at the baby girl with her hand still on his chest.

"Looks like she found a warmer spot to sleep in," Anwa said as she crawled back into bed, with a hot tea in her hands.

Nath hugged Annabella lightly. "Yes, I think she did."

"Did I tell you how much I love you, Nath?" Anwa said softly.

Nathanael smiled.

"You are a wonderful daddy, Nath," Anwa said, smiling.

"Thank you, babe," Nath replied. "Some days, I feel so useless, though, like I don't really know what I'm doing."

Anwa laughed, "We both don't know what we're doing, Nath. But I think every day we get better and better at being new parents. And I think that is all the universe expects of us." She leaned over and kissed his forehead.

Nath smiled and felt genuine happiness flood his entire body, spreading through his veins, a warmth that he couldn't quite describe. This must be what bliss feels like, he thought.

$$\text{❧} \cdots \text{❧}$$

It was late September, and the fishing was going strong, all the employees were busy with salting the excess fish. Nath was beginning to get called out to help; several of his employees had become sick with the fevers. He wasn't sure whether it was just an overnight sickness or something more serious, so he told those workers to stay home and not to touch the fish. He felt guilty about leaving Anwa alone with the baby, but she understood completely and even urged him to take care of their business.

Garth approached him early in the morning with a disturbing message. "Mikom has sent an urgent message requesting Anwa and you to visit him at Sandy Bar. His health has suddenly declined, leaving him seriously ill, and he wants to see his sister. He says that he is afraid he might die."

An eerie shiver ran up his spine. "That's terrible," Nathanael said. "When did you get the message?"

"A native boy came running into town early this morning," Garth replied. "He said it was an emergency."

"Okay," Nath replied. "I will go home right now."

Nath ran briskly to the cabin, urgency rushing through his veins. He burst through the front door, frightening Anwa with the wild look in his eyes. She immediately picked up on the emergency.

"What is it?" Anwa said. "What has happened?"

"Your brother, Mikom, has sent an urgent request for us to come visit him. He is very sick; he may die. I'm sorry, Anwa. Let's take Annabella to my parents, and we will go without her. Many people are falling sick in Gimli with fever, and now your brother is sick too. I don't want our baby getting ill."

Anwa jumped off the sofa, grabbed her light coat, packed a small shoulder bag and grabbed Annabella from the bassinet. She was shivering with anxiety. Nath ran outside to prepare the horses for travel. What is happening? Why is everyone falling sick? A shiver ran up the back of her head, and she felt slightly dizzy. Something terrible is happening, she thought.

Nath rushed back into the cabin. "Okay, the horses are ready," he said, grabbing Annabella's overnight bag. He rummaged through it, adding some spare clothes, some goat's milk and cloth diapers. Anwa watched him in a daze, rooted to the spot in the middle of the cabin. Nath looked up and saw the fearful look in her eyes. It affected him greatly. His body was racing, and now it stopped harshly. He could sense something from her; it was emanating from her being. He laid a reassuring hand on her shoulder, knowing somehow that it was useless; things were going to happen regardless of what they both did, again they were only small pieces being played in the larger puzzle of life.

"I love you," Nath reassured her. "We will face whatever is happening together, babe." He slid his fingers into her hands, squeezed them tight, then brought them up to his lips, kissing her small knuckles. He looked into her glazed eyes; they were beginning to tear. He wanted so much to fix everything for her, rearrange her emotions to happy ones, but again he was powerless; all he could do was be her rock. "Let's go, babe," Nath said, calmly. "Hand me the baby; I will take her to my parent's place. Mamma and my sisters will take care of her well, don't worry."

Anwa bundled Annabella up in a baby blanket, kissed her tiny head and handed her to Nath. They both left the cabin, slamming the door behind them. Somehow, they both knew things would never be the same again. A gust of wind flapped the door back open again, startling both of them. Nath rushed back and closed the door securely and hurried to his mom's house across the street.

※ ··· ※

The trip to Sandy Bar was surreal. Both Nath and Anwa were quiet, mulling through their thoughts and emotions with a togetherness Nath couldn't quite explain. Once in a while, Anwa would look at Nath, shrug and nod, with a weak smile. He would just know what she was feeling; it was odd like words no longer had to be spoken. She was grieving the loss of her brother already. She had no clue what Mikom was sick with or what was happening, but she just knew in the pit of her stomach that she was going to lose a loving family member. It pained her heart so much. There was a dreadful ache in the middle of her chest, and it felt like the ground was giving way from underneath her feet. The only thing holding her up was her husband's love. She looked over at Nath again; his eyes told her he was here for her no matter what, that he was stronger than both of them combined, and she melted from the sheer love that was emanating from him.

The road was rough but clear. Pebbles were on the path, with grasses and shrubs framing the edges. The horse road somehow became smaller and smaller, almost being overtaken by the bushes, as they travelled closer to the Sandy Bar reserve. It was a long trip, but much shorter than the winter trip. It only took 2 hours this time.

As they neared the end of their journey, they saw a brown haze in the sky and the smell of smoke. Anwa began to gallop the horse. Nath followed behind, slapping the horse's rump. The smell of smoke grew stronger and stronger, an acrid sting in the air. She had no clue what they were burning, but it smelled awful. Anwa's skin tingled up her arms all the way to her scalp, lifting the hairs on her arms and head. Nath could feel the urgency of her panic. All he could do was keep up. Anwa sped through the bushes, her heart pounding until finally, Sandy Bar came into view.

She was momentarily confused because officials were barring the entrance to the reserve. She stopped her horse and jumped off, confronting the officials in uniform. "What is going on here?" she shouted. "I came to see my ill brother, Mikom. I must see him!"

A large man looked down at her then glanced in the distance observing Nath tying up the horses. "Who are you, Miss? Do you live at this reserve?"

"No, I do not live here!" Anwa replied exasperated. "My brother Mikom lives here, and he just sent an urgent message that he was very ill and may die soon. I need to see him."

"Miss, I need your full name."

Nath ran up to them finally. "It's Mrs., not Miss. Her name is Mrs. Anwa Olason; she is my wife. What is the problem here?"

The large man assessed Nath and changed his tone. He addressed Nath. "Your wife, is she of Swampy Cree heritage?"

"What does that matter?" Nath snapped angrily. "We came here to see her dying brother for some last rites. Are you going to let us in, or do we need to bring the people of Gimli here to make you?"

The large man looked behind him and nodded at another man. "Just give me a brief minute." He left to talk to his supervisor, a roundish man with a preacher's collar.

Anwa was shivering with anxiety. Nath wrapped his large right arm around her shoulder, pulling her in close to him. "It's going to be alright, babe," he said. "Breathe. They will let us in." Nath kissed her head.

Anwa stared at the roundish man in charge; she thought she recognized him. She squinted and searched her memory. Finally, it made sense. She turned to Nath. "That is the Reverend! He is of Swampy Cree and British descent. When I was young, my family and I used to go to his services."

He must have overheard Anwa, because the Reverend now approached, with his hand outstretched for a handshake with Nath. "Hi, my name is James Settee, Church of England missionary, I'm the Reverend here as your wife Anwa has correctly noted. I am also serving as an intermediary between the Icelanders and the Crees."

Nath shook the offered hand. "I am Nath Olason, and this is my wife, Anwa. We came here to visit her brother, Mikom. He is very sick, and he sent a messenger to call for us, stating that it was an emergency. I heard of some strife forming between the Cree and Icelanders over land issues at the last Gimli town meeting. What is going on?"

"Yes, there have been some altercations regarding land issues, and I am trying to maintain a constant presence for my fellow natives," James stated. "And yes, Mikom is very sick. So are many others. We are trying to understand currently what is making everyone so sick. You are welcome to visit your brother, but you must take precautions. Wash your hands and destroy your clothing afterwards."

A stocky woman rushed out quickly from the crowd forming at the entrance. "You will need to be more than just cautious!" she shouted at Anwa and Nath.

The woman elbowed her way out and approached Anwa.

James Settee looked down, somewhat embarrassed. "This is my wife, Sarah Settee. She is a practicing midwife."

Sarah looked at her husband, disdainfully. "He doesn't believe me," she said. "This disease is very, very serious. I have first-hand knowledge of this terrible disease. If you were intelligent people, you would all leave this area for your own sake."

"Why? What disease is it?" Anwa asked.

"It is smallpox, my dear," Sarah replied dramatically.

"Now, dear," James interrupted. "This has not been established as of yet. You know this, Sarah. Health officials are still determining the causes and symptoms of this disease. Nothing has been declared as smallpox."

Nath hugged Anwa close to him. "When will they know?"

"We are not sure, but within the next month or so, we should have a final diagnosis."

Sarah interrupted again, "It is smallpox! I have seen this terrible disease before. Please, if you see your brother, do not touch anything, wash your hands and leave this area at once. It seems to be affecting the Swampy Cree natives quite dangerously quick and also young Icelandic children. These people die the quickest. Heed my warnings. The officials don't want to listen to me because I am an uneducated midwife and a Cree woman. Even my own husband doesn't want to listen to me."

James laid a hand on her shoulder. "When we get an official diagnosis from Dr. Lynch, we can then raise such alarms, but until then, Sarah, please do not scare the Icelanders."

Sarah rolled her eyes and stomped away.

James looked at Nath and Anwa. "I apologize for my wife's behaviour. Please go see your brother, Anwa, but err on the side of caution."

Anwa grasped her husband's hand tightly. "Ok, let's go see my brother now."

"Please follow me," James said, leading them into the reserve.

Nath and Anwa followed hand in hand. What they saw greatly disturbed them. Several people were lying in sick beds, groaning, sweating and surrounded by family. The dying were delirious, shouting things, then gasping and clutching their heads. Most people had varying degrees of skin rashes. Anwa squeezed her husband's hand again. Nath silently squeezed back.

They were led through the sickness tent, where the sick were obviously being cared for, all the way to the last area. Here is where James opened a flap and gestured for Anwa to go in.

Anwa stepped in easily, but Nath was so much taller, he had to crouch his head to get in and even then, his head brushed against the large tent flap serving as a doorway to Mikom's private area.

Several cousins and friends surrounded the bed, weeping. Anwa approached the bed, everyone turning and noticing her immediately. "Anwa!" a tall man shouted, waving at her. "Mikom has been waiting for you." He stepped aside and let her in beside the bed.

Mikom was feverish, soaked with a slick gleam of sweat all over his head and chest. He was shirtless. Along his chest and arms was a terrible skin rash. His eyes were closed, and he was groaning, shifting his head from side to side. Anwa was in shock; she was too late. He was delirious already. Mikom would never even know that his sister came to his aid.

At that moment, Mikom opened his eyes. He looked directly at Anwa, his eyes focusing, clouding over, then re-focusing again. Finally, he nodded his head knowingly. "Anwa," he whispered softly.

Anwa sat next to her brother and smoothed his hair. "Mikom, I brought some medicinal tea. Please drink it."

His eyes looked into hers. He nodded, then closed his eyes again as Anwa's hand slowly smoothed his hair, calming his anxiety. "I will try to help you recover, my brother. I will stay here and help you. I brought many herbs with me."

"No," he croaked. "I just wanted to say my goodbyes to you. You must leave soon, my sister, and go far away. I will not be on this earth for much longer."

A shiver ran up Anwa's spine upon hearing these chilling words from her dying brother. She stopped talking and just smoothed her brother's hair, over and over again. The whole room was silent, except for the weeping. Anwa did not shed a tear, though, she just calmly soothed her brother for the entire time. Mikom was lulled into a pleasant sleep by his sister's touch. His eyes closed, and his breathing became deep and steady.

Nath stood back in the crowd, giving her space, watching the scene unfold. They must have been there for over an hour before James Settee returned.

"I'm sorry, Anwa, but you must leave now," James announced.

Anwa bent over Mikom and waved her hands over his chest. "Goodbye, brother." She enjoyed a few moments of silence with her brother, their final goodbyes sealing the room with quietness.

She then stood up, turned to James and held out her hands. "Where can we wash our hands?"

James gestured to a washbasin with a freshwater barrel and soap. Anwa washed her hands vigorously, and then Nath did the same.

James Settee watched them both with compassion in his eyes. "Did you have a good visit?" he asked.

"My brother is dying, Reverend Settee," Anwa replied. "I would have liked to see him healthy and robust, to say goodbye in better ways, with him fully aware, but I am humbly thankful for being allowed just to see him and say our final farewells. I left some medicinal tea for when he wakes up, could you please ensure that he drinks the tea?"

"Yes," James responded solemnly. "I will make sure of it."

When they were both finished washing up, Nath held Anwa across her shoulders and lead them both out of the tent, following James.

As they returned to the entrance, the smell of smoke filled their nostrils again. It was a sickly acrid smell, something Nath had never smelled before.

Anwa spoke firmly to James Settee. "Whatever are they burning, Reverend?"

James coughed and cleared his throat. "They are burning the bodies and clothing. Just in case it is smallpox."

Anwa breathed in sharply and stomped out with Nath in tow. He rushed to catch up with her because she was walking rather briskly to the horses.

"Hey, babe," Nath called to her.

She continued rushing to the horses, without turning back once.

"Hey," Nath said as he finally caught up to her. He grabbed her arm. She turned to face him with tears flowing freely down her pretty face. She collapsed into his arms as he engulfed her whole body into his. Her sobs took over her entire body, heaving with convulsing breaths that left her weak and lifeless in his embrace. Nath lifted Anwa up and carried her to the tree where the horses were, slumping on the ground with her wrapped in his arms. He rocked her silently as she poured her emotions out onto him. Every heave and sob was met with a tight reassuring squeeze. Nath hugged his wife with all his love until he began to cry with her, while the stench of burning flesh still lingered in the air. It was too much for either of them to fully comprehend, so their emotions took over everything.

Anwa snuggled in Nath's arms as the tears slowly stopped and the reality sunk in. They calmly wiped their tears, stood and mounted the horses, preparing to head back home with the bad news.

CHAPTER 17

They arrived in Gimli at dusk; their eyes dry, and their emotions empty. Anwa was in a terrible state of shock. She looked straight ahead and silently led the horses to the barn. Nath was silent, too, very concerned for his wife and his family. They immediately washed themselves from head to toe in the lake, cleansing their naked bodies in a remote spot rarely visited.

Nath rubbed the soap onto Anwa's hair and her body, foaming the bubbles onto her breasts and her tummy, then she dived into the water, rinsing thoroughly. She returned and washed her husband with the soap as well, concentrating on his shoulders and hair.

After they both finished rinsing and drying themselves, they burned their clothes on the beach, walking home in clean towels.

They entered the cabin, changed into fresh clothes and solemnly went to his parent's place to deliver the bad news.

Nath spoke first. "You must take Annabella away from here. Go to Winnipeg and stay with Aunt Anita. The smallpox disease is affecting young children and Cree natives the deadliest. We cannot risk Annabella's life. You must take her before they quarantine this area. It must have come here from the Large Group."

Margret nodded. "Yes, there were some people sick on the ship when we arrived. We stayed away from them. It was first a small boy that was sick."

"I believe that small boy has died in Gimli," Nath said. "It has not been confirmed that the disease is smallpox, but it sounds like it since there have been widespread outbreaks in major ports like Halifax, Montreal, Liverpool and Quebec City. The Phoenician ship had passed through these ports with the Large Group, so we can assume that the Icelanders contracted it there and then brought it to New Iceland."

Anwa was hugging her baby while breastfeeding her, listening to her husband take control. It was a lovely sense of comfort when he took command of everything, and she always knew he made informed decisions, so she followed his lead. She didn't want her baby to go, but it was best for now. It wouldn't be long; the disease would disappear in a few months, and they could be together again. It was temporary, she told herself.

"Anwa, myself, Bea, Pabbi and Garth will stay," Nath said. "But I want my daughter to go to Winnipeg with Mamma and my sisters. It is only temporary for a few months until the disease runs its course. It will save Annabella's life. Will you do it? Pabbi and Garth can escort all the women to Winnipeg."

They all nodded in agreement, except for Emma.

"I'm staying in Gimli," Emma stated confidently. "I can help you and Anwa. I was immunized a few years ago when I worked in the hospitals back home. I will be a great asset here."

"Alright," Nath agreed. "There have been some sick fishermen, and I will need to get them isolated away from the fish supplies. Anwa will help me with salting the excess fish and storing the stocks. You can help with the sick, Emma, if it comes to that."

Everyone else agreed to leave in the morning. Anwa and Nath kissed their daughter's head, leaving her with Mamma and retreated to their cabin, still afraid of passing any bacteria to the young baby.

"Do you think we are doing the right thing?" Nath asked Anwa as they walked across the street.

"Yes, I do," Anwa replied. "It's just temporary."

"Yes, it is," Nath replied, feeling a lump forming in his throat.

By morning, the group was gone. Annabella was on her way to Winnipeg. Part of him felt afraid, part of him felt remorseful, and the other part felt relieved that she was out of harm's way. Nath wasn't too sure which part was most accurate.

They had said their goodbyes, and now it was just Anwa and him again. They were too distraught to make love, so they just retreated to their cabin and lay naked in each other's arms, releasing their inner fears and doubts, talking softly to each other. Anwa lay between his legs, her head resting on his inner thigh. She laid her hand idly on his flaccid penis, and Nath wound his hands into her hair. They talked about the decisions they have made and their future decisions to keep the town and themselves safe.

They lay like this for over two hours, comfortably hashing out details within each other's nakedness. It was a hot September evening and being naked just seemed so natural. It released all the negativity and death from yesterday. It helped unwind the brutal emotions that had racked Anwa and her husband.

It was one of the beauties of their love. It was so comfortable, like coming home. They both helped each other and gave all their love to each other, equally. It was a union.

And together, they would save the fishing company from the disease and possibly the town of Gimli. This afternoon, they would start salting the fish themselves. Just one more naked hug and kiss, then they would go, Nath thought.

They worked all afternoon and into the evening at the fisherman shed, storing the fish. Nath had told everyone who was feeling slightly sick to go home; two fishermen that had no signs of ill health had stayed on, helping them stock the fish.

Anwa and Nath set sail to secure the nets for the evening. The wind was brisk, and a chill was creeping into the late September air. They both pulled their hats on as the boat sailed north. The fishermen were setting the nets farther and farther north because they were getting less and less fish in the south basin. Several of the natives told them to go farther north. A few trips later, they discovered their nets were overflowing. The longer trips north were paying off. They had begun transporting fish to Winnipeg and selling it to the local businesses there. The fishing industry in Gimli was starting to look promising. The last thing Nath needed was to have it falter so early in its existence.

Anwa's hair was tied low in a braid along her back, and her hat covered her entire head. She stood firmly on the side of the boat, watching the wind direction in the sails. Nath observed her as he steered the vessel north. She had recovered amazingly quickly from the pregnancy; almost all the weight she had gained was already gone. Her breasts were a bit larger from breastfeeding, but this would go down too soon for his liking. She was agile and experienced with the boat; he was glad he had a wife that had such great skills. He was quite proud of her. When he introduced her to others, he stood a bit straighter and a bit taller.

The boat took an hour to reach the spot north. They eased the sheets, letting the wind out of the sails, and the boat slowed as it approached their destination. Anwa unrolled the nets as Nath grabbed the ends, dropping them in the water and securing them.

When they were done, they both prepared the boat for the trip back, adjusting the boom and checking for wind direction before straightening the sails. Nath wrapped his arm around his wife's waist. She turned and curled into his embrace, chuckling.

Nath smiled. It was the first time she had laughed for the past two days. He leaned in and kissed her soft lips. She immediately opened her mouth, accepting his tongue. Her honey sweetness stirred his groin, sending currents of desire to his penis. They will have been together for almost a year, and he still craved her body, her touch, her exquisite smell, nothing had changed.

Anwa broke the kiss. "We need to get back, babe," she said.

"Ok," Nath said. "But I want to tell you how important you are to me. I will give you anything. I would give you my life if I had to."

Anwa immediately kissed him, her soft lips pressing against his. "I would die for you too," she said.

Nath kissed her head and hugged her firmly, his arms over her shoulders. She had her arms wrapped around his waist, enjoying his smell, his touch and his entire being.

A wind gust blew strongly in the sails, flapping them crazily as if telling them to get moving. Finally, Nath released Anwa, and they straightened the sails, adjusting their position in the boat and raced back to shore.

The sun was setting beautifully on the horizon as they approached Gimli. The clouds were pinkish with purple tinges with the moon rising in the distance, a small faint outline, barely visible against the colourful sky. It was moments like this that made Nath fall in love with Gimli. The beauty was breathtaking. He never wanted to leave. They would endure whatever was necessary in order to survive and stay in this beautiful land.

As the boat neared the shore, they noticed a few people gathering at the beach. Anwa squinted, trying to make out who they were. A few seconds later, she identified her mother, Bea and a few other people. She glanced at Nath, and he nodded questioningly. She shrugged, and they both steered the sails to the shoreline.

That's when she saw the same messenger boy from Sandy Bar.

Her heart fell into her stomach. Nath noticed and grabbed her waist reassuringly. "It will be alright, babe," he said. "I'm here with you. We will get through this together. Let's get this boat to shore."

Anwa gulped down the certain fear of loss and tried to help steer the boat. As they neared the shoreline, Bea and one of the fishermen grabbed the rope, securing the vessel to shore. She immediately noticed her mother's swollen eyes of grief.

Nath looked at Anwa, concern washing over his face. "Are you okay?" he asked.

Anwa closed her eyes and hugged herself. "Not really," she responded.

Nath grabbed her arm and led her off the boat, their feet dropping onto the sand. The small crowd gathered around the boat. Her mother approached Anwa solemnly.

"He's dead, Anwa," Bea spoke wearily. "Mikom is dead."

Anwa collapsed into her mother's arms, as they hugged each other firmly, relying on one another for support. Nath wrapped his large arms around both of them as the sobs racked their bodies. He felt his own tears threaten to escape his eyes, but he swallowed them down. He must be strong for them. He would not cry.

Anwa was in the middle, and his arms reached around Bea's shoulders. Soon, more people came and joined, their hugs adding onto the small group until there were almost ten people, all who knew Mikom, Bea and Anwa. It was a town tragedy.

Mikom had saved the people of Gimli last winter with his food rations, and now he was gone. The health officials had burned his body and all his possessions; there was nothing left of Mikom to remind them.

CHAPTER 18

Two weeks later, an official named Dr. James Spencer Lynch arrived in Gimli. He was a tall slim man with a curled moustache that was in fashion these days. He arrived in early October with a small group of health workers to investigate the illness that was spreading through New Iceland. They set up in a cabin offered by Yuri, one of his guest farm dwellings.

They began conducting tests and collecting data, names and ages of the sick.

Several people had died after Mikom's death. Approximately ten people in Gimli and so many victims in Sandy Bar that there were rumours the officials would burn down the entire reserve. Anwa and Bea were appalled. They didn't understand why.

"It's to contain the virus if necessary," Dr. Lynch said. "We still are not one hundred percent certain it is smallpox, but I have been commissioned by Lieutenant Governor Alexander Morris to report on the Icelandic colony and also serve as Medical Officer. My findings so far have resulted in modifications in diet, housing and hygiene."

Anwa spoke angrily, "What does housing have to do with anything?"

"Plenty," Lynch replied. "We are currently organizing two teams of surveyors throughout the reserve, and a third construction crew that is beginning work on a colonization road to connect Gimli, Sandy Bar and Lundi to the main road network in Manitoba."

"That has to do more with politics, not health," Nath interjected.

"Not really," Lynch replied. "If a quarantine is necessary, we will need to mark the borders and send in health supplies to the affected areas."

"This is why we are noticing these iron stakes everywhere?" Bea asked.

"Yes," Lynch stated. "We are marking out the sections, quarter sections, settlements, reserves and townsites."

"That doesn't sound like the job of a medical officer," Nath pointed out.

Lynch smiled, sarcastically, "Politics affects medicine and medicine has a bearing on politics. It is just the way it is."

"This doesn't sound right," Nath said. "Can't you see that?"

"It is perfectly right, Nathan," Lynch concluded. "It is my job, and I intend to carry it out to the best of my abilities. Now, if you will excuse me, I have some meetings with the health team to set up care." Lynch moved roughly past Nath, brushing his arm, rudely.

Nath felt his temper rise.

Anwa ran her hand along Nath's arm. "Let him go," Anwa stated. "He won't listen to us. This is more about segregating than it is about saving lives. We can only do what we can for ourselves personally, keep healthy, stay away from the ill, offer herbs and isolate the food supplies. There is still so much we can do, Nath."

His blue eyes grew a slightly darker blue. "You are right," Nath replied. "I will leave it be for now. But when I get the post of assistant reeve, I can make changes happen then."

Bea looked thoughtfully at them both. "I just hope they don't burn down Sandy Bar," she said. "That would be horrific, to all of us."

Three days later, Emma started working for Lynch. She personally didn't like the man or his views, but she felt that with her immunity and her prior hospital experience that she would be a valuable asset to the team.

She was right.

But what she didn't understand was the doctor's negative views on the Icelandic colonists. He began prescribing diet and hygiene changes, while people were dying.

Emma did what she could. They had set up a mini-hospital for the sick in the center of town. At first, they had only five patients, but after only the fourth day, it had swelled to thirty. They had run out of beds, and there were rumours that people were dying in their homes. Emma was horrified. She tried to help with bringing water and cool cloths, taking temperatures and disinfecting surfaces. It was incredibly busy, and she was continually being pulled away to assist with patients, often being derailed halfway through her tasks by the chaos of the emergency hospital environment.

A few people had died in their hospital beds, all of them children. Families were reeling, weeping and hugging each other, but they fell ill too. The skin rashes were appearing everywhere.

Emma saw Dr. Lynch come out of a meeting. She approached him. "Dr. Lynch, we need to do something to contain this smallpox. What are your next steps? What are we to do?"

"We have not determined that it is smallpox with one hundred percent certainty yet," Lynch responded. "But when we do, we will begin applying quarantine to specific areas." He walked away briskly, not elaborating on when or where the quarantines would begin.

She watched his retreating backside and wished that more could be done. She sat down wearily, staring blankly at the hospital beds with patients moaning. The events of the past few days hit her with such an overwhelming awareness. It felt like an earthquake was happening, and she was powerless to stop it. She burst into tears of frustration and stress, her body heaving, and her nose swelling. She thought back to Annabella and was so happy that Nath had decided to send the baby girl to Winnipeg. She looked up and stared into the hospital beds. A young child, not even two years old, was being wrapped up in a body bag. The little boy had died this afternoon. They were burying the dead with services in the graveyard outside of town. But what she didn't understand was why they were burning the bodies of the natives and the Icelanders continued getting standard funeral services.

Life was just not fair.

❧ ··· ❧

By the end of October, Anwa and Nath had secured, stored and salted all the fish. Garth and Pabbi had returned to Gimli, lending their time and effort to the fledging fishing industry. Garth exported the fish by boat to Winnipeg twice a week, always returning the next day. There were no other fishermen, all had either fallen sick, or they were tending to their ill family members. Luckily, Nath and his family had managed to escape the disease. They washed daily with soap and even washed their clothes every few days, wearing a newly cleansed pair of pants every day. They washed their hands often, after eating, touching fish, anything. Emma stayed at the hospital. She feared that she would infect her family, so she slept on a cot in the emergency room. She sent regular updates to her family via messengers but even those people were instructed to keep their distance.

Anwa was so relieved that Nath had made the tough decision to send Annabella to Winnipeg. In Gimli, it seemed that there were more deaths and sick individuals than there were healthy people. It was chilling, every day, seeing more people wailing that their children had died in their beds. Some people did recover from having the disease, although these were mostly healthy, robust adults. But for reasons unknown, the native population was rapidly falling ill. She was frighteningly worried about her relatives and their homes in Sandy Bar; they were still burning bodies. Reverend James was a strong man, and he maintained that the integrity of the natives should be upheld.

The officials were fighting him adamantly.

Several iron stakes had been placed all around the vicinity of Sandy Bar. Several surveyors and road crews were out that way, marking everything. It angered her that roads, reserves and townsites were taking precedence at this harrowing time of widespread grief.

Anwa discussed going to Sandy Bar with Nath.

"No," Nath replied firmly. "It is too dangerous. I don't want you to get sick or any of us. We need to just stay isolated here in our cabins while the disease runs its course."

Anwa threw her hands up in the air. "So, we are just going to let the officials burn down the entire reserve!"

"I'm sorry, Anwa," Nath replied. "I know how you feel, and if I could do anything to stop this, I would. You must know that." Nath grabbed her hands in his and squeezed them. "Believe me; this is what is best for us right now. Let Dr. Lynch and Reverend James deal with this epidemic. We need to focus on staying alive, my sweetheart. I don't want to lose you."

Anwa's eyes moistened as she looked into his deep blue eyes. "It's so hard for me to accept that we are powerless, babe. I know what you are saying, and I love you, but-"

"Remember something, my dear," Nath interrupted softly. "You are more precious to me than anything. Please, we cannot take these kinds of risks."

"Ok," she said relenting. "I won't speak of it again. You're right. We need each other right now."

❧ ⋯ ❧

The following week, Sandy Bar was burnt down to the ground. The only bodies that were given a proper funeral was the chief and a few others. All that remained was a smouldering black ground of ash.

The iron stakes in the ground remained as well, reminders of the boundaries the medical officers had made. Many of the residents of New Iceland speculated this was more of a decision to create barriers between the native people and the colonists, allowing them to expand the land for Manitoba and the white settlers. It was a shameful way to conduct politics, although it was not something people fought against too valiantly. This was normal practice in these times. The popular belief was that communities succumbing to epidemics like smallpox were mostly lower class and not worthy of proper medical attention. It was sad and dreadfully untrue but universally accepted as just the way things were.

Anwa, Bea and Garth cried over tea at mamma's house; they wept for their lost heritage, their lost relatives and their feelings of hopelessness. Nath was out at the fisherman's shack with Pabbi. Anwa wished he was here. He didn't know what happened yet. Reverend James had travelled to Gimli with the bad news. His wife, Sarah, was with him. They briefly sat everyone down that had relatives in Sandy Bar and broke the news softly in a solemn service at the chapel. Afterwards, Anwa had travelled back to her mamma's home, wondering where Nath was. He had said that he was going to work at cleaning up the fisherman's shack and bring the nets in for the last time. It was getting cold with the November winds; Anwa speculated that he possibly had to work late into the night.

She was beginning to get worried now; it was getting dark outside. Anwa stood and hugged her mamma. "I'm going to the fisherman's shack to see how Nath is doing. I will tell him the horrible news."

Suddenly, the door burst open.

Everyone in the room turned their heads, staring at the door.

It was Nath. His hair was all matted and scraggly from a hard day of fishing and cleaning. "I have bad news," he said solemnly. "Pabbi came down with a fever today. I took him to the hospital. Emma is nursing him." He shuffled his feet nervously. "Dr. Lynch just told me that a quarantine is now in effect. No one can leave Gimli. The entire area of New Iceland is now under quarantine."

It was November 27, 1876. A cordon sanitaire station was set up at Netley Creek, sixteen miles from the northern border of Manitoba at Boundary Creek. The quarantine line was being enforced by a thirteen-member military garrison.

"We are here to stay now," Nath said, solemnly.

CHAPTER 19

The Netley Creek military garrison was part of a more extensive quarantine station that also operated as a hospital. Before being permitted to pass, people were forced to wait at the quarantine station for a specific amount of time. During that time, their clothes and possessions were taken and burned. Those who were determined to be infected were detained and confined to the hospital.

Resentment grew within the quarantined areas as the measures seemed harsh and overbearing. Contrarily, citizens in the neighbouring areas praised the strict enforcement. The military crackdown restricted trade and food, resulting in more hardship and malnourishment for the people affected. It was a hot topic of discussion and something both sides strongly disagreed upon during this hard time.

Anwa knew why it was necessary; to stop the spread of this evil disease, but all the same, it was terrifying being confined. They could not transport any more fish, nothing. She tried to talk to Nath about it, but he was suffering. His father was ill with smallpox and fighting for his life. Emma had confirmed the diagnosis and was at the hospital with him every day.

"It will be alright, Nath," Anwa said, rubbing his shoulders. "He is a strong adult man. Many adults are living through the disease; the children succumb the fastest, it seems. He has a good fighting chance. He will make it."

"I hope so," Nath said, sadly, as he threw more wood in the stove. It was beginning to get cold again. The December winds were growing colder and colder; even a few snowflakes had fallen yesterday.

"Come here," Anwa said, as she grabbed his arm and led him to bed. She sat him onto the bed, knelt in front of him and began to silently remove his clothing, starting with his pants and his undergarments. Next was his wool sweater, followed by his undershirt. Then she sat him down on the bed and removed his socks. He watched her silently, grinning with love when she noticed his erection.

After she finished undressing her husband, Anwa stood up and began removing her own clothes seductively; a bit slower than usual, Nath thought. While she was stepping out of her dress, Nath watched as her heavy breasts popped out of her brassiere. Her round buttocks jiggled deliciously as she removed the last of her undergarments. When she was done, Anwa smiled, standing in front of him, completely nude.

"You are the most beautiful woman in the world, Anwa," Nath stated. He crouched forward and grabbed her arms, pulling her on top of him, his erection fully hard now. He positioned her luscious hips over his penis and let her take control, sliding herself gently on top of him. Her breasts dangled in his face as his penis entered her wetness. He thrust his hips upwards so she could rock onto him. Her pelvis ground into him exquisitely. They both groaned in ecstasy, not wanting it to end.

They continued to make love for hours, the lust and passion returning fiercely similar to when they had first met. It was the most wonderful spontaneous feeling, like being lifted in the air and floating happily above the horizon. They immersed themselves into each other's senses, breathing in their natural scents and absorbing each other's touch. Nath swam in her warmth, all the while on the other side of the door, the December winds howled angrily.

Nath treasured these moments with Anwa. He kept thinking he was so incredibly lucky, and something told him that he needed to relish the sweet intimacy while it was here because nothing in life is guaranteed to stay.

※ ⋯ ※

Nath awoke with Anwa's hair matted around his arm, spread all over the pillow. He coughed and shifted his weight. Anwa murmured in protest. He grinned and shifted his weight again, trying to ease his body out of bed. He needed to urinate. Finally, he climbed softly out of bed, amidst groaning protests from Anwa.

"I need to pee," Nath said.

"Mmm," she mumbled.

Nath walked to the outhouse and urinated, feeling slightly light-headed. Must be the lengthy lovemaking, he grinned. When he finished and came back into the house, his stomach felt a bit hungry and unsettled, so he found himself some bread and put honey on it.

Anwa murmured, "Hey, come back to bed." She patted the bed beside her.

"My stomach's feeling strange. I just need to eat, I think," he replied.

Her eyes bolted open. "Are you alright, Nath?"

Nath could see the fear in her eyes. "I'm fine, sweetheart. I washed my hands after the hospital and washed my clothes. I'm just hungry, that's all."

Anwa got up immediately. "I'm going to make you some medicinal tea, just in case."

She rummaged in the kitchen and fixed her husband a herbal tea. While the water was boiling, she stood and hugged him while he was sitting in front of the stove. Nath buried his face in her warm breasts, murmuring his approval. She kissed his forehead and frowned worriedly.

When the water had boiled, she prepared his tea and sat across from him, concern on her face.

"Don't look at me that way," he said. "I'm fine." Nath sipped the hot tea.

Anwa watched for a few moments, then bent forward and placed a hand on his forehead. The shock registered plainly on her face. "You're hot!" she said alarmingly.

"It's just the tea," Nath replied.

She jumped up, rummaged for a small towel and immersed it in cold water. She returned swiftly and placed the rag on his forehead. "You should lie down, babe," she said.

"I'm fine, babe," Nath argued. "Just an unsettled tummy, that's all."

"Maybe," Anwa said softly. "Please lie down, and I will monitor your temperature. Conserve your energy, my sweetheart."

"Alright," he relented. Nath moved to the bed and laid down on his side, drinking the tea. Anwa sat down with him, sitting in the spoon of his body as he laid curled around her. She pressed her hands along his back and arms, massaging his muscles lightly. Anwa had specially mixed the tea from herbs to boost his body's ability to fight illness. She often kept these special teas on hand, just in case.

"You may begin to feel tired, just sleep if you need to, the tea does that sometimes," Anwa said.

Nath looked up at her. "Yes, I'm starting to feel sleepy."

Anwa placed her hand on his forehead again; he was heating up. Her brow wrinkled into a worried frown. She grabbed the cool towel and placed it on his head again.

Nath murmured, drowsily. "You take such good care of me, babe," he slurred, as the need to sleep overtook him. His head bobbed and finally hit the pillow as his breathing became deeper and deeper.

Anwa sat beside him, concern building in her heart. She removed the towel from his head and brought it to the sink replenishing it in cold water again. She returned and placed it on his forehead, then grabbed a thermometer and placed it in his mouth. His body was steadily increasing in temperature. Fear gripped her throat, her stomach churned crazily, and her skin tingled all over her body. She didn't want to even think of it; she didn't want to acknowledge what possibly could be happening right now. The thought was just too much to bear. Her heart would surely shatter into a million pieces. The rising despair continued to creep steadily into her body like a devil in the night, curling around her throat, threatening her most prized possession, the love of her life, her husband, Nath.

When he awoke, his body was covered with sweat. Anwa had stripped him naked and had several cold towels placed all over his body. She was applying an ointment to his skin. He had no idea how long he had been sleeping, but he still felt quite tired and completely exhausted. He was disorientated. He knew that he was in his home with Anwa, but he didn't know what time it was, or whether it was summer and he had to retrieve the fishing nets or if it was the middle of winter and settlers were dying from the cold weather.

He opened his eyes wider, then noticed Anwa boiling water and mixing herbal tea. He tried to speak, but his voice was gravelly. A groan came out instead.

She whipped her head around at the noise. Her hair swished and flipped onto her shoulders as she swung around and raced to his side.

"Oh my God, Nath," Anwa shrieked. "How are you feeling, babe?"

He opened his mouth to speak, but nothing legible came out, just a creak and a groan.

"I will get you some water!" Anwa raced to the cupboard, grabbed a cup and filled it with fresh water. She ran back, sat on the bed, grabbed the back of his head and tilted the water to his lips. Nath drank the water greedily. It felt like heaven to his throat; it cooled his tongue, his neck and his esophagus. When the cup was drained empty, she ran to get more, returning to fill his eager mouth with the rejuvenating liquid. "I have some more tea that I would like you to drink," she said. "I have cooled it with some water to keep your fever down. Here, drink this next." She grabbed a canteen of the medicinal tea from the bedside table and offered it to his lips. Nath's eyes glowed as he drank the honeyed tea. When he finished, Anwa placed her hand on his forehead, her brow wrinkling with anxiety. He was still very hot! His last temperature reading was 101 Fahrenheit; it had steadily climbed higher and higher.

Nath moved and shifted his body upwards, so his back rested against the wall. His voice finally worked. "How long have I been sleeping?" he croaked.

Anwa began weeping; the flood gates had opened. "Two days," she replied. All the pent-up energy that she had used to save his life in the past two days came rushing back into her, shaking her emotions like a scatter bomb. She cried and hugged him fiercely. She had hardly slept for 48 hours, constantly checking on Nath.

He hugged her weakly, his body sticky with sweat. "Babe," Nath asked softly. "Do I have smallpox?"

"Yes," she whimpered. Anwa threw the blanket off his body and showed him the lesions that started appearing on his arms and torso. "I have been washing, drying and applying an ointment to the lesions. I have been doing everything that I can, babe. Please don't leave me. I need you; I can't live without you. Do whatever you need to do, Nathanael, but just don't die on me."

Nathan held Anwa's body close to his; her head rested on his shoulder. He saw the lesions on his arms, they were red, some oozing, but some looked healed as well. The ointment must be working, he pondered. Another thought entered his mind, but he was too sick, the thought fleeted away, and weariness took over again. Although it disturbed him because he knew the thought had been important. He strained to open his eyes and tell her something, but he couldn't remember what; so, he just said something else, something that he needed to tell her also.

"You are the love of my life, Anwa," he said. "I will never leave you."

Then he fell back asleep.

❧ · · · ❦

Anwa cried on his chest all night, her tears mixed with his sweat and her emotions mixed with her thoughts. She couldn't bear the thought of losing him. Her entire body shuddered just by the notion of such a horrible thing. Nath meant everything to her. She couldn't even describe it to others because it was something most people have never experienced before.

She could feel him; she could sense his thoughts, his actions before he did them and his feelings before he said them. She felt so intricately connected to him that even when he was away for a few days, she still could feel his being, his passions, his everything. She would dream in colour sometimes, and he would always be in those dreams. They would be making love, sharing naked intimacy and talking about their fears. Everything was so close and connected with them both that losing him would be like losing half of her own life.

Anwa hugged Nath fiercely and willed her energy into him to save him from this dreadful smallpox. She prayed every night that he would be spared. She didn't know how to pray, but she just begged and pleaded, whispering prayers spontaneously during the day and night. She had not left the house in over three days. She had not told anyone of Nath falling ill. She hadn't really even thought about it; her whole focus was helping him live. She wasn't sleeping or eating well. Her tummy was full of constant anxious butterflies. She wasn't functioning in any other sense but being Nath's nurse.

Her eyes began to droop, and she fell asleep for a few hours, while memories of Nath flooded her dreams.

❦ ··· ❦

The sand filtered through his fingers. She watched as he smiled coyly at her. She knew that he wanted to kiss her. She felt so drawn to Nath. As she leaned in and felt his hands along her waist, he shifted his weight closer to her. He was so handsome, she thought. The sunrise was so breathtaking; it was a perfect moment for a kiss. But something stopped them.

Someone shouted. Anwa didn't understand what was going on. The clouds were coming in over the horizon, thick storm clouds. She tried to touch Nath, but he was getting farther away from her. She tried to stop it, but her arms wouldn't work. The shouting started again.

Then she awoke.

Garth was shouting on the other side of the door. "Anwa! Open the door! Are you alright? We haven't seen you for days. Open up, or we are breaking down this door!"

She groaned. "Okay!" she replied weakly. "I'm coming."

Anwa pulled her drained body from the bed and propelled herself to the door. She felt strangely lightheaded and unsteady like the floor was going to give way underneath her feet. She made it across the room and jiggled the lock, not entirely understanding why it wouldn't open. Finally, she concentrated and unlocked the door.

Bea and Garth stood with a worried frown curling their eyebrows. She could not understand why they would be concerned about her. It was Nath everyone needed to worry about instead.

"Anwa!" Bea shrieked. "You need to sit down. Oh my, sweet, baby girl." Bea rushed into the cabin as Garth lifted Anwa off her feet and laid her on the bed beside Nath.

"I was just sleeping," Anwa said, drowsily. "I don't know why you are all worried about me. It's Nathan; he has smallpox. I've been nursing him all this time. His lesions are getting better. I noticed that he was waking more often too."

Bea looked with concern at her daughter. "Anwa," Bea said, calmly. "We haven't seen you in a week! Why didn't you tell anybody?"

"Oh," Anwa answered. "I don't know why. I wasn't thinking about that. I have just been so upset and consumed with helping Nath get over this horrible illness that I guess I just forgot to take time out to tell you. I was so afraid of leaving him. I can't lose him, mamma. I can't. He means everything to me." Anwa burst into tears, sobbing uncontrollably into her hands.

"Oh, baby girl," Bea said softly. "You are a good wife. There is only so much that you can do. You are not a miracle worker. If Nath survives, he will survive. If he doesn't, it will be extremely painful, but life still goes on."

"No," Anwa replied. "You don't understand. He has my heart and my soul. I cannot live without him." Anwa looked up briefly, her eyes swollen and red, as Bea massaged her back lightly.

Bea hugged her daughter warmly as the tears burst out of Anwa's body, shaking her entire small frame. "It's going to be alright," Bea reassured her.

The sobs continued and flowed out of Anwa as if a river had flooded its banks. All the uncertainty and sleepless nights caught up with her. Not knowing if he was dying or living, or if her medicinal treatments were even helping, played with her sense of hope. The pent-up emotions flooded out of her, racking her small body. Bea held on tight, wrapping her strong arms around her frazzled daughter.

She looked over her shoulder at Garth. "Honey," Bea asked. "Could you please get her some water?"

"Yes," Garth replied, grabbing a cup, then filling it with water and returning to where they both sat.

Bea grabbed the cup, offering it to Anwa. "Anwa," she said softly. "Drink some water."

Anwa looked up and nodded. Bea tilted the cup to her lips.

"What's going on?" a gravelly voice asked from behind them.

They all turned around in shock.

Nath sat himself up on the bed. "What is all the commotion about?"

"Oh, my God!" Anwa shrieked. "Nath! Baby! You are back!" Anwa jumped from her mother's arms and rushed into the bed with Nath, hugging him fiercely. "Oh my God, Nath, I thought you were dying in my arms. I was so upset. I wanted to just die with you. Thank you! Please don't ever go away again. I felt so alone, so deserted, so useless." Anwa sobbed onto his tummy as her arms wrapped around his waist.

Nathan looked down at her, running his hands along her hair. "Baby, it's alright. I told you I wasn't going to die. Baby, I'm here, it's alright. Breathe." He continued to pat her hair and touch her shoulders, smoothing his hands back and forth along her skin, until she calmed down. "Baby, look at me," he said.

Anwa turned her head and looked up at him, her head still resting on his bare tummy. The lesions did not spread to his abdomen, and they were healing on his arms. He placed his hands on both sides of her face. "You saved me," he said, in wonder.

Bea and Garth were pleased. Sometimes adults did live through the disease, but they usually did not recover as quickly as Nath did. Usually, it took four to six weeks before the lesions began healing and even then, sometimes there was permanent scarring.

Anwa smiled brightly. She was on a rollercoaster of emotions, her crying turned to laughter, then returned to tears. She still felt weak from no sleep and little food, but she was strong enough to hold onto her husband. Nath shifted in the bed, pulling her with him.

"I need to urinate," Nathan said.

Garth immediately grabbed his arm and helped him to stand. He curled an arm under Nath's armpits and supported him. They staggered to the back door, then Nath grabbed onto the door frame and urinated in the snow-dusted brown grass. When he was done, he walked back into the cabin, astonished at the mess. There were pots everywhere, homemade tea bags, washcloths, plates and cups. Anwa must have stopped everything just to take care of him. He felt so incredibly grateful, but he also felt sad and guilty that he had put Anwa through such a terrible ordeal. Even now, he looked at her sitting on the bed, her hair was bedraggled, and her clothes were dirty and smelly. Actually, it was the same clothes she had worn when he had first fallen asleep.

Then he remembered!

"Anwa," he said. "Have you been washing your clothes, washing your body? You must have, right? You knew that it was important that you protect yourself from this disease. Tell me, you did. I tried to remind you when I was sick, but I was too ill to remember. Please tell me you did."

He knew the answer before she said it. Anwa looked down at her filthy hands. "I did wash my hands the first few days," she responded. "But I lost track of time. I was very drowsy. I hardly slept; very tired. I didn't even know how much time had passed until Garth almost kicked down the door today."

"How much time has passed since I first fell ill?" Nathan asked.

"It's been over a week since we heard from either of you," Garth answered.

"We were very worried," Bea confirmed. "We should have come earlier, but the entire town of Gimli is locked down. Everyone is being told to stay at home. You should drink some water, Nath. You still look unsteady. I will make some soup for both of you." Bea rummaged through the kitchen, finding spices, some potatoes and dried meat.

Nath walked gently over to the bed and sat down gingerly with Anwa. "Babe, I need you to change your clothes and wash yourself. I know you are tired, but please do this. I am getting better. After you are cleaned up, you can sleep. I am here to stay, don't worry."

"Okay," Anwa's eyes darted around the room for her clothes. She felt quite disorientated from lack of sleep. Finally, she found her chest and removed some clean garments.

Garth stood. "I will go and leave you with some privacy," Garth said.

Bea started heating the soup on the woodstove. "The soup will cook for a bit," she said. "I will be back in a little while. Wash up, Anwa." Bea grabbed a large pot of water and placed it on the stove. "There, the water is warming for you to cleanse with now. We will return soon. Nathan, please help her."

"I will," he said gently.

When the door closed, Nathan helped Anwa remove her dirty clothes. He threw them outside. The clothes would be burned. He removed her socks as well and her undergarments, throwing them out the back door in a pile. Her body was thin, he noticed. She had not eaten well in the past week. He immediately felt another wave of guilt that he had made her suffer so emotionally. There was little he could have done about it; nevertheless, he still felt remorseful.

He hugged her naked body against his partially clothed body. He awoke only wearing undergarments. It felt so good to feel her skin against his.

"Babe," he said softly. "I know you don't want to hear this. But after you wash, you shouldn't hug me anymore until I am fully healed. I will ask Bea to help us clean up the house too. Disinfect as many things as we can." Nath lifted her chin up and looked into her eyes, searching them. "It's important. This illness is contagious."

"Yes, I know," Anwa replied. "I won't kiss you, but I cannot stop hugging you, Nath. I will wash every time I hug you. Right now, I need your skin against mine more than ever."

Nath kissed the top of her head. "We will see."

The water was steaming, so he poured some into the washbasin, mixing it with lukewarm water and soaked a sponge into it. He grabbed the soap and washed his wife's naked body all over. His large hand rubbed soap bubbles onto her calves, her thighs, her beautiful breasts, her neck, her tummy and her vulva. He washed every spot as he felt his energy slowly returning. He soaked the sponge again and rinsed her entire body. Anwa leaned over and washed her face in another clean basin. Then Nathan soaked her hair in the large bowl, massaging a bubbly soap onto her hair and kneading her long hair against her scalp. She moaned; the feeling was so exquisite. Nathan massaged her scalp until all her hair was full of bubbles. He then immersed her hair in the basin, rinsing it clean. Afterwards, he changed the water and rinsed her hair once again.

"You didn't eat well," Nath pointed out. "You are thin, baby."

"I couldn't eat, Nath," Anwa said. "My tummy was too upset."

"Let's eat some soup together then," Nath said.

"Good idea," Anwa agreed.

Nath poured the soup into two bowls, while Anwa dressed into clean clothes. They both silently ate the soup, slurping the warm luscious liquid into their mouths. They were ravenously hungry. Nath grabbed a second bowl and ate that as well, drinking a whole two glasses of water with it.

Bea knocked. "Is it alright to come in now?"

"Yes," Nathan bellowed at the door.

"Oh, my," Bea said, astonished. "The colour has returned to both of your faces! You both needed that soup!" Bea laughed heartily. "I am glad that you are both getting better." Bea started washing some pots and putting things away.

Nath coughed, clearing his throat. "Bea, I have a favour to ask," he said. "Could you please help us disinfect the cabin?"

"Of course," Bea replied.

"But after we are done," he said. "I want you to burn your clothes. I will be burning Anwa's clothes and my own in the firepit tonight. You can just add them to the fire."

"Is that really necessary?" Bea asked.

"Yes, it is," Nath answered. "The last thing I want is any of you getting sick as well."

❧ · · · ❧

Bea helped clean the next morning. Garth came over too. They all scrubbed the cabin down, burning clothes and sheets. They even cleaned the outhouse.

"This cabin is as clean as it is going to get," Bea said, brushing a lock of hair from her eyes as she scrubbed the floors.

Nath smiled, "Thank you for helping us. I don't think we could have done it without you. Anwa is still weak. So am I. It will take a while for both of us to recover."

Anwa walked in from the fire. "I burned everything," she said tiredly. "Are we all done now?"

"Soon," Nath answered.

Anwa looked at him, wearily, and stepped towards the bed. "I'm feeling weak, babe."

Nathan looked up immediately, alarm bells going off in his head. She didn't look well; her steps were fragile, and her face was gaunt. "Lie down, babe," he said, as he finished cleaning the last cups. He could feel something was wrong; he would put her in bed soon after he finished with the cleaning.

Then he saw her falter.

Anwa gazed at him with a faraway look in her eyes. Nath rushed to her. He threw down the cup he was holding, leaving it clattering on the floor. He was too late. She teetered as a wave of dizziness assaulted her, then swayed and instantly crumbled to the floor.

"Oh, my God!" Nath shouted, grasping to catch her, barely cradling her head before it hit the wood floor. He crouched, curling his arms under her knees and shoulders, picking her up and bringing her to the bed. He laid her down gently and crawled in the bed with her, concern all over his face. "Babe, don't do anything else, please. We will finish everything. Are you okay?"

Anwa's eyes opened lazily. "I feel awfully dizzy," she said. "Maybe it's just all the weight that I had lost." Her eyes searched his for answers.

Nath ran his hands along her hair. His heart flipped inside his chest, fear gripping him in the most menacing way. He was terrified of her getting smallpox, absolutely terrified. His throat felt constricted, and his breaths came out short and shallow. "I want you to rest. Please, Anwa. Don't do anything else. I can't lose you to this smallpox. I think we've cleaned the virus out of our home now. Your mom and I will finish. Rest, my sweetheart."

"Okay," Anwa said, laying back on the pillow. "I'm tired. I think I will go to sleep."

"Good," Nath said, his brow wrinkling in worry. "I love you."

"I love you too," Anwa murmured back as she fell asleep quickly.

Nath watched her as she turned onto her side and curled into the pillow. He stood and looked at Bea. "I'm worried," he said.

"I know," Bea said. "So am I."

Chapter 20

They both slept soundly that night wrapped in each other's arms. They slept for over ten hours! When Nath awoke, he felt Anwa stirring.

"Babe," he said. "How are you feeling?"

"Better," Anwa murmured, her eyes opening. "I just needed a good nights sleep." She kissed his lips.

He kissed her back with a closed mouth, then pulled her away. "I know you don't like this," he said. "Neither do I, but we can't kiss no more, at least for a few days. I'm contagious, babe."

"Okay, babe," she replied. "I understand."

Nath hugged her one more time warmly then stepped out of bed. "I will make some tea," he said.

Anwa rolled over and murmured.

He looked at her body, curled up within the mass of blankets and sheets. His heart thumped loudly in his chest. He loved her so incredibly, more than anyone in his life. She had nursed him and healed him. The sores were still on his arms and his face, but they were improving, some scabbing over, some fading.

He didn't know whether it was the medicinal tea that she had given him or just the sheer power of her love that had healed him, but whatever it was, he was so entirely grateful for this second chance at life. He suddenly became quite emotional; his eyes swelled up with tears as he watched his lovely wife snuggle into the blankets. He would do anything for that woman. She was his angel.

When the tea was ready, he walked up to her, patting her butt and offering her the hot tea. "Here, babe," he said. "Drink."

She rolled over and sat up; her face quite pale. "Thanks, babe," she said, tipping the tea to her lips.

"Are you alright, babe?" Nath asked. "You look very pale."

"Still a bit dizzy," Anwa answered.

"Baby," Nathan said, his voice cracking. "Don't get sick, please. Let's do everything we possibly can. Okay? I can't lose you."

"Okay," Anwa said. "I will wash my hands. But I do feel quite dizzy, so please help me up."

"Drink your tea first," Nath said. "Then, I will help you up."

They sat on the bed in silence, sipping their teas. When they had finished, Nath pulled his arms under hers and helped her stand. They walked over to the washbasin; Nath stood firmly by her side as she washed her face, brushed her teeth and cleaned her hands.

"Do you feel better?" Nath asked, with a worried frown.

"A bit," Anwa answered. "Still dizzy."

Nath smoothed her hair and helped her back into bed. "Don't get sick, please," he pleaded.

"Babe," Anwa said softly. "I know you don't want me to be sick, but if I am, please don't ever take me to a hospital, like Mikom was. I want to stay right here."

Nath hugged her and laid close beside her, worry creeping into his heart like a devil in the night. "I will do as you wish," he replied solemnly.

The next day, Anwa developed a fever.

Nath felt the floor fall from beneath his feet. His heart panicked, and his mind raced. He told himself that if his body could make it through this illness, then so could she. But something was wrong; something was different; he could feel it in his bones. He didn't know what it was, but Anwa wasn't progressing with the illness like Nath did.

He fed her the medicinal tea and layered cool cloths on her. The lesions hadn't even appeared yet, and she was already getting very sick. Her entire body was burning up. Sweat covered her head, her chest; even her hair was wet with sweat. Nath tried talking to her, but her responses came out as feverish mumbles.

"Babe," Nath said softly. "Fight this. You are strong. If I can do it, so can you."

Anwa's eyes opened briefly. "It's so hot in here," she mumbled.

Nath's heart stopped as she spoke. "Babe," Nath replied. "Drink." He put a cup of water to her lips as she gulped the liquid down quickly. "I will cool some tea and give that to you as well. Hold on."

He rushed into the kitchen area, mixing the hot tea with cold water and returned, but she had already fallen back asleep. He tried waking her, but she didn't respond. His entire body lit up with worry, goosebumps travelling all over his arms and legs; even the hair stood up on his head. He panicked. The room started to spin. What was he supposed to do?

Someone was knocking on the door. "Yes," Nath shouted at the door. "Come in, come in."

Bea opened the door.

She immediately saw the worry on Nath's face, then noticed Anwa's crumbled form on the bed. "Nath!" she said. "What happened?"

"She kept saying that she was dizzy," Nath cried, tears streaming down his cheeks. "She just fell asleep without drinking her tea. She won't wake up. I don't know what to do, Bea."

Bea walked to the bed and laid a hand on Nath's leg. "I will go get Emma," she said. "We will fight this. I will go right now." She left in a panic, slamming the door behind her.

Bea ran to the hospital as fast as she could, her steps urgently propelling her. She burst into the emergency tent. "Emma! Emma!" she shouted.

Several people turned their heads at the commotion. Then a voice responded.

"Bea?" Emma shouted back. "What is it?"

"Oh my God, Emma," Bea shrieked, collapsing in grief, tears flowing freely down her face. "It's Anwa," she said, her voice cracking. "She's sick. My baby girl won't wake up. Please help us. Come now, please. Save my daughter."

"Oh my Lord," Emma said, grabbing Bea by the arms. "Sit, I will come right away. Let me pack a bag." Emma threw several items into her nurse's bag immediately, panic and dread filling her heart.

Emma grabbed the bag and left the hospital with Bea, stopping to rinse their hands in a vinegar solution. They checked out of the exit station and hurried to Nath's house.

Several minutes later, Emma and Bea burst through the door. "Nath! Oh, my Lord. Are you alright?" she shrieked.

"Bea told me that you had smallpox, and now Anwa is ill. What are the symptoms?"

Nath closed his eyes tight. When he reopened them, they were wet with tears. "Two days ago, she fainted. She complained about dizziness ever since. Then just this morning, she started developing a fever. She is covered in sweat now. I fed her the medicinal tea that she had given me. I put cool clothes on her, but she has hardly awakened. I even cooled the tea. She has a very high fever. She fell asleep before drinking her tea this morning, and I couldn't awaken her. I don't know what to do, Emma. Please help me."

Emma washed her hands and approached the bed. She lifted the sheets. "She hasn't developed the lesions yet," she said.

"No, she hasn't," Nath said. "I have looked."

"Well, sometimes they don't appear for a few days," Emma stated.

"What can we do?" Nath said.

"Be with her," Emma responded. "Stay by her side, keep her cool, awaken her with cool cloths and feed her honeyed water often, continue cooling the tea and give her that as well. She will awaken abruptly, when she does, feed her fluids as much as possible. If you can, feed her small amounts of lukewarm soup. I will stay with you, Nath. Although, Bea, you must not be here. I know its hard, but you may get sick too. We will allow occasional visits, but you must wash your entire body and burn your clothes afterwards. This is very serious; please be cautious."

Emma continued to examine Anwa for lesions. She found the thermometer and stuck it under her tongue; Anwa hardly moved. Emma was alarmed. She had only seen this response in a few other people, specifically Swampy Cree natives and they succumbed quickly to the disease. Doctors were not sure why, but they hypothesized it was because Icelanders had several years of immunity. Smallpox had spread throughout Iceland in the early 1700s; some Icelanders were even vaccinated, but the Swampy Cree were completely without any prior exposure to smallpox. This particular native community was greatly isolated from the surrounding world, not having much contact, even with the government. They existed quite peacefully, hunting and fishing up in the Interlake basin of Lake Winnipeg, very similar to societies that live on islands. They succumb quickly to communicable diseases because their immune systems have not developed the required antibodies over the generations to fight disease. Emma continued her exam and pulled the thermometer out of Anwa's mouth. It read 102 degrees Fahrenheit!

"Nath," Emma said softly. "Come here, please."

She showed him the thermometer. "She has a very high fever. One hundred- and three-degrees Fahrenheit is when we will need to admit her to the hospital."

"She doesn't want to go to a hospital," Nath said, expressing Anwa's wishes strongly. "She said this."

"Okay," Emma said. "If that's her wish." Emma paused and placed the palm of her hand on Nath's shoulder. "Nath, I need to tell you something that might be very hard for you to hear. Please sit down."

"What?" Nath said, nervously. "I made it through smallpox, and so can she. I cannot lose her. She cannot die."

"Sit down, please."

Nath gazed down dejectedly and sat his buttocks on the edge of the bed at Anwa's feet. He laid a large hand on her foot, massaging it absentmindedly.

"Nath," Emma said softly. "The Swampy Cree community was decimated. For some reason, that the doctors do not fully understand, the native people here were powerless against this disease."

"No," Nath replied. His mouth twisted in an injured state; his lip quivered, but he controlled it by mashing his lips together.

"Listen to me, Nath," Emma continued. "I'm your sister. I love you, but you can be stubborn. You have to hear me out. I have been at the hospital for the past two months. I have seen all sorts of sick people with smallpox. Do you trust me?"

"Yes," Nath responded. He shifted both his hands to Anwa's foot as if he could somehow hold onto her this way.

"Nath," Emma said softly. "I know Anwa is Swampy Cree. You know this as well. Bea may be the last of the Swampy Crees after Anwa." Emma laid her hand on Nath's knee. "I'm sorry, Nath. Anwa doesn't have much chance of surviving this. Her body is quickly succumbing, and her fever is growing by the minute."

Nath looked down at his toes. He didn't want to listen to Emma anymore; she was wrong. This couldn't be happening. It was not possible; he could not lose Anwa. How could he possibly live without her? It was just a notion that simply was not comprehendible. What about Annabella? She would never even remember her mother. No, it was inconceivable. This could not be happening.

He didn't realize that he was crying. But suddenly, Emma was beside him on the bed, holding him tightly in her arms. "It will be okay. I will be here with you, Nath. I will stay here as long as you need me to."

Nath sobbed heavily, tightly gripping his sister, his head wedged into her shoulder. All the events of the past two weeks came rushing through him. He questioned if it was his fault, what he could have done to prevent it. He thought of his dad getting the disease, the hospital and his own struggle to survive smallpox. It all felt surreal as if someone had written a play, and he was only an actor, and none of this was real.

Emma patted his back and smoothed his shoulders as he sobbed heavily into her neck. She gripped him tightly, letting him release all his pent-up emotions. "Pabbi made it through too, just so you know," Emma said. "He is not doing as good as you, but he is recovering. He will live."

Nath heard her words and nodded, unable to speak at the moment. His heart was breaking unbearably, shattering into tiny pieces. He felt as if he might die with her, but he somehow knew that he would not. Life was unfair, he thought.

He heard Emma talking again. His brain wasn't sure whether he wanted to listen to her words anymore.

"Nath," Emma said. "I know it's hard. But you should say your goodbyes soon. Most Swampy Cree natives perish within five days."

CHAPTER 21

Nathan slept with Anwa all day and all night. He rarely got out of the bed. He wanted to cherish every moment he had left with the love of his life. He fed her, he gave her water, but she rarely opened her eyes. She would open her mouth and accept the liquids, but he felt her slowly slipping away from him. He didn't know what else to do but strip himself naked and press his skin to hers; maybe he could transfer his energy, his immunity through her skin to help her fight. He hugged her tight all through the day and night; sometimes, he would change her position so she could rest her head on top of him, curling her neck and shoulders into the crook of his arm.

She started developing the lesions the next day. Each time he saw one, he spread the ointment on them. He examined her body every day and treated each lesion as they appeared, washing them clean, then applying the medicated cream she had made.

"Hey, Babe," Nath said. "I know you can hear me. I love you, Anwa, and I'm going to try to take care of you the way you took care of me. I'm using the same ointment cream, the same medicine tea and the same love that you showed me. Stay with me, Anwa. Please."

Nath's fingers spread the cream on each lesion, gently dotting it on and then rubbing the medicine into her skin slowly. She rarely turned anymore. He felt like he would die with her if she left him. His entire being felt like it was on survival mode like someone had flipped a switch, and all he could do was hold onto these moments. His world slowed down to every minute and every second. He bent down and kissed her forehead, then laid a cool cloth on her head. She was still sweaty and hot. Her body was burning up.

He turned her onto her side and noticed more lesions on her back, he dotted them with the cream as well, massaging it in gently. He wanted to transfer his energy, his health, his everything into her body to help her fight. He felt that just touching her constantly would do this. He heard Emma's words in his head but refused to accept them. The talks of death were a constant dark demon in the back of his mind that he refused to let in. Hope constricted his throat; he must believe that she will live. He couldn't grasp any other knowledge than that.

He fell asleep in her arms on the fourth night. He had her body wrapped up in his embrace, his entire being trying desperately to transmit his love into her to help her survive. They slept soundly like this for a few hours, arms and legs entwined together.

Sometime during the night, he awoke abruptly, with the darkness surrounding them. Emma was asleep on the other bed. The cabin was quiet. He wasn't sure what had awakened him, but he heard a noise, a groan or something. He strained his ears to hear anything unusual.

Anwa moaned.

He straightened up in bed. "Baby, are you awake?" he said, hope ringing in his words.

Anwa's eyes opened. Nath curled over her, their eyes connecting in the dark, searching each others' gaze. "Hey, babe, I'm here," Nath said reassuringly. "How do you feel?"

Anwa's voice came out as a croak.

"I will get you water!" Nath jumped up and fetched a cup of water, holding it to her lips. She sipped the refreshing liquid greedily. Nath's heart jumped into his throat. Hope flooded his constricted lungs. He was actually holding his breath while she was drinking; when she had finished, he let out a deep exhale.

"How do you feel, babe?" Nath asked again.

Anwa looked deeply into Nath's eyes once again, and he knew. "Nath," she said weakly. "I need you to know something." She swallowed momentarily, then continued. "Babe, you are the best thing that's ever happened to me. I need you to know that. I love you more than life itself. I have been trying to fight this, but I don't know if I am strong enough. I feel very weak, babe. And I just wanted to let you know that I want you to raise our baby girl as best as you can. Kiss her and hug her a lot. Tell her when she grows up that I'm sorry that I never got to be a mother to her throughout all her ups and downs. And tell her that I love her so much." Anwa's tears fell onto Nath's hands as he held her hands in his. Anwa leaned into him, and they kissed. A soft, gentle, passionate kiss, her honey mouth opened, and his tongue found her warmth.

Nath laid her head back onto the pillow, and they kissed like this for quite a while, just enjoying the intimacy. Nath imagined they were kissing on the beach, sand in their hair, laughing as the summer wind blew over the top of their naked bodies. Anwa's hands fluttered to his chin as she lightly ran her hands along his jaw, caressing his beard briefly. Nath broke the kiss and stared into her eyes.

"What we have," Anwa said softly. "Other people don't always experience it. We have something extraordinary, Nathanael. It's more than just love; I can't even describe it. It's transcendental. No matter what happens to me, Nath, I will always be yours; I want you to know that. But if we must say goodbye for now, then we must. I believe this is something that's not within our control. I love you, Nathanael."

Nath looked deep into her eyes, kissing her once more, relishing in her honey kisses. Then he smoothed her hair from her eyes. "And I love you, Mrs. Anwa Olason, more than I have ever loved anyone in my life. Even though I don't want to believe it and I don't want to say it, I will. Goodbye, my sweetheart." Nathan knelt his head onto her lap and cried heavily, shaking with the sobs.

"Goodbye, my sweet Nathanael," Anwa whispered.

Nath hugged her abdomen fiercely, and she cried with him, her tears dropping on his head. They stayed like this for hours, sobbing in each other's arms until they both cried themselves to sleep. They both flitted in and out of romantic dreams of sunrises, moons, waves and beaches; images of what once was and what may never be again.

In the morning, Nathanael awoke, and Anwa was dead, curled up in his arms like an angel. He sat up and rocked her body tightly in his arms, tears streaming down his face. He sobbed recklessly, rocking her lifeless body back and forth, kissing her hair over and over again. He held her head firmly in his arms and continued swaying her, while his tears flowed like a river onto her hair. His body heaved as he cried and cried, unable to comprehend the consequences, the future, unable to understand anything but this last moment.

Emma awoke and stumbled over to the bed. She looked at Anwa's lifeless body. "Nath," she said. "Oh, Nath, I'm so sorry."

Nath looked up at Emma, his face swollen with tears. He didn't say a word. There were no words to say. He had just lost the love of his life.

PART TWO

1877 - 1883

CHAPTER 22

His boots crunched on the hard snow as his angry footsteps propelled him through the forest. Branches caught on his coat as he fiercely brushed them away. The buried leaves and twigs snapped under his wrathful feet. The wind howled through the trees, urging him to turn back, not to go this way. But he wouldn't listen. He was angry, sad, emotional and out of control.

Life was cruel, mean and downright, cynical. The snowflakes whipped at his face as he crashed through the bushes. His mind was frayed and out of control. He didn't want to think; he wasn't even capable of rational thought right now. His emotions were taking control of his body and his mind. At this moment in time, he was reckless, and concerns for his own safety were nonexistent. He felt so lost, so defeated, that anything could happen right now, a wolf could attack him in the forest, a storm surge could whisk him out to sea, and he would just let it take him.

He half walked, half ran, stumbling here and there, picking himself back up and surging forward. He had no idea where he was going, he just fled. His thoughts were wild, and his feelings raw. He had cried for a month, every day, every hour. It was useless; nothing was to be gained from this outpouring of grief.

This morning something had snapped in Nath's mind, his grief turning into raw anger. Everyone was so concerned about him, asking how he was. Emma had moved in with him, cleaning, forcing him to eat and keeping him company. He appreciated the companionship, but he was just tired of hearing the pain in people's voices as they asked how he was doing.

How did they think he was doing? He knew it wasn't right to think so bitterly, but to his emotional mind, it was normal, it was expected, it was the only reaction that he had left.

Emma stayed, but everyone else had begun to filter out, accepting the tragedy of loss that so many townsfolk had been through as well.

Nath brushed another branch aside brutally as he crashed through the forest, intent on physically exhausting himself.

He didn't see the snow-covered fallen log in front of him.

His boot connected with the rotting log, throwing him off balance, and he flew recklessly into the air, landing on his right knee and his hands.

Nath cursed as pain seared into his knee. He looked down. His pants were torn open at the knee, blood spreading slowly from the wound.

He cursed.

The pain somehow felt unnaturally good to his soul, like somehow, he can validate that his body was now feeling the pain that his heart was experiencing in such awful frequency.

He grinned crazily and pulled the leather bag from his shoulder. These trees were always in the way anyways.

He reached inside the bag and pulled out an axe. It was a good axe; he had sharpened it and took good care of it over the short time he was in New Iceland. It had been a lifesaver, actually. The axe was used to build the many homes the settlers had erected. He had felled many trees with this well-honed axe.

He gripped the handle and picked the tree closest to him. It was a tall oak, probably 30 feet high. The trees out here grew very tall, but the trunks were slim. The wild forests were so thick and overcrowded, the trees perpetually caught in a state of competition for the sunlight, never having a chance to thicken at the base, having no choice but to grow taller and thinner. They looked like giant toothpicks with a bunch of branches at the top.

He threw his leather bag down onto the snowy ground and wielded the axe. He swung it mightily over his shoulder and aimed for the slim base. It connected into the narrow trunk with a loud thud. It stuck firmly into the base of the tree. Angrily, he wrangled it out and swung the axe again in the same spot, making another clean cut. He repeated this several times until he heard the large tree branches sway at the top. He pushed the tree away from him. It didn't budge. He looked up and surveyed the top of the tree. It was a large tree; he should be more careful. What he was doing was dangerous; a little voice inside his head screamed. He ignored the voice and swung the axe again with all his might. His forearms and shoulders bulged, sweat beginning to form on his face.

He heard a crack.

He stepped back, then rushed at the tree with all his weight, smashing his shoulder against the wood.

The tree swayed but still did not fall.

He rushed the tree again, pushing with all his strength, the testosterone pulsing furiously through his entire system.

The tree cracked loudly and fell, slowly at first, then picking up momentum as it screamed to the ground opposite of where he stood. It smashed against several bushes and branches on its way down, leaving a path of destruction.

Finally, the tall oak crashed onto the snow-covered ground with a mighty thump, bouncing and sending a cloud of snow up in its wake. Nath smiled aggressively.

He hadn't come here to cut down trees, nor did he even know why he had brought the axe with him. It was just a physical reaction to an emotional breakdown.

He turned and surveyed the trees around him. The forest was impossibly thick; he was a small piece in an enormous puzzle. He didn't care. He swung his axe at the next tree closest to him. It was a thin dying aspen that was clearly failing to compete with the other hardier trees for sunlight. His axe connected with the trunk satisfyingly; he wiggled it out and swung it again, his shoulders bulging with the effort. The axe sliced back into the aspen with a loud thud.

The tree swayed helplessly.

Grinning, Nath rushed the tree, and it fell, whistling through the air and landing on the snow, bouncing even higher.

Nath stood proudly, wiping his brow. The sweat was collecting on his face now, the physical exertion evident. He removed his coat and his sweater, working at the next tree. With only a thin undershirt on, Nath swung, sliced and carved at the trees, cursing at the more stubborn ones. Sweat poured from his body, soaking his shirt and his face. Even though it was the middle of winter, the exertion was extreme, even for a man as big as him. The temperatures had dropped, and the frigid snow had done nothing short of strengthening his resolve.

He continued for most of the afternoon, wielding his axe, felling trees, big and small, thin and dying, healthy and robust.

He didn't care. He was wild and out of control. He grabbed branches and pulled them out of the ground with his bare hands when they scratched his shoulders. He sliced and then kicked dead trees over. He unleashed all of his energy at the trees, the environment, the very things that had been his nemesis since he landed here.

His hand scraped against a sharp branch, drawing blood. He growled and let out a visceral bellow. He punched crazily in the air, his fist accidentally connecting with a solid tree trunk. His knuckle snapped, the sound reverberating painfully through the forest. The very same knuckle that Anwa had healed over a year ago, an event so recent but yet so distant.

He shouted angrily, waving his broken fist to the sky, the blood sliding down his arm, combining with his sweat-soaked body. The anger bubbled up inside of him, breaking his barriers of restraint.

He hollered at the skies, his voice ricocheting throughout the forest.

"Why?" he roared furiously. "Why!"

He threw his axe into the closest tree and slumped down onto a log. He held his head in his hands for several moments; then, as if he had just thought of something, he stretched his neck up to the tops of the trees. The trees swayed in the wind as if waiting for his next question.

"Why her and not me?" he shouted, tears beginning to fall from his eyes. He didn't want to cry again, but the tears wouldn't have it any other way. "Why not me!" he shouted one last time, as the sobs took him over, and he slumped in despair, his head in his hands, surrounded by a graveyard of fallen trees.

CHAPTER 23

Emma stood at the door, her hands on her hips. "Where have you been? You disappeared for an entire day," she said, her eyes pleading with him. "Nath, please, let me look at your hand."

Nath was slumped onto his bed, propped up by the back wall, looking down at his bloody knuckle. He glanced up at his sister. "I was just out letting off some steam," he replied.

Emma stepped closer. "Will you let me look at your knuckle?" she asked.

Nath looked at the door and then stared at Emma. Anwa wasn't here anymore; he reminded himself. It was ridiculous, but sometimes it was as if he forgot and he just expected her to come barrelling through the door at any moment.

Emma tilted her head to the side. "Are you alright, Nath?" she asked.

His eyes flashed angrily. "No!" he yelled. "I'm not alright. Far from it! I'm sick and tired of everyone asking me that."

Emma stiffened and turned to leave. She took three steps and placed her hand on the doorknob.

"Don't leave," Nath said quietly. "I'm sorry." He stood and walked towards her.

Emma turned and ran to him, hugging him fiercely. Her tears dropped onto his shoulders. "It will get better, Nath. I'm so sorry."

Nath hugged his sister back, but the tears were dried up in his eyes now. He just stared ahead blankly. "I don't know if it ever will get better, Emma. What could ever possibly make things better?"

"You have a daughter, Nath," Emma said. "We will get her from Winnipeg as soon as the quarantine is over."

"Yes," Nathan said softly. "Annabella. I will get her as soon as it is safe for her to return here."

Emma pulled away from him and touched his knuckle. "Let me set that and wrap it," she offered.

"Okay," he relented, slumping down onto the low rocking chair that Anwa used to breastfeed Annabella on every day.

Emma pulled her nurse's bag open and dabbed iodine on the wound. She cleaned the entire wound and then pulled out the gauze to wrap it. She rolled up a small piece of fabric and handed it to him. "Bite on this hard," she said. "I'm going to set it now."

Nath placed the fabric between his front teeth and clamped down. Emma firmly pushed until the bone snapped into place. Nath stifled a curse, then felt his arm go weak with pain.

Emma grabbed his face. "It's done," she said. "All better now. Let me wrap that knee too. It looks like you fought someone. Did you get into a fight?"

"No," he replied stonily. "Nothing like that."

Emma nodded. She knew her brother. If he wasn't going to tell her what happened, then she needn't bother because he would never talk.

"Okay," she said. "I'm going to clean up that knee, wrap it and apply some ice. You are going to have to change into some short pants. I'll wait outside."

"Wait," Nath said. "I will change, but first, will you find out from Dr. Lynch when the quarantine is expected to be lifted?"

"I will," Emma said softly. "I'll ask tomorrow."

❧ ···❧

Nath wandered around the streets of Gimli the next day. It was deserted. Everyone was either locked in their homes, dying in the hospital or working tirelessly at the hospital. So many people had perished. Many residents were talking about leaving as soon as the quarantine is lifted. The number of dead was declining, though, so it meant the epidemic was ending soon, or so they dared to hope.

It could also be the result of mostly everyone dying or surviving; the disease ultimately exhausting itself throughout the community. The people left, like Nath and Pabbi, were the lucky survivors. They were like the walking dead in a ghost town.

The only other presence in the town was the military. It angered Nath to see them. He understood why they had to quarantine the lands of New Iceland, but he recognized that it was also politically motivated. Everyone could see this; it was that obvious.

The government was using the smallpox epidemic as a convenient way to colonize the white people away from the native people. They no longer intermingled. No natives were in the town of Gimli, except for Bea. Nath didn't understand this type of racism; he never understood it. It just simply didn't calculate in his head.

All the surveying and stakes in the ground were being used to separate the natives into reserves. The white people, mostly Icelanders, claimed the rest.

It was not right, Nath thought. He resolved that if he ever had a chance as an assistant reeve or as a reeve himself, then he would try to invoke change. He was not any better or worse than the native people. His brother in law, Mikom, was a native, Anwa was native, so was Bea. He loved them all dearly.

Most importantly, Annabella was half Swampy Cree too. He would be the person to fight for her rights. And he would do that to his death, he thought.

He walked past the Hudson Bay trading post; it was empty, the windows boarded up. A soldier stood by the entrance. Nath glared at the military intruder, his heart empty.

"When is this quarantine going to be over?" Nath asked, smiling at the soldier.

"Not sure," the soldier responded. "Probably a couple more months. We still have a long road ahead of us."

Yeah, burning down Swampy Cree villages takes some time, Nath thought sarcastically. But Nathan did not utter another word and just nodded, his eyes gazing across the horizon.

This place called Gimli is a very lonely stark place now.

Emma returned home utterly exhausted, working double shifts for several weeks now. She opened the door and collapsed onto her bed.

She glanced at Nath, "Where were you yesterday? You didn't come home again."

"Nowhere," Nath answered. "Just need some time alone, away from everything."

"Are you alright?" Emma asked concern sketched across her face.

"No," Nath stated solemnly.

"I'm worried about you, Nath," Emma said.

"Don't be," he responded. "I don't think that I will ever be alright again. But I'm here. I'm not going anywhere."

"Okay," Emma said.

The room grew silent as brother and sister sorted out their thoughts. Do people ever recover from a death in the family, Nath wondered? The room grew darker as the night began to descend upon the small cabin.

Nath looked at Emma from across the room. "It feels like a prison here," he said.

"I was just going to say the same thing," she replied, lifting her feet onto the pillow, propping her tired toes up.

"Did you find out when the quarantine is going to end?" Nath asked.

"Sort of," she answered. "Dr. Lynch said another few months, maybe as long as six months. There are still a few cases coming in every day. Not as much as before, but smallpox is still here. It's not safe for Annabella yet."

Nath frowned, his eyebrows creasing angrily. "I really hate this smallpox," he said. "I really do."

"I know, Nath," she said. "So do I, so do I."

CHAPTER 24

The summer heat soaked into Nath's body as he pulled the day's catches in. It was mid-morning, but already the sun was beating down on his back. He searched his boat for a shirt and pulled it over his shoulders. The summers could be so blistering hot, although the winters are always a formidable cold tundra. A land of extremes, Nath thought. He had loved his New Iceland once. Now, he wasn't so sure. He would stay, but he wasn't sure how long he could live in this desolate town. Well, he thought, we will have to wait and see what the future holds.

The sun was shimmering against the calm lake. The heat of the sun was beating down on his shoulders and his head. The gentle breeze could fool you out on this lake. It would blow in your face, cooling you down while your skin burns to a pinkish-red colour. It was all so deceptive and cruel.

Nath missed his baby daughter. They were not allowed any contact with the outside world, so he had no clue how she was doing. He wondered if she had already learned to walk, how many words she knew, and what kind of personality she had. Would she be more like her mother, kind and strong, or more like her dad, stubborn and outspoken?

Nath pulled and pulled until the entire net flopped into the boat. He counted approximately 20 fish, mostly whitefish. He was hoping to catch the more elusive pickerel fish, they were tastier, and many people seemed to be asking for this particular fish.

Oh, well, he thought, it is food.

He clubbed the fish, prepared them and stuffed them into a salted container. When he was done, he relaxed, lying back in the boat, staring at the cloudless sky. The water lapped at the boat rhythmically, gentle waves nudging the stern ever so slightly.

Nath felt calm and relaxed with the sound of the lapping; it lulled him and nourished his soul.

He fell asleep briefly, nodding off to the soothing rhythm of the waves.

When he awoke, all he could think about was his baby daughter.

He adjusted the sails and steered the rudder, turning the boat around to go back. It had drifted off course quite a bit. He didn't know how far he had glided, but it was farther south than he wanted to be.

Nath adjusted the sails to the optimum position, aiming to get the boat returning to shore as fast as possible. There was little wind, so he relied on his expertise with sailing to maximize the wind that he had.

Luck was on his side, just as he adjusted the sails, a gust of wind in the middle of the lake carried him scurrying towards the Gimli shoreline.

With the wind gusting in his face, he could see the worn pier in the distance. He would have to fix the dock again, he thought. He would try to fix it better this time. Nath mulled over the possible ways to make it sturdier and less subject to water damage. It would take some ingenuity, but he was confident they would all come together to find a solution.

Nath held the rudder straight and steered the boat into the delipidated pier. He could make out a small woman on the dock, waving.

He squinted against the setting sun and strained to see who it was. He angled the boat slightly, approaching the dock, and realized that it was his sister, Emma.

She waved happily, standing on her toes excitedly. What the heck is making her so happy, he thought? Her enthusiasm was infectious, and he felt himself smiling for the first time in many months.

The boat floated closer to the pier as Nath threw the rope to Emma. She caught it and tied the boat to the large wooden pole, pulling him in.

"Nath!" she screeched excitedly.

"What has made you so excited?" Nath said, chuckling from her contagious spirit.

Her blue eyes lit up like sapphires. "The quarantine is over, Nath!" she yelped. "It's finally over! We can go to Winnipeg and get Annabella, Mamma and Eva! We can have our lives back now."

Nath smiled broadly. For the first time in six months, his heart lifted with hope.

Nath pulled the reins on the horses, steadying them and attached the carriage at the back. Emma had her bag already packed, but Nath just threw a bunch of clothes haphazardly into his leather bag. He was going to get his baby daughter finally; he was going to see her today. The excitement and love washed over him like a thousand little cupid arrows, penetrating his chest straight into his heart.

They both decided that they were not going to wait until tomorrow morning. Nath had checked in with Pabbi and told him they would be travelling to Winnipeg immediately. Pabbi encouraged them to go and bring back their loved ones. There wouldn't be enough room in the carriage for them all, so he chose to stay at home. The smallpox had left Pabbi with a strange weakness in his arms. He had fully recovered but still struggled with this mysterious weakness. The doctors said it was just something that happened to some people. It was like a permanent side effect.

"Okay," Nath said. "Are you sure that you'll be alright?"

"Yes," Pabbi answered. "I will be fine. Don't worry about me. Hurry, bring my wife, daughter and granddaughter back. Get out of here already!"

Nath and Emma hugged Pabbi and loaded up the carriage. As they rumbled down the street, he noticed a lot of activity happening, people outside, people talking, and people on horses. He wondered what was happening.

Emma chatted excitedly as they approached the military stop at the outskirts of Gimli near the hospital. Dr. Lynch was standing there in a tall white coat. As the carriage slowed down, the military personnel waved them to the side, pointing to a clearing.

"What do you think is going on?" Nath asked his sister.

"I don't know," Emma said. "Dr. Lynch told me this morning that they were lifting the quarantine. I pulled off my nurse's hat, rushed home, packed and went straight to the dock."

"Well, I don't know what is going on," Nath said. "But I sure don't like Dr. Lynch. He's been a bigot, a naysayer and a backstabber. I can't wait until he leaves our land."

Nath slowed the carriage to a stop as he waited for the soldiers to approach the riding seats.

"Dr. Lynch would like to have a word with you," the young soldier said.

"Is that so?" Nath said, dauntingly. "About what?"

"I don't know, sir," the soldier replied. "I'm just following orders. We are pulling out, but it seems like the rest of the town wants to do the same."

Dr. Lynch walked up to the carriage. "Nathan Olason," he said, with an air of authority. "I need to have a word with you in private."

"Whatever you have to say can be said right here in front of everybody," Nath replied, coldly. "I have nothing to hide."

Dr. Lynch looked nervously at Nath and then caught sight of Emma beside him. "Emma," he said, acknowledging her. "Why are you both leaving so soon?"

Emma opened her mouth to speak, but Nath held up a hand, silencing her. Nath turned his gaze back to Dr. Lynch. "The quarantine is lifted, correct, Dr. Lynch?" he asked.

Dr. Lynch stood defiantly. "Yes, we received orders to lift the quarantine this morning," he replied. "Hear me out, Nathan. A large number of people seem to be leaving, a sort of exodus. It's not something we had anticipated. I would like to ask for your help to talk some sense into the remaining residents. The town will be deserted at this rate." He looked at Nath, then glanced at Emma, trying to garner support from her.

Nath narrowed his eyes, trying to remain calm. "Do you know why that is, Dr. Lynch?" Nath asked calmly. "Because you and your soldiers have effectively imprisoned us in our own country for over eight months whilst your military personnel drew borders around the white settlements and the native settlements. I can understand the quarantine, but even that should have been implemented much earlier. When Sarah Settee initially diagnosed the disease as smallpox, the quarantine should have been immediately enforced."

"She is not a licensed practitioner!" Dr. Lynch shouted indignantly.

"She has more experience than anyone here regarding smallpox," Nath said. "I believe she was a midwife who had dealt directly with smallpox before. Nobody listened to her."

Dr. Lynch interrupted angrily, "We cannot take the word from an unlicensed practitioner, female and part Cree, too, I must say!"

Nath felt his blood boil. He took two deep breaths and disembarked slowly.

Emma glanced at her brother, "Nath, tread carefully," she warned.

Nath landed with a thud firmly on both feet. He took two large menacing steps towards Dr. Lynch. The two soldiers immediately came to attention, sensing conflict. Nath waved a reassuring hand at them. "No need to worry, men," Nath said. "I only have a few words to say; then I will be on my way."

Dr. Lynch took several steps backwards, his face turning a pale colour. He stood defiantly but farther away, out of harms reach. "Well then," Dr. Lynch said, more gently. "Say what you have to say, Nathan."

Nath nodded, pleased that the soldiers had paid attention to his deescalating words. Then he grinned at Dr. Lynch, gratified that the man wore a complete expression of fear on his ashen face. "Firstly, Dr. Lynch," Nath said, calmly. "We have been waiting for the expiry of the quarantine to pick up my baby daughter in Winnipeg. No one will stop me. My baby daughter is currently the most important person in my life, more important than even myself right now. I have been waiting for this moment to retrieve her." Nath paused for effect, then continued. "Secondly, my sister and I are amongst the original settlers of Gimli, and we intend to return. I call this land home, and I am going to Winnipeg to retrieve the remaining members of my family. I don't know where everyone else is going, but that is for New Iceland to resolve once we can establish a stable government. And I can assure you that I will be part of that emerging government."

Dr. Lynch quietly listened, no longer interrupting, knowing that Nathan was speaking the truth. He had heard that Nath was already being voted in as the next possible assistant reeve.

Nath smiled coldly, as he continued, "Lastly, if you and your medical staff had been more concerned about saving lives rather than burning down the native villages and creating borders to segregate the native reserves from the white settlements; you would have heeded Sarah Settee's warning, placed the quarantine back in September and maybe saved hundreds of lives in the process!" Nath's voice had risen steadily throughout his emotional tirade, although now, he lowered his voice to almost a whisper. The soldiers had both taken several steps closer to hear him, but also to be prepared for an altercation. "And maybe," he paused, "My wife wouldn't have died." Nath stared at the doctor with a face of stone, his voice returning to normal, acceptable levels. "Now, Dr. Lynch, it was very nice chatting with you, but we really should be on our way.

And as for you personally, doctor, you should be gone before I get back. You are not welcome here any longer."

Nath nodded at the military personnel. "Thank you, soldiers, for keeping your cool. Please do us all a favour and escort the doctor out sooner rather than later."

With that, Nathan hopped back into the riding seat, whipped the reins, and the carriage jerked out of Gimli onto the main road south to Winnipeg.

CHAPTER 25

The carriage bounced and jostled along the gravel road for hours. The heat from the early afternoon sun beat onto their heads and shoulders as brother and sister spoke about the journey ahead of them.

"Have you ever been to Winnipeg yet?" Emma asked.

"Other than when we first arrived, no," Nath replied. "I have not travelled to Winnipeg since. But I know where my Aunt Anita lives. She has been the most gracious person throughout this crisis, sheltering Annabella, Mamma and Eva. I will be in her debt for saving my daughter's life."

"Yes," Emma said. "It was one of the best decisions you made."

"If I would have known about how the disease affected the Swampy Cree," Nath said, looking down briefly. "I would have sent Anwa too."

"She wouldn't have gone," Emma replied. "You know that."

"You're right," Nathan said silently, the carriage jostling them over the rough roads. "She would have stayed by my side."

Nath looked over the rough road ahead, with all the purple flowers growing along the sides. It was such a beautiful area in the summer, he thought.

"Things are going to get better, Nath," Emma said. "It has too; there is no other way but up from the bottom."

"True," Nath replied solemnly.

❦ ⋯ ❦

Several hours later, they stopped the horses for a rest. Nath pulled the reins over to the side of the road, parking the carriage at a small clearing. Emma fed the horses hay while Nath departed with two water buckets to fill from the lake.

As soon as he returned, the horses drank eagerly from the buckets. He joined Emma on a picnic blanket, and they ate lunch, musing about the future.

"I wonder if Annabella has learned to walk yet?" Nath asked.

"Oh, probably," Emma replied. "She will be eleven months old now. She should be walking or close to it by now."

"I wonder how she looks," Nath said. "When I sent her to Winnipeg, she was just a newborn, only two months old. She has grown up since then, maybe even developing some unique facial characteristics. I wonder if she looks like Anwa or if she looks like me."

"I don't know," Emma replied, munching on some fish and turnips. "Often, babies look a bit like both parents."

Nath chewed the salted fish thoughtfully, swallowing a mouthful. "Do you think I will be a good single father?" he asked. "I'm a little worried. I don't know anything about being a female. How am I supposed to raise a girl into a woman? I don't even know where to start."

Emma smiled, "You will be a perfect daddy, Nath. Just let your fatherly love guide you. The best parents are the ones that care the most. When it comes from that special part of your heart, Nath, you will find a way to make it all happen."

"I hope you are right," Nath said, smiling. "I'm really looking forward to having her in my arms."

"I know you are," Emma said as she laid back onto the blanket, letting the sun warm her skin.

Nath laid down beside her as they both looked up at the puffy white clouds. They shaped and reshaped with the high winds, sometimes shifting into faces and objects. Emma pointed out a man's face; then it changed into a woman's body. Nath laughed as they shared this special moment as brother and sister.

"What do you think is ahead of us now?" Nath asked.

"I think it will be a long rough road to recovery," Emma replied. "I can't lie. It might not be easy, but it's the right road now. I think the worst is over."

"I hope so," Nath stated simply.

"We should leave soon," Emma said. "Your daughter is waiting for you."

Nath and Emma packed up their picnic and hopped back into the riding seat, snapping the reins as the horses lurched forward.

❧ · · · · ❧

They trotted into Winnipeg, the carriage creaking and jostling along the wide main street. Anita's house was not far. The journey was long, the horses were worn, and they were all ready for a much-needed rest.

Nath snapped the reins, urging the horses to go on. A few more blocks and they would be there. He had never travelled much in Winnipeg, but he knew the address and directions. They would be turning right along the next side street. Nath's heart blossomed with hope as the horses pulled them closer and closer to their destination.

As they rumbled down the street, Nath's pulse quickened. Aunt Anita's house was near, he knew. Nath pulled back on the reins, slowing down the horses. He peered at each property, looking for the right number. Her house was number 34. They passed number 30, then 32, and as they rolled up, Nath pulled the reins to a halt in the front of 34.

It was a quaint little property with a tiny fence, a large yard and a sturdy brown log house. There was a beautiful vegetable garden in the backyard as well as the customary outhouse farther back. Nath hopped off the riding seat and walked towards the house, his heart beating loudly in his ears.

A small boy came running along the side of the house, with two other children chasing him. He barrelled right into Nath's legs, oblivious to the obstacle in front of him. The boy looked up at him, bewilderingly, said excuse me and continued running, his followers in hot pursuit.

Nath laughed and knocked on the large wooden door. He heard several creaks and groans from the floor joists, then finally, the door was pulled open by a sweet older attractive woman in her forties. "Hello," Anita greeted him. "What can I do for you?" She narrowed her eyes suddenly, cocking her head to the side. "I have never met you, but I have seen you before. Umm, in pictures, I believe."

"Hi, Aunt Anita," Nath introduced himself, holding his arms wide. "It's Nathan, Annabella's dad."

"Oh, my God!" Anita shrieked, hugging him fiercely as Emma stepped up the walkway behind him. "Nath! You're alive! We were beginning to worry that everyone had perished. We couldn't send word; we didn't hear from anybody. Gimli was under strict quarantine!"

"We survived," Nathan said strongly. "They just lifted the quarantine this morning. We left as soon as we could."

"Oh, my Lord!" Anita cried. "Come in and rest. Have something to eat! I see that you have met my mischievous boy William and his brothers."

"Yes," Nathan laughed. "They almost ran me over!"

Anita peered over his shoulder. "Emma!" Anita squealed. "Come in, come in!"

Emma walked in, hugging Anita. "So nice to see you again," Emma said warmly.

"We are here to collect my family and take everyone back to Gimli," Nath said softly. "Where's Annabella, Mamma and Eva?"

"Mamma and Eva are in town right now, buying some food from the market," Anita replied. "But Annabella is here."

As Anita stepped aside, a small girl crawled into the main living area as they spoke. She gently propped herself up, grabbing tables, chairs, anything she could find to help stabilize her attempts at walking. She looked up briefly at Nath, locked eyes with him, then promptly fell down on her butt hard. She pouted, embarrassed at her failure to walk. Stubbornly, she pulled herself up again.

Nath rushed into the room and bent down to Annabella, with a huge smile spreading across his face. "Hi, sweetheart," he said. "It's daddy."

Annabella looked inquiringly at his masculine rough face. "Ma?"

Nathan smiled. "Yes, baby girl," he cooed. "I am your mamma and dada." He laid out his hand to help her stand. She looked down at his large hand and placed her tiny fingers on his palm, using him as leverage to stand up again.

She stood feebly, slightly teetering, almost falling on her butt again, but she held onto her father's hand fiercely, her tiny fingers curling over his thumb and somehow managed to stay standing.

Nath smiled broadly, immensely proud of his baby girl, tears quickly filling his eyes. "Bella," he said, his voice cracking. "You are the cutest baby girl I have ever seen."

Annabella looked up at her dad's face, her confused blue eyes piercing through his.

"You have my eyes," he said wondrously. "And your mamma's dark hair." He smoothed her hair from her eyes, placing the thick locks behind her ears. They walked together, Nath crouched on his knees and Annabella using him as a walker. "I love you, my baby girl. I missed you so much."

Emma and Anita watched in silence as father and daughter bonded for the first time in nine months. Both women cried tears of happy joy.

Finally, Nath sat down on the floor and let Annabella crawl onto him. She climbed onto his back, his arms and then pulled on his hair forcefully.

"Ouch!" Nath cried happily.

Bella grinned and laughed sweetly. She pulled at his ears next.

"Hey!" Nath laughed heartily.

Then she pulled his shirt and climbed on him again, stumbling and almost falling. Nath grabbed her just in time and pulled her over his head as she slid into his lap. She pushed herself up indignantly and stomped away, falling down three times.

Nath had tears of joy falling freely down his face, watching his stubborn baby daughter's attempts at walking. Finally, Annabella reached her great auntie. Anita scooped her up and walked two steps with her before she began wriggling out of her grasp.

"Okay, okay," Anita cried as she placed Bella down on the floor. "Go on your own then!" Anita glanced at Nath. "She's a willful one!"

"She is!" Nathan exclaimed, happily.

Anita waved Emma in, closed the door and sat on the sofa. "Where's Anwa? Is she still in the carriage?"

Nathan looked down to the floor, momentarily paralyzed.

Emma spoke for him, "Aunt Anita, we have bad news."

Anita's face paled, and she grasped her hands over her mouth. "No," she said.

"Smallpox claimed Annabella's mom in January," Emma said softly.

Nathan continued looking down at the floor, not raising his head once.

"It has been very hard for Nathan," she said. "It's been a long rough road for him. And for all of us. We are still grieving."

"Oh my god," Anita said. "I'm so sorry, Nath."

"I'd prefer not to talk about it," Nath said softly, still looking down at the floor. "I'm here to get my baby daughter. She's the only thing I have left."

Anita hugged Emma and patted Nath on the shoulder. "Okay," she said. "I will get her clothes and pack everything up for you."

"Thanks," Nath said solemnly. "I mean that. I owe you, Auntie, for saving my daughter's life. If you ever need anything, I am the man to call."

"It was the least I could do," Anita responded. "No need for indebtedness." She turned and walked down the hall, flipping open luggage containers and filling them with baby clothes. She called out, "I will pack some infant cereal recipes for you as well. I will give you what leftovers I have; the oats should last a few days."

"That would be wonderful!" Nath answered back as Annabella returned to him, climbing into his lap.

Emma smiled, "She's so cute, Nathan. She knows that you are her daddy."

"I'm glad," he said. "I was worried about that."

Annabella looked up at Emma and broke into a huge smile. They both laughed. "It's time to take you back home, my sweetheart," Nath said softly.

❧ · · · ❦

The next morning, Nathan finished packing the last piece of luggage in the carriage. It was full. Mamma, Annabella and Eva were sitting snugly in the carriage, waving to Aunt Anita. Nath hugged her warmly, thanking her again and hopped into the riding seat with Emma.

He snapped the reins, and the carriage rumbled forward. Nath glanced at Emma. "This wasn't the way I had envisioned picking up my baby daughter. Anwa should be here with us. It was only supposed to be temporary. Life isn't fair."

Emma ran her hand along her brother's arm. "Everything will be alright, Nath," she said. "When you aren't given a choice, you just have to live with what you have and be grateful. Annabella is alive and well. We should be thankful for this."

"Yes," Nathan replied. "You are right. I don't know what I would have done without her. I love that little girl so much;

it feels like my heart is going to jump out of my chest. Last night, I got all choked up when she fell asleep in my arms. She's my sweetheart."

"She is, Nath," Emma agreed. "Let's take her home."

The carriage rolled onto Main Street and clambered out of the city, the horses leading the splintered family back to Gimli.

CHAPTER 26

"Da!" Annabella shouted.

The sun had just risen, and Nathan lazily crawled out of bed, rubbing his eyes. He shuffled half asleep over to Annabella's small bed. "What is it, Bella?"

"Dada!" she shouted. She was standing inside the railed bed. Nath sniffed and smelled the awful feces scent.

"Alright," Nath said. "Time to change your bottom." He shuffled lazily over to the dresser, grabbing a cloth diaper and pins. He returned to her bedside, rolled her on her back and changed the smelly garment. "Ah, Bella. How a little girl like you can emit such rancid smells is beyond me!" He cleaned her up with a wet rag, wiping her from front to back like his mamma showed him to. Then he wrapped the clean diaper onto her, fastening it with the two pins.

"Okay, my sweet," Nath mumbled. "Time to go back to bed. Daddy needs sleep."

"Me sleepy too," Bella announced proudly.

"Love you, Bella," Nath said. He smiled, kissed her on the forehead and returned to bed.

"Luv, dada," Annabella shouted back as the early dawn closed in upon the small family. The sun rose slowly over the snow-covered landscape as they both drifted back to sleep.

Time passes by so quickly with a baby in the house, Nath thought.

Before he realized hours had elapsed, Annabella awoke again. "Da!"

Nathan was already awake, pouring himself a hot tea. He whisked her out of her bed and placed her on the floor. She ran mightily across the room. She had mastered the art of walking within a few weeks of bringing her home. Now, six months later, she was running! She had long black wavy hair just like her mom, but her eyes stayed blue so far. He knew that the colour could change as she grew older, but so far, she miraculously retained his eye colour. He knew it was extremely rare, and he was delighted to have such a unique, beautiful daughter.

"Me hungry," Bella stated rather abruptly.

Nath lifted her up and placed her into the feeding chair, giving her a bottle of milk. She sucked on the nipple, drinking half of its contents.

"Daddy's going to make your oats now," Nath said. "Please sit still, Bella."

"Da," Bella said loudly. "Me luv, dada."

Nathan smiled, his eyes gleaming with love for this tiny little girl. "I love you, too, my sweetie," he replied, stirring the oats on the stove. He handed her small pieces of hard-boiled egg on a plate. She picked them up daintily with her tiny fingers, then stuffed them in her mouth.

"Good girl! Yummy!" Nath said brightly, impressed with her improved eating skills.

He stirred the oats for a few more minutes, added maple syrup and then scooped the runny cereal into a small bowl. He sat down in front of Annabella and lifted a spoonful it into her already opened mouth. She swallowed and opened her mouth again; she was a hungry young girl. He spooned another small amount into her mouth, wiping her chin with the spoon. She immediately swallowed and opened her mouth again. Nath continued feeding her until she finished the entire bowl.

"What a good girl you are!" Nath exclaimed, cleaning up the table and removing her cloth bib.

He placed her down on the floor while he cleaned up.

A male voice sounded on the other side of the door. "Hey, Nathan!" Several knocks followed.

He recognized the voice. "Come in, Viktor!" Nath shouted.

Viktor walked in with his little nephew, Joshua, Aron's baby boy. The boy was born one month before Annabella. Josh immediately ran over to Annabella, handing her a crude wood toy. They played happily, shouting at each other, laughing and eventually hitting each other.

"Bella!" Nath hollered. "Be nice!"

Joshua looked hurt, then sulked into the corner. Bella soon followed him, kissing him on the head. "Bella, sorry!" she said loudly.

"That's better," Nath shouted, laughing.

Viktor sat down at the table with a happy grin. He had good news to share. Some Icelandic people had decided to stay during the exodus, and New Iceland was in the process of developing a government to try to keep more people from deserting. Elections were scheduled to be held in late 1877 with the hope of finalizing a constitution in early 1878. The idea was that the entire territory of New Iceland would now be called Vatnsthing, or Lake Region. The area would be divided into four divisions; the district Vidinesbygd, which included Willow Point and Gimli, Arnesbygd, Fljotsbygd, and Mikleyjarbygd, encompassing Arnes, Icelandic River and Hecla Island, respectively. A five-person council, consisting of a reeve, an assistant reeve, and three council members, were expected to govern each of the districts. The members would be scheduled to meet regularly and decide over issues within their regions. It was an exciting new change. They would finally have a chance to govern their own lands.

"Nathan, you are being considered for reeve in the district Vidinesbygd, right here in Gimli," Viktor announced.

Nathan mused thoughtfully, "I don't know if I will have the time to devote to the position of reeve. I have my hands full with Annabella right now. She is my first priority. I will have to approach the council and ask for the lesser position of assistant reeve."

"I'm sure we will all be happy with that," Viktor announced. "This is good news! We can actually govern our own people now."

"Yes," Nathan nodded in agreement. "But if there are no people left to govern, then what will we have left?"

"True," Viktor responded. "But it still is a good start for a brighter future."

Nathan smiled, "Maybe so."

They drank their teas while the babies played happily. After an hour, the screaming started again, and Nath had to grab Annabella, soothing her, as Joshua yelled nonsense baby garble at her. What the fight was about this time, they had no clue! Nath chuckled and kissed her forehead while she hugged him, her tears absorbing into his shirt.

Viktor stood, sweeping Joshua into his arms. "Okay, well, I better get back and take Josh home to my brother's place.

It looks like he's ready for a nap. It's wonderful to see you again, Annabella!" he cooed. "Nath, things are looking up. It's a good day."

"Yes, it is," Nath replied, smiling as Viktor left the house, closing the door behind him. He hugged Bella and rocked her silently as she murmured into his shirt. It's not the New Iceland government that made him happy and gave him life again, he mused. It was this little bundle of feminine spirit he held in his lap that had breathed life back into his soul. Annabella, his baby girl, was his angel.

CHAPTER 27

Nathan pulled the fishing boat into the harbour, tying it onto the dock. It was a beautiful early morning in the late summer of 1883. Lots of changes were happening in Gimli. Catastrophic flooding in 1880-81 had ignited an exodus that had left only 100 people in all of New Iceland, vast amounts of people emigrated to Winnipeg and even farther south to Dakota and other southern regions. New Iceland continued to struggle as a distinct nation, although, many people believed that the Icelanders would benefit from becoming an official part of Manitoba and Canada. In 1881, the New Iceland government disbanded, and the province of Manitoba had grown to encompass all of New Iceland along with other northern areas.

Nathan and his family stayed in Gimli, valiantly building new homes and fishing every day. By July, they noticed that several people would request fish from their boats. Nathan began salting and selling more fish than ever. Nathan, Garth and Pabbi built a larger fishing hut to store the fish, opening its doors to the public just two weeks ago. So far, it was busier than Nath had ever thought it would be. Several people began returning to Gimli for work. The fledging logging and fishing industries were attracting many people back to the shores of Gimli; even Nath was thinking of hiring a few new people again. Groups of families were slowly returning to New Iceland.

Things were finally improving; he could feel it in his bones. But his heart was still numb. He never dated not even one woman since Anwa's death. He simply wasn't interested in pursuing a woman at all. He went to Winnipeg several times and met several women who clearly thought he was handsome, but something was always missing. He didn't know what, but it was like a piece had been taken from him. He just couldn't fathom filling the gaping hole in his heart with someone other than Anwa. Everything just failed to compare to the love they had shared. Instead, he just buried his grief and hardly noticed women anymore. The only little female in his life was his baby daughter, and he was okay with that.

Nath stood and inhaled the fresh morning air. He then pulled the nets out of the boat and wrestled them towards the drying racks in the early morning sun.

"Daddy!" Annabella shrieked, running along the beach with her long black hair flying behind her. Her seven-year-old body was so much larger than she had ever been as a baby, and her energy was incomparable to any other children. As she grew older and older, Nath noticed so much of Anwa in her appearance. Her skin was a light tan, half white and half native. She had the stubbornness of the Olason's deep in her veins, though.

"Bella," Nath said, smiling broadly. "Did you finish your homework?"

Several schools had been built nearby to accommodate the young children in Gimli.

"Yes, Pabbi," Annabella said sweetly.

"Good!" Nath replied warmly. "Help me with these nets then, sweetheart."

Bella eagerly grasped the long side of the nets as both father and daughter gently draped them over the drying racks. Nath adjusted them expertly and looked back at the boat. "Could you help me unload the fish, too?" he asked.

Annabella clutched her fishing gloves; they were the smallest size Nath could possibly find, but still floated on her hands like giant mittens. She seized the fish with her dad, throwing them roughly into pails. They worked together like this for over an hour until Garth arrived, tugging the buckets inside the fishing hut.

Nath put his arm around her affectionately and hugged her gently. "Thanks for helping out, Bella."

"Hey, Dad," Bella asked, sweetly. "I have a question for you."

Noting her sweet coercing tone, Nath smiled suspiciously. "What is it?" He wasn't expecting a lot from her; she was only seven. Although he was impressed with her ability to help with the fishing hut, he was quite proud of her.

"Well," she said. "I thought maybe you could take me out fishing with you. Like in the boat, I mean, in the middle of the lake. You could teach me how to fish. I would be a great helper!" She smiled her sweetest smile and clasped her hands behind her back.

"A fishing boat is not a place for little girls," Nath answered rather abruptly.

Annabella's eyebrows pinched into a frown. Her lips pursed together. Then she nodded as if something just became very clear to her. "Mamma used to fish," Bella said defiantly. "You told me that she even taught you how to fish! She was a girl!"

Nath laughed, "You are right. That is true. But she was eighteen years old, not seven."

Annabella turned and stomped away angrily. She walked halfway to the house when she realized something. She turned back and ran back to the dock. Nath looked up, startled.

"How old was Mamma when she first learned how to fish?" Annabella asked.

"Oh," Nath said. "I don't know. She learned to fish with her family in the Swampy Cree reserve."

Garth grabbed a pail and nodded at Annabella. "Anwa learned to fish at your age, Bella. Around seven years old, maybe a bit younger." Garth paused, glancing at Nath. "Sorry, but it's the truth."

Nath laughed and cleared his throat. "So, you won," he said, smiling. "But how do we allow you to go fishing while you are still going to school?"

Bella smiled broadly, "I will go in the early mornings with you and late evening only. I will still go to school and do all my homework too." She rocked on her feet, proudly and energetically.

"Okay," Nath replied chuckling. "When do you want to start fishing?"

Annabella shrieked and bounced into his arms, throwing him backwards in the boat. Nathan laughed as she peppered him with kisses. "Tomorrow? Can we start tomorrow morning?"

"Yes," he laughed heartily, hugging her fiercely.

She leaped enthusiastically off of him and skipped back to the cabin. "I'm going to do all my homework right now!" she yelled back.

Nath smiled as her small form skipped along the sand, disappearing into the cabin. *My baby girl wants to learn fishing;* he mused happily. It might not be a perfect life, but, at this moment, he felt like he was the luckiest father in the world.

THE END

The saga continues with Nath and his family in

BOOK TWO

OF

▦ THE OLASON CHRONICLES ▦

Final Note to Reader

Smallpox lasted for an estimated 12,000 years globally. The first possible cases were traced as far back as 10,000 BCE in Asia. Smallpox killed approximately one-third of patients who acquired the virus; the lucky survivors were often scarred permanently and sometimes left blinded for life. Pockets of epidemics flared throughout the years. In 1717, inoculations began, but smallpox continued to persist, spreading by travel and immigration. In 1796, Edward Jenner, a training physician in the UK, created the first widely adopted vaccine, but sadly many isolated communities did not have access to it.

Countless aboriginal communities perished, including the Swampy Cree reserve in Manitoba. The Swampy Cree had no immunity and were never vaccinated; they were decimated.

In 1959, the WHO organized a mass immunization campaign. It took eighteen years to eradicate the disease. In 1977, the last case of smallpox occurred in Somalia. The immunization campaign was a success.

Currently, two stores of smallpox virus remain in the entire world. To safely guard against bioterrorism, the virus is now held securely at CDC's headquarters in Atlanta, USA and another facility in Koltsovo, Russia.

The events in my story are derived from an 1875 Icelandic immigration account that I used fictitiously to create my saga. I have attempted to keep my story as real as possible, inserting facts to bring my story to life. Some timeframes have been intentionally skewed to fit events into my story. All my characters are fictitious, with the exceptions of the following historical individuals:

Sigtryggur Jonasson, Icelandic entrepreneur.

James Settee, Church of England missionary, mixed Swampy Cree and British ancestry.

Sarah Settee, Cree English wife of James Settee.

Dr. James Lynch, medical officer at Gimli during the pandemic.

The story of the Gimli Icelanders is truly a story of heroes, resilience and heartbreak. I came across the history several years after I purchased my cottage in the beautiful RM of Gimli. I began talking to my neighbours and slowly discovered that mostly everyone had a mix of Icelandic, native and Ukrainian in their background. My sons and I visited the museum in Gimli, and we were enthralled by the immigration saga. It took a few years after, but *The Strong Amongst Us* began slowly forming in my mind, and it soon developed into a deep heartfelt passion for making this story known to the world.

Currently, two flags are erected at Willow Island, formerly called Willow Point. One is a flag of Canada and the other is the flag of Iceland. In 1890, a New Iceland festival started and continues to this very day.

I would like to thank the New Iceland Heritage Museum in Gimli, Manitoba, for the wealth of information, the insight and the soul-inspiring displays of the Icelandic people.

I would like to thank Atina A., fellow writer and close friend, for being there for me when the conflict in the novel was too much for my heart to take, bringing me back down to earth and helping my emotions to settle.

I would also like to thank all the individual Reddit and Twitter followers that have faithfully followed me on this journey in completing this amazing novel. Without this constant encouragement and engagement, I may not have finished this book. I gratefully appreciate the support; even though I have not met many of my followers, you are in my mind and my heart, which is like finding gold.

And most importantly, thanks to my teenage sons; for pitching in when I was juggling too many balls at once, for understanding why mommy was up until 2 am writing, my absences travelling to the cottage and marketing in New York City, but most of all, for listening to my excited rants and emotional outbursts while writing. It was definitely a roller coaster ride for all of us. I love you both so much, no one else in the world touches my heart like you two boys do.

And lastly, thank you to all my readers, you give my life meaning.

Don't miss the captivating sequel

THE STRONG WITHIN US
BOOK TWO

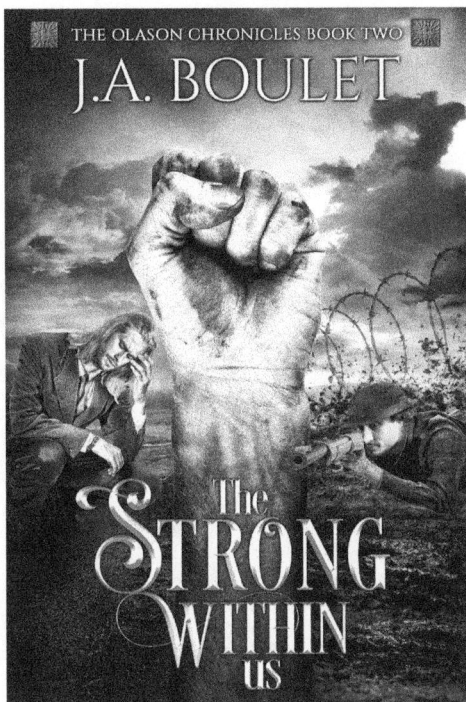

Coming soon in Fall 2020

J. A. BOULET was born and raised in Western Canada. Both her parents were landed immigrants from Hungary, a direct result of the mass emigration during the 1956 Hungarian Revolution. J. A. Boulet was born many years later as a Generation Xer and a first-generation Canadian. She started writing poetry at the age of five and subsequently progressed to short stories and novels. Writing has always maintained a strong current of passion throughout her life. She recently left her career in finance to pursue her dreams of being an author. She currently lives in Canada with her two teenaged sons and a pet crested gecko named Mossio.

You can learn more at:

Website: jaboulet.ca
Twitter: @ love_walk_life

CPSIA information can be obtained
at www.ICGtesting.com
Printed in the USA
BVHW070718150720
583536BV00008B/112